The Great Deceiver

Also by Elly Griffiths

THE DR RUTH GALLOWAY MYSTERIES

The Crossing Places
The Janus Stone
The House at Sea's End
A Room Full of Bones
Dying Fall
The Outcast Dead
The Ghost Fields
The Woman in Blue
The Chalk Pit
The Dark Angel
The Stone Circle
The Lantern Men
The Night Hawks
The Locked Room
The Last Remains

THE BRIGHTON MYSTERIES

The Zig Zag Girl
Smoke and Mirrors
The Blood Card
The Vanishing Box
Now You See Them
The Midnight Hour

OTHER WORKS

The Stranger Diaries
The Postscript Murders
Bleeding Heart Yard

FOR CHILDREN

A Girl Called Justice
A Girl Called Justice: The Smugglers' Secret
A Girl Called Justice: The Ghost in the Garden
A Girl Called Justice: The Spy at the Window

ELLY Griffiths

The Great Deceiver

QUERCUS

First published in Great Britain in 2023 by

QUERCUS

Quercus Editions Ltd
Carmelite House
50 Victoria Embankment
London EC4Y 0DZ

An Hachette UK company

A CIP catalogue record for this book is available from the British Library

HB ISBN 978 1 5294 0 990 1
TPB ISBN 978 1 5294 0 991 8
EB ISBN 978 1 5294 0 993 2

10 9 8 7 6 5 4 3 2 1

Typeset by CC Book Production
Printed and bound in Great Britain by Clays Ltd, Elcograf S.p.A

Papers used by Quercus are from well-managed forests and other responsible sources.

For Dennis's other granddaughters:
Giulia, Sheila, Ellie and Katie

PART 1
April

CHAPTER 1

Tuesday, 12 April 1966

Max Mephisto always dressed carefully for a rendezvous with a woman, even if said female was only two days old. Check suit with the new thinner lapels, white shirt, narrow tie. He paused in the hallway to select a trilby. Men were going out without hats now but Max, although he liked to think of himself as a modernist, could not quite bring himself to do this.

He walked briskly down the stairs, ignoring the lift (he wasn't in his dotage yet). In the entrance hall, light was glowing through the stained glass in the front door and Alf, the concierge, was dozing on his chair. He straightened up to a full salute when he heard Max approaching.

'Good morning, Mr Mephisto.'

'Morning, Alf.' Max was grateful that the man didn't know that he was also known by the frankly ridiculous title of Lord Massingham. He had a feeling that Alf would enjoy that one far too much. As it was he liked to salute and remind people that he'd been in the Royal Army Ordnance Corps ('The Sugar Stick Brigade').

'It's a lovely one,' said Alf. He gave Max an enquiring look as if to say, 'off somewhere nice?' but Max just responded with a vague smile. He liked to keep his life private and, besides, explaining his errand would involve saying the word 'granddaughter'.

Leaving a plainly disappointed Alf behind him, Max stepped out into the sunshine. He was about to walk towards Kensington High Street in search of a cab when someone shouted, 'Max!'

Max turned. Something about the voice seemed to drag him backwards, through velvet curtains, stage doors, vanishing cabinets and digs that smelt of rain and cigarettes. He had to rub his eyes before he could focus on the figure hurrying towards him: grey hair, threadbare suit, anxious expression.

'Max. Thank God I caught you.'

'Ted?' said Max. 'Ted English?'

Max was proud of himself for remembering the man's real name when it was his stage name that was clamouring to be heard. Ted was another magician. The Great Something. With a pang, Max thought of his old friend Stan Parks, also known as The Great Diablo, dead now for two years.

'I've got to talk to you,' said Ted. 'I've just come up from Brighton.'

By the looks of him, he'd run all the way. But Max was intrigued, despite himself. He had a soft spot for Brighton. He often thought that he and the south coast town had a lot in common: both smart on the outside but with something steelier and less charming lurking backstage. Plus, many of his friends lived there.

'I was just on my way out,' said Max. 'My daughter's had a baby.' There, he'd said it. 'I'm on my way to visit her in the maternity hospital.'

'Ruby Magic's had a baby?' Ted seemed temporarily distracted. Ruby would be pleased that he remembered the name of her TV show.

'Yes. A little girl.' No name yet. Ruby said that she and Dex were still arguing over it.

'Please, Max. Just a few minutes. It's . . . it's a matter of life and death.'

Now Max was definitely interested. He steered Ted past the gawping Alf and into the lift. He didn't look as if he'd manage the stairs. As the iron cage creaked upwards, Max suddenly remembered Ted's stage name.

The Great Deceiver.

DI Bob Willis and WDC Meg Connolly stood outside the seafront house and breathed deeply. Sea air is good for you, Meg's mother always said, but today the exercise was more to do with expelling the stench of death.

'You never really get used to it,' said the DI after a few minutes.

Meg was grateful that the DI acknowledged what they'd just seen. She had been involved in violent cases before. Just last year she had investigated the death of a show-business impresario and had nearly got herself murdered for her pains. She had seen a dead body then but it had been recently deceased. She had never before been in a room where a body had lain for two days. The pathologist, Solomon Carter, thought that Cherry Underwood had been stabbed on Sunday night. It was now Tuesday and she hadn't been missed because there was no show on Monday. But fellow lodgers in the boarding house had noticed the smell and, eventually, the landlady had used her skeleton key. She had fainted, right into the arms of Ida Lupin, strongwoman.

'We need to check everyone who was in the house on Sunday night,' said the DI, still expanding his chest like someone in one of those advertisements on the back pages of the newspaper. *Shamed by your poor physique?*

'Yes,' said Meg. It would be a long job because the boarding house was full of people performing at that week's Old Style Music Hall show on the Palace Pier.

'What was her act again?' asked the DI. Meg knew, from station gossip, that the DI's wife had once been part of a troupe that performed naked tableaux. Perhaps this accounted for his embarrassment when discussing anything theatrical now.

'Magician's assistant,' said Meg. 'The act was called The Great Deceiver.'

DI Willis grunted. Meg thought that it was a noise of disgust but, a few minutes later, he said, 'I once knew a magician called The Great Diablo. Lovely chap.'

'Was he a friend of Max Mephisto's?' asked Meg. This might be a gruesome murder case, but she still couldn't get over her fascination with the famous magician.

'They were good friends once,' said DI Willis. 'Served in the war together. With the super too.'

The fact that Max was a friend of their superintendent, Edgar Stephens, only added to his mystique.

'Do you think Max knew Cherry?' asked Meg.

'He wouldn't be bothered with an act like that,' said the DI. 'Max is a Hollywood star now. He's beyond all this.' He waved at the building behind them, which was certainly looking shabby in the spring sunshine, the wrought-iron balconies leaking rusty tears. 'Come on,' he said, as if Meg had been keeping him waiting. 'Let's go and find out who killed Cheryl.'

'Cherry,' said Meg. It seemed very sad that you could be murdered and still people wouldn't get your name right.

CHAPTER 2

'Have you got anything to drink?' asked Ted.

Max glanced at the clock on the mantelpiece. It was only ten a.m. But he opened his drinks cabinet. It occurred to him that Ted must have taken a very early train from Brighton.

He poured a whisky for Ted, who downed it in one gulp. Max refilled the glass, resisting the temptation to have one himself. Nothing says 'devoted grandfather' like turning up at a maternity hospital smelling of alcohol.

'It's Cherry,' said Ted, after a few seconds. 'She's dead.'

Max waited. He wondered if he was meant to know who Cherry was.

Ted drained his glass. The whisky didn't seem to have had much effect and Max thought he remembered rumours about Ted having a drink problem. It happened to lots of old pros but Max was determined that he wouldn't be one of them. He stopped himself from offering Ted another drink. He didn't want the magician to drink himself into a stupor. Not without telling his story first.

But Ted suddenly seemed to pull himself together. He said, 'Cherry was my assistant. A good one too. I went to see her in her digs on Sunday morning. Just to go through the act. Well, this morning her landlady telephoned. Cherry's been murdered. Stabbed to death in her bedroom. They've just found her body today.'

'My God,' said Max. 'How terrible.'

'Yes,' said Ted. 'She was a lovely girl. And to think . . .'

He produced a large handkerchief with a flourish, as if he was about to perform a trick, but, instead, blew his nose loudly.

'I'm sorry,' said Max. He remembered when Ethel, who had once worked with him, had been brutally murdered. You become close to your assistants. You travel with them, rehearse with them, perform twice nightly. On stage, you need to be able to communicate without words. That was why Max had worked so well with Ruby.

Ted emerged from his handkerchief and his voice changed, became businesslike.

'You know the head of the Brighton police, don't you?'

'I do,' said Max, suddenly wary.

'I want you to go and see him,' said Ted. 'Everyone will think I did it. Tell him I didn't.'

How do I know that you didn't? Max wanted to say. Instead, he tried for a soothing tone: 'I'm sure the police won't jump to any conclusions . . .'

'Please,' said Ted. 'I didn't do it. She was like a daughter to me.' And he started to cry in earnest into the handkerchief.

Meg's first interview was with the owner of the house, Linda Knight. She wasn't anything like Meg's image of a seaside landlady. She was quite young, for one thing, and rather stylish. Linda had dark hair, cut in a chin-length bob with a heavy fringe, and was wearing a skirt that, if not quite a mini, still ended halfway down her thighs. Meg was conscious that her uniform skirt was slightly too short when she was sitting down and that, as usual, she had a run in her tights. But, thank goodness for tights. Meg still remembered the agony of stockings, the annoyance when a suspender broke, the chance that someone would see an inch of goose-pimpled thigh when you sat down.

'Blimey,' said Linda. 'What a morning. That poor girl.' She had a distinct cockney accent, which made Meg like her even more. Meg knew that her own voice betrayed the fact that she was born and brought up in Whitehawk, one of the poorest areas in Brighton.

'Can you take me through what happened?' said Meg. 'I know it's hard. I'm sorry.'

'That's OK, love,' said Linda, 'it's your job. Shall I ask Annie to bring us some tea?'

Meg had no idea who Annie was – the maid, perhaps – but she was all for the idea of tea. Linda went to the door and shouted downstairs, then came back to sit opposite

Meg, knees neatly together. They were in what Linda called 'the lounge', a room with rather startling red walls. It had probably once been a grand drawing room but now the paintwork was peeling and the marble fireplace had been boarded up and replaced by a three-bar electric heater. Two faded sofas faced a large television set. Only the sea view, displayed in the French windows, was unchanging and magnificent.

'When did you suspect something was wrong?' asked Meg.

'I didn't see Cherry on Monday,' said Linda, 'but that wasn't strange in itself. I thought she was probably rehearsing. She didn't come down to supper but I just thought that she might be out with friends or a boyfriend.'

'Did she have a boyfriend that you knew of?'

'No, but I didn't know her that well. She'd only been here a few days. Some of the others – Bigg and Small, Ida – are regulars. But Cherry hadn't been in the business that long.' Linda dabbed her eyes with a small lace hankie.

'Do you know what Cherry did before becoming a magician's assistant?'

'She said something about working in a shop. She was from up north somewhere. Sorry, I'm not being much help. I try to chat to the guests but I don't want to pry.'

'Let's go back to Monday,' said Meg. 'When did you first start to worry?'

'It was the smell,' said Linda apologetically.

The miasma still pervaded the house, even though

Cherry's room was, at this very moment, being cleaned by two stalwarts sent from the police station. The sea breeze, which made the velvet curtains rise like sails, couldn't entirely blow it away.

'I smelt something on Monday night,' said Linda. 'But I thought it was the drains. Sorry, I know that's horrible . . .'

'When did you think it might be something else?'

'This morning the smell was still there. It seemed to be worst on the second floor landing and I thought it was coming from Cherry's room. I knocked and there was no answer. I shouted Cherry's name. There were a few of us gathered there by then. Me, Annie, Ida, Bigg and Small – the double act – Mario Fontana, the singer. Eventually I got my key and opened the door. She was on the floor . . .'

Linda stopped and blinked.

'Take your time,' said Meg.

'There was blood on the bed and on the carpet,' said Linda, 'and the smell . . . I almost fainted. Ida caught me. Mario brought me a glass of water. Then I pulled myself together and telephoned the police.'

The call had come in at eight-thirty. Meg and the DI had been on the doorstep at eight-forty-five. Now, according to the clock on the mantelpiece, it was half past ten.

'Did you telephone anyone else?'

'I rang Cherry's partner, Ted. I thought he might know her next of kin but he said he didn't. Then he rang off. Useless article. Probably drunk.'

Ted English was top of Meg's list of suspects. She asked when Linda last saw Cherry.

'It must have been Sunday lunchtime. I always do a roast. Cherry came to the table but she didn't eat much. She said she had a headache and didn't feel well. She went back to her room before dessert.'

'Did you see her again that day?'

'No. I put out sandwiches and cocoa at six but not everyone comes down for that. And, as Cherry said she was ill . . .'

Solomon Carter thought Cherry had been killed on Sunday night, something about blood clots, room temperature and decomposition of the body. The DI had gone quite green listening to him. Meg asked if Linda had seen anyone strange entering the house.

'No, but people are free to come and go. I don't lock the front door until about midnight. It's not like some lodging houses. I mean, we're not in the fifties now. Things have changed. I'm a modern woman. I don't care who my guests have in their rooms.'

Meg was all for being a modern woman but this liberal attitude was going to make the investigation more difficult.

'Can you make me a list of all your lodgers? Everyone who was here on Sunday and Monday?'

'Okey-dokey,' said Linda. Then, without warning, her face crumbled. 'It's just so awful . . . poor Cherry.'

Annie, entering with the tea, looked accusingly at Meg.

*

'She's beautiful,' said Max.

The baby was still crumpled and cross-looking but, even so, Max thought he could see Ruby's perfect features there. He remembered when his son Rocco was born, finally being allowed onto the ward and seeing Lydia holding him like a Madonna. Max had cried then, for almost the first time since adulthood. Of course, he hadn't been there for Ruby's birth, hadn't even known of her existence until she was twenty and applied to be his assistant. Back to magicians' assistants again. Surreptitiously, Max crossed his fingers to ward off the evil eye.

'Has she got a name yet?'

'Poppy,' said Ruby, reaching out to reclaim her daughter.

'Poppy?'

'Yes. It's nice, isn't it? Goes well with Ruby. Dex wanted Marguerite after his mother. Imagine!'

'Imagine,' said Max. He would have preferred Marguerite. 'How is Dex?' he asked.

'Oh, fine. They don't let fathers in until the next day but he stayed here all night, sleeping in the corridor. He whistled our favourite tune so I'd know he was there. When he saw her, he cried.'

Max felt a wave of fellow-feeling for the man who wasn't quite his son-in-law. Dex Dexter might be divorced with two children but he loved Ruby. If it had been up to him, they would be married by now. He wondered how the nurses had treated Ruby, knowing that she was unmarried and that the father of her baby was a black jazz musician. Of course, Ruby was famous and fame trumped most things. Max wasn't sure about prejudice though.

He asked about the care in the hospital. 'Oh, they've been nice enough,' said Ruby. 'Asking for my autograph and all that. I did hear two of the nurses speculating on how dark the baby's skin would be though.'

Poppy's skin was the colour of weak tea. Her eyes were tightly closed but Max assumed they would be brown like Ruby's. And like his. People had often speculated that Max – with his dark hair and Italian complexion – might have 'black blood somewhere'. But Max's blood was the same colour as everyone else's.

The private room was full of flowers. Max could see a gigantic bunch of lilies and wondered if they were from Dex. Max didn't like lilies. He liked to boast that, unlike most pros, he wasn't superstitious, but lilies were ill-starred flowers. By dint of squinting, Max read the card on some pink roses. *All love, Mummy and Daddy.* Gavin French wasn't Ruby's father, Max thought, with a surprising stab of anger. But he was pleased that Ruby's mother had sent flowers. She hadn't been wild about the whole illegitimate baby thing either.

'Has Emerald been to see you?' he asked.

'Yes,' said Ruby. 'She came yesterday. She said that Poppy looked like her.'

'I think that's a good sign.' Emerald wasn't Max's biggest fan, something to do with getting pregnant by him at the age of twenty-two, but Max hoped that the slight rift with Ruby would be healed.

'I think so too,' said Ruby, but she didn't seem too concerned. There was something self-sufficient about Ruby, sitting up in bed in her gorgeous dressing gown trimmed with swansdown, cradling her baby in her arms. Max sensed that she didn't care much what he, Emerald or even Dex thought. It was Ruby and Poppy now.

Feeling awkward, though he couldn't have said why, Max said, 'Do you remember an act called The Great Deceiver?'

'Magician?' said Ruby. 'A bit seedy? I think I met him in Hastings once, when I was working with Ray. I remember, because that was the first time I met Pal.'

'I saw Pal on the television recently.'

'Please,' said Ruby, with a sudden shiver. 'Not in front of my daughter.'

On cue, Poppy opened her eyes and started to cry.

CHAPTER 3

Superintendent Edgar Stephens looked at the list in front of him.

Linda Knight – landlady
Ida Lupin – strongwoman
Geoffrey Bigg – comedian
Perry Small – comedian
Mario Fontana (aka John Lomax) – singer
Annie Smith – live-in maid

The names, with their aliases and job descriptions, brought on an unexpected wave of nostalgia. They evoked the glory days of variety: playbills, 'Sold Out' boards outside theatres, Max Mephisto's name in lights. Those acts had almost disappeared now, existing only in nostalgic TV programmes like *The Good Old Days*. Even the show on the pier was billed as 'Old-fashioned family fun'. It claimed to be touring the country. Edgar wondered if Cherry's death would end the run before it had begun.

'Bigg and Small were the same size,' said Meg. 'It was a bit of a shock.'

WDC Meg Connolly could never remember that, when she was with superior officers, she was not meant to speak until spoken to. Edgar didn't mind much but Bob's ears went red, always a sign of embarrassment. But Edgar was always interested in what Meg had to say and besides, if they followed protocol, she wouldn't get to speak at all because everyone in the room outranked her, apart from her fellow DC, Danny Black. The other officer present was an older sergeant called Barker. He'd once been part of a team with DS O'Neill, a relic of the bad old days of policing, who was rumoured to enjoy beating up suspects as well as leering at all the women in the station. Thank goodness O'Neill had retired at the end of last year, not without some persuasion from Edgar. Barker was far less objectionable without him.

'Are these all the people resident in the Marine Parade house?' asked Edgar.

'Yes,' said Bob, 'but the landlady said she didn't keep tabs on who came and went. She said she was modern that way.' Bob sniffed. Although he was only thirty-seven, nine years younger than Edgar, Bob clearly disapproved of the modern world. The sixties had come too late for him. He was set in his ways now.

'What about Cherry's partner, Ted English? Have you been able to contact him?'

'DC Black went to his digs,' says Bob, 'but Mr English is apparently in London for the day.'

'He went to London as soon as he heard that his assistant had been murdered,' said Edgar. 'That sounds suspicious to me.'

'He'll have to be back for tonight's performance,' says Bob.

'The show's still going on?' Edgar knew that pros were a tough breed but this seemed to be bordering on the tasteless.

'Apparently so.' Bob at his most wooden.

'We'll send someone to the theatre,' said Edgar.

'Can I go?' asked Meg.

Edgar approved of Meg's keenness but this sounded a bit too much like she wanted a treat. Besides, it might be dangerous for her to go on her own. Edgar remembered sending Emma to watch a variety show once, in similar circumstances. She had nearly died as a result.

'No. DS Barker can go.' To soften this snub, he asked Meg to summarise her interviews with the occupants of number 84 Marine Parade.

'They were all in the house for Sunday lunch,' said Meg. 'Then Bigg and Small went for a walk. Ida Lupin went to see her mother in Worthing. Mario Fontana – he's not Italian, by the way – took a bus to Beachy Head. To see the view, apparently. They were all back in the house by six p.m. when Linda Knight served sandwiches. Cherry didn't appear but Linda didn't think that was odd because she'd said she had a headache earlier.'

'And no one saw a stranger entering the house?'

'No. Mario said that he heard voices in Ida's bedroom but that could have been the wireless. I checked and she has a set.'

'Might be worth following up all the same,' said Edgar. 'What time did Ida get back from Worthing?'

Meg consulted her notes. 'She said she got back about five but Mario heard voices at around four, he said.'

'And no one heard a girl being murdered?' said Bob, sounding personally offended, as he often did when confronted with terrible events. 'When did Carter think the attack occurred?'

'Between nine and midnight.' Edgar looked at his notes. 'I think that's as specific as he can get. It does seem strange that no one heard anything.'

'Most of them watched television after supper,' said Meg. 'That was probably quite loud. My dad always turns the volume all the way up. And there's the wireless too.'

'If the assailant took the girl by surprise,' said Barker, 'she might not have had time to cry out.'

This was a valid, if unsettling, point.

'Let's check on them all again,' said Edgar. 'Mario's bus trip sounds a bit odd too. Talk to the bus company. See if there are any witnesses. Anything from the scene, DI Willis?'

Edgar knew that his team teased him for his preoccupation with the 'scene'. He always insisted on taking photographs and dusting any available surface with fingerprint powder. 'One day,' he told his sceptical officers, 'we'll be able to identify a murderer by a single hair.'

'A couple of fingerprints were found,' said Bob. 'We'll match them against the files.'

Edgar had watched the fingerprint experts at work, leaning over the black-and-white photos with a magnifying glass, examining loops, whorls and arches. It was fascinating but, unless they had a match on file, ultimately pointless.

'Murder weapon?'

'Carter thinks it was a kitchen knife. Not found at the scene.'

'I checked with Annie, the live-in maid who does the cooking,' chipped in Meg, 'and she said nothing was missing from the kitchen.'

'Any news on next of kin?' Edgar asked Bob.

'The cleaners found a letter from her parents in Cherry's room,' said Bob. 'They live in Cheshire. The local police will be with them now.'

'Poor people,' said Edgar. He could just imagine the encounter. 'You're too sensitive,' his mother used to tell him and, sadly, this trait didn't seem to improve with age.

When his officers had left the room, Edgar's secretary, Rita, told him that Max Mephisto had telephoned. Edgar was mildly intrigued. He wondered if Max was calling to tell him that Ruby had had her baby. That didn't seem likely though. Edgar had once been engaged to Ruby but this episode was rarely mentioned by any of the people involved. Edgar was happily married to Emma, his former DS, with whom he had three children. Ruby had become a star and now seemed to be having a baby without the complication of a husband.

'Max. Sorry to miss you.'

'Your secretary said you were in an important meeting.'

'Rita likes to make everything sound dramatic.'

'Was your meeting about the murder of a girl called Cherry Underwood?'

'How the hell did you know that?' People often said that Max had magic powers but Edgar had never seen proof of it before.

'Cherry's stage partner, a man called Ted English, came to my flat today. He's convinced that he's the main suspect.'

'I'm certainly anxious to speak to Mr English,' said Edgar.

'That's why I'm calling. Ted said that he was getting the one-thirty back to Brighton from Victoria.'

Edgar looked at his watch. Two o'clock. 'I'll send an officer to the station.'

'Are you going to arrest him?'

'Not immediately. As I said, I'd like to talk to him. What sort of a man is he?'

'Inoffensive, I'd say. Got a reputation for drinking a bit too much. Ruby described him as seedy. I saw her this morning. Did you know she'd had her baby? A girl called Poppy.'

'I didn't know. Do pass on my congratulations. Mine and Emma's.'

'I will. She seems very happy. But Ruby reminded me that Ted – his stage name is The Great Deceiver – was part of a group of magicians that worked the south coast circuit. The Great Raymondo was another one.'

'They all like to call themselves "the great", don't they? Like dear old Diablo.'

'He was great, in his way. Have you ever heard of a man called Gordon Palgrave? Known as Pal?'

'That rings a bell.'

'He's reinvented himself as a television presenter but he used to be a magician. And he's a very nasty piece of work. Lots of rumours about forcing himself on young girls, promising to make them famous if they slept with him. That sort of thing.'

'He sounds vile.'

'He is. I just thought, if Ted was part of that set, he might not be as innocuous as I thought.'

'I wonder why Ted came to you? It seems like he took the train to London as soon as he heard about Cherry.'

'Misdirection,' said Max. 'He is a magician, after all.'

CHAPTER 4

Meg was disappointed with her first sight of Ted English. He came into the station flanked by Danny and DS Barker looking, whatever the DI said, very much like he was under arrest. English was a thin man with sparse grey hair. His nose was dripping and he looked too scared of his escort to wipe it surreptitiously on his sleeve. Barker hustled the magician into the interview room. Meg hoped that they let him have a handkerchief.

Meg was still in the incident room, typing up the morning's interviews, when English was ushered out, this time escorted by Danny alone, who winked at Meg as he passed. She hoped that she wasn't blushing. It wasn't that she fancied Danny, she told herself, it was that her fair skin coloured very easily. 'You're a typical Irish colleen,' DS O'Neill used to say, before moving on to other, more personal, remarks. Meg, along with every other female in the building, was delighted when he retired.

The DI, who'd been sitting in on the interview, came out

to say that Ted English hadn't been charged with anything but had been advised not to leave the area.

'He can't,' said Meg. 'The show's on the pier this evening.'

The DI gave her a look. 'I'm aware, WDC Connolly. DS Barker will be attending.'

Barker looked smug. 'He seemed a shifty individual to me, sir,' he said.

'And English had no real alibi for Sunday night,' said the DI. 'Said he went back to his lodgings but no one there could vouch for that. We'll have to keep an eye on him.'

'Surveillance?' Danny sat up straighter.

'Let's keep him under observation,' said the DI. 'No need to make it a secret operation either. If we station a panda car outside his lodgings, it'll make Friend Ted nervous and nervous men make mistakes.'

'I wonder who's going to stand in for Cherry tonight?' asked Meg.

'I'll let you know,' said Barker with a wink that felt very different from Danny's earlier.

But maybe Meg had misjudged the older man. When the DI had left, Barker leant over Meg's desk. 'Want to come to the show tonight? I know the manager. I could get another ticket.'

Meg did want to. Very much.

Edgar arrived home to find his wife and three children in front of the television. Edgar had initially been against buying a set but, last year, a stint of enforced babysitting had convinced him of the benefits of children's TV. But it was unusual to see the whole family – Emma, ten-year-old Marianne, eight-year-old Sophie and Jonathan, not yet three – watching together at seven p.m. Even the baby was staring transfixed at the screen as a man with a startling white quiff was shouting, 'Hug or Hit!'

'Hallo,' said Edgar.

Only Emma turned and smiled.

'Hit!' shouted Marianne.

'Hug!' yelled Sophie in the falsetto that meant she was on the verge of laughter or tears.

'Hit! Hit! Hit!' chanted Jonathan.

As Edgar watched, the man with the quiff approached a nervous-looking woman in a miniskirt. He was carrying a large rubber hammer. The studio was full of people yelling and strobe lights flashing on and off. The man turned and faced the camera. He smiled and, to Edgar's mind, it was the most sinister facial expression he had ever seen. A scroll appeared in the background saying, 'HUG'. The man advanced on the woman and wrapped both arms round her. The audience cheered.

'What on earth's this?' said Edgar.

'*Hug or Hit*,' said Marianne, in the world-weary tone she had recently perfected.

'It's Pal's show,' said Emma, standing up. 'There's a singer – usually a woman – and the audience decides whether Pal hugs her or hits her with the hammer.'

The name Pal was striking its own hammer peal in Edgar's head.

'He looks an odd character,' he said. The man still had one arm round the woman as the credits rolled.

'Oh, he's foul,' said Emma equably. 'Do you want your supper? We've had ours.'

Emma bribed the girls to give Jonathan his bath and went downstairs to heat up the leftover hotpot. Watching his wife moving, slightly abstractedly, around the basement kitchen, Edgar remembered where he'd first heard of Pal. He was the ex-magician that Max had called 'a nasty piece of work'. He told Emma as she put the gravy-stained plate in front of him.

'Careful. It's hot. Pal certainly seems a bit odd. That hair, for one thing. It's snow white, you know. He dyed it so that it looks better on TV.'

'Max said he was part of a rather seedy group of magicians.'

'Is this linked to the murder?' said Emma. 'The one in Marine Parade. Sam was telling me about it.'

There had been nothing about Cherry's death in the papers yet but Sam, Emma's partner in the detective agency, was a freelance journalist who always knew the stories before they made it into print.

'Possibly.' Edgar couldn't see any point in denying it. 'The dead girl was a magician's assistant.'

'Like Ruby was,' said Emma.

'Oh, Ruby's had her baby,' said Edgar. 'Max told me. A girl. I've forgotten the name.'

'That's wonderful.' Emma looked genuinely pleased. Whatever her past feelings towards Edgar's ex-fiancée, the two women now got on rather well. 'We must send flowers.'

'Max is a grandfather,' said Edgar. 'I wonder what he thinks about that?'

'He'll hate it but he'll carry it off all right,' said Emma. 'I wonder whether Ruby will get a nanny. I'm sure she'll want to go back to acting and I know she's not living with Dex.'

Edgar often wondered whether Emma secretly wanted a nanny. She'd had one herself and, while she always insisted that she wanted to bring her children up without live-in help, Edgar noticed that references to 'Dear old Brownie' were more frequent these days.

A yell and a splash came from upstairs. Emma went to investigate and, almost immediately, the telephone started ringing from the hall. Before Edgar could swallow his scalding mouthful, Marianne had galloped downstairs and Edgar heard her say, 'Brighton 28097.' Marianne loved answering the phone.

Edgar cooled his mouth with some water and stood up. But Marianne was shouting, in a very different voice, 'Mum! It's Sam!'

That meant the call would take a long time. Edgar finished his supper and went into the kitchen to wash up. He'd just finished when Emma appeared in the doorway.

'What did Sam want?' Edgar dried his hands on a tea towel.

'Cherry Underwood's father has just rung her. He wants us to take the case. To find her murderer.'

CHAPTER 5

Meg sat in the bedroom she shared with her sisters, Aisling and Collette, and surveyed their joint wardrobe without enthusiasm. What on earth could she wear to the theatre tonight? Eighteen-year-old Aisling was more fashionable but she was quite a bit shorter than Meg, who was almost six foot. Aisling's minis would look downright indecent on Meg. Collette was only twelve so she didn't count and, anyway, all her clothes were hand-me-downs from her sisters. Meg's third of the wardrobe was full of slacks and boring skirts, most of which had their hems hanging down or needed dry-cleaning. The only outfit that was even slightly smart was the black dress she'd worn to her grandfather's funeral four years ago. She wished that she could go to the show in her uniform but that would rather defeat the object of being undercover.

Meg got out the black dress. It was wool with a high neck and long sleeves. 'You can't go wrong with black,' Meg remembered Emma saying once. Emma had been the first woman detective sergeant in Sussex and was still a legend at Bartholomew Square station. But she was also undeniably posh and presumably had rooms full of theatre-going clothes. It wasn't that Emma looked exactly stylish. Not like Ruby Magic, whom Meg had met once and who often appeared in Aisling's fashion magazines. It was just that Emma always looked like she was wearing the right clothes for the right occasion. Maybe that was just upper-class confidence, something that was in short supply in the Whitehawk council house Meg shared with her parents and three siblings. Before Marie had married and Declan and Patrick moved out, there had been nine of them there. The youngest, Connor, had shared with his brothers but now had a room of his own, aged only ten. 'It's so unfair,' his sisters wailed. 'He's a boy,' their mother had replied inexorably.

The dress seemed a lot tighter than it had four years ago. Meg didn't think she'd got fatter but maybe she'd 'filled out' as the woman in the brassiere-fitting department of Hanningtons once put it, causing Aisling to collapse into giggles. Meg thought of herself as flat-chested – unlike Aisling – but maybe she wasn't really. Still, at least the dress was long enough. Meg had already reached this height at the age of thirteen, which had made her last years at school rather trying.

Meg added black tights and her flat, everyday shoes. She wished she had a brooch or one of those scarves that women like Emma are born wearing. She compensated by putting her hair in a bun and using some of Aisling's mascara and lipstick. Her face, in the bathroom mirror, didn't look too bad but she couldn't see the rest of herself. Her mother regarded full-length mirrors as self-indulgent, if not actually sinful.

'That's my lipstick,' said Aisling, when Meg presented herself in the kitchen.

'You shouldn't be wearing make-up at your age,' said Meg's mother, Mary, from the gas stove. 'I like to see young women as God intended them.'

'Naked?' said Aisling. 'Like Adam and Eve before the Fall?' She was the clever one and went to the grammar school. She was about to take her A levels, which in itself seemed an amazing achievement.

Connor and Collette laughed. Padre Pio, the budgerigar, joined in. Mary waved her spoon at all of them, spattering a few drops of gravy like holy water.

'If that's how you're going to talk at university, Aisling,' said Mary, 'you'd be better off entering a convent. The Little Sisters of Mercy have a vacancy, I believe.'

'God forbid,' said Aisling.

'Aye,' said Mary. 'Very likely He does. Leave Meg alone. She looks very respectable. You can borrow my good green coat, love. It's still cold in the evenings.'

Respectable, thought Meg, hunting for the coat in the cupboard under the stairs. She hadn't thought she looked that bad.

*

DS Barker didn't comment on the dress, or the coat, but it would have seemed strange if he had. Barker didn't wear uniform for work so he looked the same as usual, tall and thin with teeth that always looked slightly too big for his mouth. His nickname at the station was 'Chubby' but Meg had never asked why. Hers was 'Long Meg', which was apparently the name of an ancient witch who got turned to stone. Could have been worse, she supposed.

At first they stood in the lobby, not speaking, and Meg wondered if they were going to spend the whole evening in silence. Then Barker turned and walked away. Just when Meg decided that he'd abandoned her, he appeared again, carrying a programme and two red drinks.

'Thank you very much,' said Meg. The programme was a pound so this was surprisingly generous. She thought of a music hall song her dad used to sing about a 'dirty dog' stealing a man's girl while he went to get the 'nuts and the programme'. She giggled and Barker asked what was funny.

'Nothing. What's the drink?'

'Bloody Mary. Get it down you. The show's about to start.'

Meg's mother said 'Bloody' was a wicked swearword because it was a shortening of 'by Our Lady'. Also, 'Bloody Mary' was the disrespectful title Protestants used for Good Queen Mary, who'd restored the Catholic faith after Henry VIII. All these factors made Meg a little nervous of the drink but she took a cautious sip. It tasted awful, like juice that had gone off. Should she say something?

'What's in it?' she asked.

'Just tomato juice. Drink up, there's a good girl.'

It must be on the turn, like the NHS-supplied welfare orange juice Meg used to have as a child when it got left in the sun. Meg tried not to breathe in as she drained the glass. She didn't want to appear rude.

'Let's go,' said Barker, putting his empty glass on a nearby ledge.

Meg followed him, feeling slightly unsteady. Declan was always saying that the piers would collapse into the sea one day. She hoped it wouldn't happen tonight.

Meg had been to the Palace Pier Theatre before. When she was six, a Catholic charity called the Knights of St Columba had organised a trip to the pantomime for local children who might not otherwise have afforded such a treat. Meg, Declan and Patrick had actually been driven into Brighton by their parish priest, Father Costello. Aisling was too young and Collette and Connor hadn't even been born yet. The show was *Aladdin*, starring Max Mephisto as Abanazar. Meg could still remember the delicious thrill of fear when the wizard appeared on stage, firecrackers exploding from his voluminous sleeves. Perhaps that was why she was still a bit scared of Max.

The theatre was imposing too, with its intricate metal archways – now rather rusty – and minarets designed to echo the famous Pavilion. Inside, it was easy to forget that you were suspended over the sea. It was a proper auditorium, with balconies and gilt carvings and velvet curtains. Meg and Barker made their way through the excited crowds. They were in the first row of the circle. 'Lou said we'd have a good view here,' said Barker. 'It's wonderful,' said Meg. She was pretty sure that the Knights had been in the cheaper seats.

The orchestra was playing 'Sussex by the Sea' and Meg found herself swaying to the music. She really must get a grip and behave more like a policewoman. Barker didn't seem to mind though. 'They play this at Albion matches,' he said. 'It's a grand tune.'

But soon the lights dimmed and a voice offstage intoned, 'And now – courtesy of Larry Buxton Enterprises – a night of good old-fashioned entertainment. Please welcome the stars of the show!'

The curtains opened and the stage was suddenly full of people, waving as the band played 'Happy Days Are Here Again'. Meg thought she saw Bigg and Small but the other stars were unrecognisable under the lights. They trooped off, still waving, and a more soulful tune began. Meg opened her programme and managed to make out the first act: The Dancing Snowflakes.

It was very pretty, thought Meg. The stage was dark apart from shapes like lace doilies projected onto the backcloth. The dancers, in white floaty ballet skirts, swayed and twirled. Meg clapped enthusiastically at the end but Barker remained slumped in his seat. Perhaps ballet wasn't his thing. Aisling had once longed for ballet lessons but it was an 'extra' at school so their parents couldn't afford it.

Next to perform was Mario Fontana. He had a loud, operatic voice and, when not singing, spoke in what was obviously meant to be an Italian accent. Meg, who had interviewed John Lomax yesterday, found this rather disturbing. Lomax was from Birmingham, he'd told Meg, and he'd spoken in a flat adenoidal way that reminded Meg of Liverpool, a town she'd visited last year. Fontana got a big hand for his final number '*O Sole Mio*' and departed blowing kisses and shouting, '*Bella! Bella!*'

Next, a large cabinet was wheeled onto the stage and, accompanied by a drum roll, the offstage voice announced: 'And now, for your delectation and wonderment, The Great Deceiver!' When the small man in a dinner jacket appeared, there was a ripple of laughter. Did Ted English mean his appearance to be an anticlimax? wondered Meg. There was no sign that the act was meant to be funny. She watched closely. After all, the magician was their number one suspect. Next to her, Sergeant Barker also sat up straighter.

The Great Deceiver started off with a few card tricks that were visible only to the front rows. Then he juggled with some balls before making them disappear one by one. This was quite clever but the flashes of light and clashing of cymbals distracted Meg, making it hard to concentrate on what was happening. Then, to another drum roll, the magician asked the audience to applaud his 'lovely assistant'. Meg leant so far forward that she was peering over the edge of the parapet. A woman marched onto the stage. She had long blonde hair and her figure, in a spangled dress, was curvaceous, but she was at least a head taller than English. Another ripple of laughter. Something about the woman seemed familiar to Meg. But where would she have met such a glamorous creature?

After a few twirls, the woman went into the cabinet and Ted, with obvious effort, revolved it. Then – drums again – the door was opened to show that it was empty. This time there was genuine applause, generous enough to get the man and his wardrobe offstage. There was no sign of his assistant.

The curtains closed for the interval. 'What do you think?' asked Barker.

'I liked the dancers,' said Meg, 'and it was quite clever how he made the girl disappear.'

'She was an Amazon, if you like,' said Barker. 'Did you know that Amazon warrior women used to cut their tits off? Want another drink?'

'No thank you,' said Meg. She couldn't face another glass of the awful red stuff. Also, did he just say 'tits'?

'Go on,' said Barker. 'It's your night off.'

This wasn't, strictly speaking, true. As far as Meg was concerned, she was still working. But she was worried about offending her colleague. Maybe you always had to accept a drink if one was offered? Barker was looking at her in a strange way. She couldn't work out if he was angry or not.

'Thank you very much,' she said. 'But could I have lemonade this time, please?'

Barker pushed his way through the crowds to the bar, leaving Meg standing by the door. The small space seemed very full of people, all talking in loud confident voices.

'Traditional entertainment . . .'

'Rather trite, to my mind . . .'

'Definitely not a lyrical tenor . . .'

'Quite an Amazon . . .'

There was that word again. Meg didn't think she'd ever heard it before. She flattened herself against the wall and observed the drinkers. There had been a few families in the audience but here it was all older people, mostly very well-dressed. No one her age and, she was willing to bet, no one from Whitehawk either. There were some fur coats and quite a few bow ties. People from Hove, she guessed. Then Barker was back with two more Bloody Marys. Meg's heart sank even as she thanked him.

'Here's mud in your eye,' said Barker.

Was that some kind of toast? 'And in yours,' said Meg, trying to be polite. She took a sip. It tasted even worse this time.

'I suppose this is all new to you,' said Barker. 'The theatre and all that.'

'I came here when I was six,' said Meg. 'Me and my brothers.'

Barker made no answer to this so Meg thought she'd better carry on the conversation.

'Have you got any brothers and sisters?'

Barker drained his glass. 'Got a sister but I haven't seen her for years. I bet you've got a big family. Mick used to say you were typically Irish.'

Mick was DS O'Neill's first name. Meg could just imagine the way he'd said this. She was saved from answering by the bell ringing for the second half.

'Drink up,' said Barker.

Meg managed to swallow the rest of her drink but, for a second, was genuinely worried that she'd be sick. The bar, with its red walls and gold furniture, seemed to spin like the waltzer on the pier. She had to grab Barker's arm to stop herself falling. To her surprise, he patted her hand. 'Good girl. Let's get back to our seats now.'

The orchestra was playing as they edged their way back along the row. Then the curtains rose and the disembodied voice was intoning, 'Please welcome – Ida the Strongwoman.' A woman in a fur bikini strode onto the stage. It was her walk that gave her away. Meg looked at Barker. 'That's her!' 'Shh,' said someone in the row behind. Meg's whisper must have been louder than she intended. But there was no doubt that Ida had done a quick change from being English's lovely assistant.

Her act was better than his. She tore up telephone directories and called for volunteers from the audience and then lifted them into the air. There was lots of laughter and, when she lifted a young man right above her head, actual gasps. Ida left the stage to the loudest applause yet. The dancers then appeared again, this time dressed as Cossacks, doing a lot of crouching and kicking out their legs with their arms folded. Then there were two gymnasts who were proficient without being very entertaining. Next was a man who sang while riding a unicycle. Meg was starting to feel rather dazed, or maybe it was the effect of the single, spinning wheel. She couldn't really see the point of the act. You couldn't do it yourself but why would you want to?

The final act was Bigg and Small. Meg assumed it was the coincidence of the names that had brought the comedians together because, as she had pointed out earlier, they were exactly the same size. The audience loved them though and shouted out the punchlines to their jokes. Meg didn't follow it very well. Her head was aching now and her stomach was churning. She was relieved when the show was over and they were singing the national anthem.

Outside, the fresh air made her feel slightly better. Lights were twinkling in the arcades but the sea was dark on either side of them. It must have rained while they were in the theatre because the planks were slippery. Meg tried to walk in a straight line but she must have been staggering because Barker took hold of her arm and steered her through the crowd.

'Thanks so much,' said Meg, when they reached the

pavement. 'I've had a lovely evening. My bus stop's over there.' She pointed in the general direction of the Aquarium.

'I'll give you a lift home,' said Barker. 'I'm parked in the Old Steine.'

Meg wanted to say no but somehow she seemed incapable of resisting, as if her willpower had leaked away with the remains of the vile red drink. Besides, Barker was still holding her arm. He manoeuvred her across the main road, past the Albion Hotel and into one of the dark alleyways that led to the bus station in Pool Valley. Was Barker parked here, amongst the Southdown buses? Meg turned to ask the question and, to her horror, saw Barker's large teeth approaching her face.

'Give us a kiss,' he said throatily.

'No!' Meg backed away and found herself pushed up against a brick wall. Barker's lips were on hers and his hand was fumbling under Mum's good green coat. Thinking of her mother gave Meg extra strength. She pushed harder and managed to get Barker's face a few inches away.

'Prick tease,' said Barker, who seemed to find her resistance amusing. He lunged again and this time managed to get his hand under her dress.

Something Declan had once told her came into Meg's head. Swiftly she raised her knee, aiming it between Barker's legs. Now he roared with real anger. 'Bitch!' But he was also doubled up in pain so Meg made good her escape.

Her mind had cleared and her one thought was getting as far away from her colleague as possible. She careered through the narrow streets, twisting and turning until she reached the bus terminus. It felt like sanctuary; lights glowing in the transport café and in the parked green vehicles, drivers and conductors calling out to each other. The 1A to Whitehawk was waiting there, like a faithful charger. Although not, strictly speaking, allowed to let passengers on, the driver opened the doors for Meg. This act of kindness made her cry all the way home.

CHAPTER 6

For the first time in her working life, Meg considered pretending to be ill. 'Pulling a sickie,' her brothers called it. Sometimes, at school, she'd said she had a headache to get out of French but Madame Smith just used to tell her to walk round the field and come back to class. Her mother was even less tolerant of illness and injury. 'Offer up your suffering,' she'd say, if you fell and hurt yourself. 'Our Blessed Lord fell three times on the way to Calgary.'

But Jesus did not have to face a man who had tried to kiss him. Although didn't Judas kiss Jesus just before he betrayed Him to the Romans? Last night felt like a betrayal too. *Made a pass.* Is that what DS Barker had done? It sounded too trivial, too lacking in contact. Ships that pass in the night. Meg wondered whether she should ask Aisling's advice. Her sister read lots of magazines. She might be able to reassure Meg that what happened last night was nothing to worry about it. 'Goodness, Meg, you are slow,' she imagined Aisling saying. 'That sort of thing happens all the time in the modern world.' No, she couldn't give her younger sister the chance of talking to her like that.

She did, however, ask Aisling who, or what, Amazons were.

'They were warrior women,' said Aisling, her mouth full of toast. 'They used to ride into battle like men. Legend has it that . . .' Aisling lowered her voice, 'they cut off their right breasts because that made it easier to use a bow and arrow.'

Both Aisling and Meg glanced at their mother, hoping she hadn't heard, but Mary was tempting Padre Pio with a piece of cuttlefish.

'Come on, *mo chuisle*. There's a good boy.' Mary never used Irish endearments on her children but, as she often said, the pet bird caused her less trouble.

Cutting off their right breasts. That's what Barker had said, though he'd used a different word. Even with this gory detail, Meg decided she liked the idea of the warrior women. If they could ride into battle, she could face DS Barker.

But, as soon as she saw him, her courage failed. Barker was talking to the desk sergeant in the lobby as Meg came into the station. They stopped their conversation as she entered. She wanted to say Good morning, in a breezy tone, the way Emma Holmes would say it, but her tongue seemed to be stuck to the roof of her mouth.

'Young girls today,' she heard the desk sergeant say. 'No manners.'

As Meg descended the stairs to the CID room, she heard footsteps behind her. She could feel her heart beating faster but she didn't look round. At the foot of the staircase, her pursuer caught her arm.

'High and mighty this morning, aren't we?' said DS Barker.

'Let me go,' said Meg.

Barker swung her round to face him. 'Let's get this straight, girlie. If you complain about me, I'll tell the super that you went to the theatre against his orders. And you'll get the sack.'

Once again, his face, and his horrid teeth, were very close to hers. A blob of spittle hit Meg's lapel. Using all her Amazonian strength, she shook him off, and marched into the women's cloakroom.

Emma paused at the doors of the Bartholomew Square police station. She'd worked there for five years and, in that time, she'd caught a child murderer, prevented a terrorist attack and almost been killed herself. She'd had to give up work when she married Edgar, who'd been her boss. She still resented this, just as she resented the fact that Bob, who'd been her friend and colleague, had progressed smoothly through the ranks to become Detective Inspector. Acquiring a wife and children had not slowed Bob's ascent. They'd accelerated it, if anything, establishing Bob as a family man, steady and respectable. He'd even taken up golf.

But now Emma was back. She and her journalist friend, Sam Collins, had set up a detective agency and had already solved several cases. She had arranged to meet Bob today to get some background on the Cherry Underwood murder. It would be a slightly tricky meeting, she knew. Bob wouldn't want any interference with the police investigation but, on the other hand, Emma thought he might welcome any insights she could offer. She'd been the one with the ideas when they worked together. Not that Bob was stupid. He was an astute and careful police officer. It was just that he distrusted brilliance on principle.

'How did Cherry's parents find out about us?' Emma had asked Sam last night.

'Cherry's mother, Dolores, was on the stage herself. She knows Verity Malone.'

Last year, Emma and Sam had investigated the murder of Verity's husband, the theatrical impresario Bert Billington. The case had left Emma with a few unanswered questions but Verity had been delighted with Holmes and Collins. She was a supporter of the Women's Liberation Movement and, in her words, liked to surround herself with clever females. Emma could understand why Verity had recommended them but not why Cherry's parents felt the need to employ a private detective agency.

'They think the police will be biased,' said Sam. 'Apparently Ted English, Cherry's stage partner, kept going on about being friends with Max. And they know that Max is friends with the chief superintendent.'

'Do they know that I'm married to the chief super?' asked Emma.

'I told them,' said Sam. 'I felt they ought to know. But it didn't put them off. If anything, it made them think we'd have inside information.'

So that was why Emma was visiting her old workplace. She walked through the lobby, which was part of the town hall and had smart chequerboard tiles and statues in niches. 'Good morning,' she called out to the desk sergeant, who obviously recognised her. But, as Emma descended the steps to the subterranean police headquarters, she entered a different world. The smell of damp hit her with a blast of nostalgia: shivering in front of an electric fire knowing that snow was falling outside and two children were missing; watching Ruby sashay her way into Edgar's office; working alone at night with the building's ghosts all around her. The offices and cells had actually been condemned in the 1930s. Edgar said that they were going to move to new headquarters soon but Emma would believe that when she saw it.

Edgar was at an area commanders' meeting in Croydon, which would make things a little less awkward. But, as Emma walked through the open-plan area, one of Bob's more Neanderthal sergeants shouted, 'Well, if it isn't Mrs Super.' Emma ignored him and made her way over to Meg's desk.

'Hi. How are you?'

'OK. How are you? And the kids?' The two women had

become friends after a trip to Liverpool on the trail of Bert Billington's killer. Emma thought that Meg looked rather pale today and there were dark circles under her eyes.

'They're fine,' she said. 'Growing up fast. You must pop in and see them one day.'

'I'd love that. Are you here to see the DI?'

'Yes,' said Emma with a smile. 'Got to keep Bob on his toes.'

Meg laughed, although she looked round rather nervously. The loutish sergeant was leering over at them. Emma longed to tell him to get on with his work (using the upper-class voice that worked well in shops sometimes) but contented herself with a hard stare. Then she said goodbye to Meg and knocked on Bob's door.

'Come.'

'Are you too important now to add the "in"?' said Emma, entering the room and shutting the door behind her.

'I don't know why I said it like that.' It was encouraging that she could still make Bob blush.

'Maybe it was something you saw on TV.'

'Have you just come here to laugh at me, Emma?'

'No, I can do that from the comfort of my own home.'

They were both grinning.

'Would you like a cup of tea?' Bob's hand hovered over his phone as if to summon one of his minions.

'No thanks. Who's that man outside? The one who thinks he's hilarious?'

Bob looked towards the frosted glass in the door. 'Barker.

DS Charlie Barker. They call him Chubby, for some reason. He's all right. Harmless. Not like Mick O'Neill. Remember him? Absolute liability. The super had to lean on him to retire last year.'

'Did he?' Emma didn't always hear about Edgar's ruthless side. Though she knew it existed.

'I shouldn't have said anything.' Bob backtracked immediately.

'I've forgotten it already,' said Emma. 'Let's talk about Cherry Underwood instead.' She gave Bob a wide 'all colleagues together' smile.

'I can't talk about an ongoing murder investigation,' said Bob. 'You know that.'

'As I said on the telephone,' Emma continued, regardless, 'Cherry's parents have asked us to investigate the case. I think it might help both of us if we shared some background information. Obviously, I wouldn't expect you to divulge anything confidential.'

Bob looked sceptical, but maybe he was confused by the word 'divulge'.

Emma thought she would start by offering some information of her own. She got out her notebook. 'Cherry's parents, Dolores and Iain, live in Ellesmere Port. Dolores used to be on the stage. She was a dancer and once appeared in a show with Verity Malone. It was Verity who recommended Sam and me.'

'That makes sense,' said Bob. He'd had his own encounters with the one and only Miss Malone.

'Cherry was twenty-one. She liked dancing and horse-riding and baking cakes with her mum. She went to a grammar school and did fairly well in her O Levels. She left school at sixteen to work in a draper's shop. There she met a man who offered her acting work. She travelled to London and appeared in various slightly dodgy revues. She met Ted English last year and performed as his assistant several times. Her parents were pleased because they thought of Ted as a respectable magician. He'd even been on television. Cherry has an older brother, Michael, and two younger sisters, Susan and Daisy. They're devastated by her death.'

She knew that Bob, who had a good heart, would be moved by this last bit.

'It's a terrible crime,' he said. 'All we know is that Cherry booked into 84 Marine Parade on Saturday the ninth of April. She was going to stay for six weeks, for the full run of the show on the pier. Ted English visited her on the morning of Sunday the tenth, supposedly to go through the act. The landlady, Linda Knight, saw him leave but couldn't be sure that he didn't come back. She says that she runs a modern establishment, where people are free to come and go.'

This was said with extreme disapproval.

'And Cherry was found dead yesterday morning? Tuesday morning?'

'That's right. The landlady noticed a smell coming from her room. She forced the door and saw . . . saw the deceased. It was very distressing for her.'

'Have you got a list of the people staying in number 84?'

Bob sighed. 'WDC Connolly has. I suppose you might as well see it.'

'Thank you. Is Ted English your main suspect?'

'Wouldn't he be yours?'

'I suppose so,' said Emma. 'What would be his motivation though?'

'Lust?' suggested Bob. The Old Testament word was typical of him. 'Cherry was a very pretty girl. Ted doesn't have an alibi for the rest of the Sunday. Claims he was alone in his digs but no one there can corroborate that. We're watching him closely. He's still performing in the show. DS Barker went to watch it last night.'

'Bully for DS Barker. Did he note anything of interest?'

'English had a new girl assistant.'

'That was quick work.'

'Exactly. We don't know who she is.'

'Did Cherry have a boyfriend? Anyone pestering her?'

'Not that we know of. Did her parents say anything about a boyfriend?'

'There was a boy back home but they didn't think Cherry had seen him for years. She didn't visit very often.'

'Makes me glad I don't have a daughter,' said Bob although his wife, Betty, had once confided in Emma that she'd like to 'try for a girl' after two boys.

Emma thought of her own daughters, exuberant Marianne and serious Sophie. She prayed that they would never meet a man in a draper's shop and succumb to the bright lights of the stage.

Meg was still working at her desk. From the back, her shoulders had a hunched, defensive look, even though the room was now empty. Emma asked for the list of residents, adding that DI Willis had said she could have it. Meg produced a sheet of paper and Emma copied down the names. Then, on impulse, she said, 'When's your lunch break? Do you want to meet for a sandwich? There's a new coffee bar near my office.'

Meg hesitated and then smiled for the first time. 'I'd love to,' she said.

CHAPTER 7

Emma's office was in The Lanes, a twisty knot of streets between the Pavilion and the Palace Pier. Once the province of dusty antiques shops, over the last ten years the area had been taken over by coffee bars exuding steam and jazz. Holmes and Collins Detective Agency was over a jewellery shop called Midas and Sons. It consisted of one room and a windowless kitchen and sometimes Emma thought it was the place where she was happiest.

Today, Sam was out on a story – she still kept up her freelance journalism – and Emma had the place to herself. She could hear music playing in the hairdresser's below. 'Downtown' by Petula Clark. The sun had finally angled its way round to the window and shone on the old wood of the partners' desk. Emma tidied up – Sam created more mess than the children – and made herself a coffee, then got out her notebook and wrote:

Cherry Underwood Investigation.
Wednesday 13th April
Day 1
Meeting with DI Bob Willis. Ted English is his main suspect . . .

She was so preoccupied that she was almost late to meet Meg. She'd specified Sukey's because it was the nearest. Also it wasn't as noisy as the Cottage on Middle Street or as smoky as the Zodiac, where Emma's friend Astarte sometimes did horoscopes in the evenings. Meg was already there when Emma arrived, looking out of place in her uniform, surrounded by long-haired art students and girls in micro-minis. Emma hoped that she, in her new blue jeans, fitted in better but, when she spoke, she knew that she'd blown her cover. The fashion nowadays was for a transatlantic mumble, punctuated by the word 'man', but Emma was never going to lose her Roedean vowels.

'Sorry I'm late.'

'You're not really. I was early.'

'Have you ordered?' Emma picked up the laminated menu.

'Not yet.'

Meg opted for cheese on toast and Emma for soup. She went up to the counter to order and heard two beehived girls repeating 'Soup of the day', in what was obviously meant to be her voice, before collapsing into giggles.

'You should have let me do the talking,' said Meg.

'In that uniform? You'll have them thinking it's a raid.'

Meg laughed but Emma still thought that she looked strained. Meg's expression was usually one of alertness and interest, her eyes bright, but today she looked down and fiddled with the checked tablecloth. Even her hair looked different. Usually it was fighting to escape from her bun or ponytail. Today, it was flat and lank-looking, pulled back from her face.

'Are you all right?' said Emma.

'Of course,' said Meg.

'Are you sure?'

To Emma's surprise, tears sprang into her companion's eyes. 'It's so stupid,' she said.

'I bet it isn't.'

Meg wiped her eyes with the back of her hand. 'If I tell you, will you swear not to tell the super?'

Emma knew she should say, 'Well, that depends . . .' but, instead, she answered immediately, 'Of course I won't tell him.'

'I went to the show on the pier last night with DS Barker,' said Meg. 'He was the one in the incident room just now. I wasn't meant to go but Sergeant Barker got me a ticket. I thought it was so nice of him. And he was nice to me – he bought me drinks and all that. Then he offered to drive me home. We were walking towards Pool Valley and he . . . he tried to kiss me.'

'Oh my God,' said Emma.

'I said no,' said Meg quickly, as if she was afraid of not being believed. 'But he kept on. So I kicked him in the . . . well . . . somewhere not very nice.'

'Good for you,' said Emma.

'He didn't say anything today,' said Meg. 'And nor did I. It's just . . . I feel so stupid. He must have thought, because he bought the tickets and the drinks, that I'd let him kiss me. I don't even know why he wanted to. He and O'Neill were always making jokes about me being too tall and too clumsy.'

Emma clenched her fists under the table. She wanted to go back and punch Barker right in the middle of his smug, toothy face. With an effort, she controlled her voice. 'You have to tell Bob,' she said. 'He'll give Barker the sack. I know he doesn't like him.'

'No!' Meg almost wailed. The waitress, approaching with their food, looked alarmed. Emma tried to smile reassuringly at her. When the woman had backed away, Meg said, 'Barker said to me today that if I complained about him I'd get the sack. I wasn't meant to be at the theatre, you see.'

'But that's blackmail,' said Emma, feeling her blood rising again. 'Don't let him get away with it. Tell Bob. Tell Edgar. I'll come with you, if you like.'

'No,' said Meg again. 'They'll side with him. Everyone always blames the girl. When two men followed Aisling home, Mum said it was because her skirt was too short.'

'Look,' Emma put her hand on Meg's arm, 'it wasn't

your fault. Barker had no right to kiss you when you didn't want to be kissed. He's older than you and a higher rank. That puts him in a position of power, which he abused. He was taking advantage. You said he bought you drinks. Did they have alcohol in?'

'I don't know,' said Meg. 'They were called . . .' she lowered her voice, 'Bloody Marys. And they were horrible.'

'Bloody Marys have vodka in them. He was trying to get you drunk. Please let me tell Bob. He'll be on your side, I promise.'

'No,' said Meg, so loudly that the beehives started giggling again. 'The thing is,' she said, in a quieter voice, 'I noticed something at the show but I can't tell anyone, because of not being meant to be there. I tried to tell DS Barker at the time but he wasn't listening. '

'What was it?' said Emma, detective senses tingling.

'Ted English did the show with a new assistant but I recognised her. She was Ida the strongwoman. She's staying at Cherry's lodgings.'

'Did Ida tell you that she knew Ted? When you interviewed her?'

'No,' said Meg. 'It's a clue, isn't it?' And, looking more cheerful, she tucked into her cheese on toast.

'Where does Emma think you are?' asked Max.

'Following up on a story,' said Sam. 'And maybe I am. "Behind the scenes with Max Mephisto."'

Max laughed and sat up. 'Behind the scenes and under the covers.' He reached for his dressing gown.

'The *News of the World* would love it,' said Sam.

She sounded a little too excited about the idea, in Max's opinion. He didn't think that Sam would ever write a story about him, but he wasn't completely sure. That was one of the things he liked about her. He was never quite certain of her feelings for him. There was really no need for them to keep their relationship secret. Both were free agents and, though the sixteen-year age gap might raise some eyebrows, it wasn't exactly unprecedented. Max's former wife, Lydia, was exactly Sam's age. But Sam seemed to delight in keeping their meetings clandestine.

Max headed for the bathroom. He'd had a powerful shower specially installed when he bought the flat. He liked to shower several times a day, which, according to Sam, bordered on neurosis. But hot water and Italian aftershave always revived him. Max wondered what Sam would say if she knew that he'd also tried to purchase a bidet, an item apparently unknown to London plumbers.

Reappearing at the bedroom door, towelling his hair dry, Max said, 'Want to go out for lunch? There are a couple of good Italian restaurants on the High Street.'

Sam was still lying in bed. 'I'm not sure that I feel like eating.'

Max was always shocked when she came out with remarks like this. Not as shocked as he'd been when she requested tomato ketchup in Da Bruno's though.

'What do you feel like doing?' Max touched Sam's cheek and received a faint, but definite, electric shock. That had been when he first realised he was attracted to Sam, two years ago, when she'd brushed against his arm and he'd felt that jolt of static. He wondered if he was, after all, up to another love-making session.

But Sam sat up and started pulling her ill-assorted clothes towards her: black camisole, white shirt, black jumper with cut-outs on the sleeves. Her knee-length boots had been abandoned in the hall.

'Let's go for a walk in the park. We can talk about my new case.'

'Are Holmes and Collins righting wrongs again?' said Max. He wanted to light a cigarette but Sam said that the smoke made her cough. He contented himself with reaching for his silver case. *For MM with love, LL.* He really should get another one.

Sam was pulling on her baggy checked knickerbockers. 'A woman's been killed. A magician's assistant. Emma and I have been employed by her parents.'

'Cherry Underwood,' said Max.

'Yes,' said Sam. 'How did you know?'

'I know her stage partner, Ted English. I wouldn't say we were friends exactly but he came round here on Tuesday morning to tell me all about Cherry.'

'On Tuesday morning? Her body had only just been found.'

'Ted was very distressed.' Though whether this had been grief or fear of being accused, Max couldn't say.

'Cherry's parents don't trust the police because Ted's told them you're his best pal.'

The word 'pal' gave Max a twinge of unease. 'That's very far from the truth,' he said. 'In fact, I rang Edgar yesterday to tell him that Ted had been to see me. Also, to warn him that Ted was part of a very disreputable set.' He had to laugh at the suddenly alert look on Sam's face. 'Look at you,' he said, 'Lois Lane on the scent of a story.'

'I'm not Lois Lane,' said Sam, reaching for her jacket. 'I'm Clark Kent. And you can tell me all about the disreputable magicians on our walk.'

Ted English was renting a room in Charlotte Street, about fifteen minutes from the Palace Pier. Emma walked there after parting from Meg at the restaurant. She thought that Ted would probably be in, preparing for the night's performance. The road was a grand Regency terrace leading up from the sea but the boarding house had been painted a rather startling blue and Emma thought that it was probably beginning to embarrass its neighbours. There was a 'vacancies' sign in the salt-streaked bow window and Emma wasn't surprised when her knock was answered quickly. A woman in a pink overall opened the door.

'Looking for a room?'

'Not exactly,' said Emma. She was fascinated by the woman's cigarette, which was almost half ash. How could she keep it balanced like that?

'What do you want then?' It wasn't exactly a warm welcome.

'Is Ted English in?' asked Emma.

'Are you with the police? Because we had the police round here yesterday. I said to them, "this is a respectable boarding house". Ted will have to leave if that goes on.'

Cherry's murder hadn't hit the papers yet but Emma was sure that it would be in that evening's *Argus*. She was also sure that Ted would be out on his ear by then. If not in police custody.

'I'm not with the police,' she said. 'I'm just a friend of Ted's.'

'You don't sound like a friend of his,' said the landlady but she stepped back to let Emma in. The ash on her cigarette trembled but didn't fall.

'Ted!' yelled the landlady. 'Visitor! You can go into the front room,' she said to Emma, making it sound like a concession.

Emma didn't think she'd ever been in a more depressing room, despite the bay window and the blurry sea view. There were two armchairs with dirty anti-macassars, a boarded-up fireplace and a large aspidistra on an octagonal table. Emma sat down, thinking it looked friendlier, but tried not to let her spine touch the back of the chair. The orange wallpaper seemed to be closing in on her.

Ted English, who appeared a few seconds later, looked almost as unprepossessing as the room. He was a smallish man with grey hair, wearing a stained brown jumper and beige trousers. His first question echoed the landlady.

'Are you with the police?'

'No.' Emma stood up and extended her hand. 'My name is Emma Holmes. I'm a private investigator employed by Cherry's parents.'

Ted's handshake was limp and sweaty. His breath smelt of alcohol imperfectly masked with peppermint. 'It's a nightmare,' he said. 'Poor Cherry.' He sank into an armchair and Emma lowered herself into the other.

'Mrs Grant will have me out of here as soon as it hits the papers,' he said. 'The police say I can't leave town. I'll be sleeping under the arches at this rate.'

'It must be awful,' said Emma in her most sympathetic voice.

It seemed to work because Ted's eyes filled with tears. 'And, tonight,' he said, 'I've got to go on stage with an assistant who's twice as tall as me.'

'Ida Lupin?'

'That's right. Mind you, I'm very grateful to Ida. She stepped in at the last minute. She's a trouper. But it was a bit of a disaster last night.'

'Won't the show's organisers,' Emma wasn't sure of the word, 'give you some time off? After all, your assistant has just died.' She didn't want to say the word 'murdered' in case it set Ted off again.

'Fat chance,' said Ted. 'The show's one of Larry Buxton's. He's the producer and he's a hard man. If I don't appear on stage tonight, I don't get paid. It's as simple as that. I'm not a rich man.' He gestured at the room as if it proved this, which it probably did.

Thinking of the surroundings made Emma ask, 'Why didn't you stay at Marine Parade with Cherry?' She hadn't seen Cherry's lodgings but they had to be better than this.

'I had a falling-out with Linda Knight a few years ago,' said Ted. 'She's not one to forget.'

Making a mental note to ask more about this argument, Emma said, 'Can you tell me about Cherry? I know it's difficult but, at this stage, any background information is helpful.'

'Cherry's parents,' said Ted. 'Do they blame me?'

'Yes' would be the honest answer but Emma contented herself with, 'They're very upset.'

'They're good people,' said Ted. 'Respectable people. Even though her mum was on the boards herself. Her dad was a milkman. He said to me, "look after my little girl".' Ted was crying again and Emma felt her own eyelids aching. She'd only spoken to Dolores and Iain Underwood on the phone but she could imagine them very clearly. Their pain though was literally unimaginable.

'How did you meet Cherry?' she asked.

Ted wiped his eyes with a large, grubby handkerchief. 'We were introduced,' he said, 'by Pal.' Despite the tears, this was said with some pride.

'Pal?'

'You must know Pal. Gordon Palgrave. He's on TV all the time now. Have you seen *Hug or Hit*?'

'My children watch it.'

'He's a genius, Pal. Well, Cherry was his assistant for a while. Then, when he had bigger fish to fry, he introduced her to me.'

'Cherry's mum said that Cherry's show-business career began when she met a man in a shop. Was that Pal?'

'I don't know,' said Ted. 'All I know was that Cherry was getting involved with some rather dodgy people. Flesh shows, that sort of thing. Pal rescued her. He's got a heart of gold. He gave Cherry work and, when he decided to concentrate on TV, he passed her on to me.'

Passed her on to me. Did Ted really not know how this sounded? And Emma would be the judge of whether Pal possessed a heart – as well as a head – of gold.

'When did you last see Cherry?' she asked.

'On Sunday morning. We went through the act. She was shaping well. Then I left her to her lunch – Linda does a good roast, whatever else you might say about her – and came back here. No such home cooking from Mrs B, of course.'

'How did Cherry seem when you said goodbye?' asked Emma quickly, before Ted started moaning about the landlady again.

'Fine,' said Ted. 'In good spirits. I didn't see her on Monday because that was a rest day. Just the band call in the morning, to run through the music for the act, you know. Then, yesterday, Linda rang me ...' The handkerchief went to his eyes but was this 'Walrus and Carpenter'-style, to hide some other expression?

'When did you ask Ida to be your assistant?' asked Emma.

'She offered,' said Ted. 'We know each other from way back. She's a good sort, Ida.'

Emma was planning to call on Ida Lupin next but, when she looked at her watch, it was nearly three, time to collect the girls from school. Before she left, she asked Ted about the name 'The Great Deceiver'.

'It was after a chap called The Great Diablo. Ever heard of him?'

'I knew him,' said Emma. She had been fond of Diablo, even though he had tried to give Marianne a bottle of whisky for her seventh birthday.

'Well, he was quite famous in his time. And he was part of some top-secret espionage unit in the war. With Max Mephisto, no less. Everyone wanted to be "The Great". Ray picked "The Great Raymondo" but you can't really make Ted, or Edward, into a stage name. Pal suggested "Deceiver" but it's a bit of a nightmare because no one can remember if the e goes before the i.'

Wasn't 'the great deceiver' also one of the names for the devil? Satan was the father of lies. Emma was deep in thought as she walked up the hill towards the school.

CHAPTER 8

Number 84 Marine Parade certainly looked more salubrious than Ted English's lodgings. It was part of a handsome row that also contained the house belonging to Emma's psychic friend, Astarte. The boarding house was not the smartest in the street but, unlike Mrs Grant's place, it wasn't yet letting its neighbours down. Emma noticed a couple of local reporters sitting on the low wall outside. The *Evening Argus* had run the story of Cherry's murder last night. It hadn't given the address but Emma knew that journos were an enterprising bunch. Even so, she hoped that the press attention wouldn't become too intrusive. She remembered a previous case where the press had dubbed the murder site 'the house of horrors'. She hoped, partly for Astarte's sake, that the same wouldn't happen to Marine Parade.

Linda Knight, who opened the door, was definitely more prepossessing than Ted's landlady. She looked smart in an orange pinafore over a green checked shirt. Emma admired her green tights, even though they looked a bit like the costume for a principal boy playing Robin Hood.

'Hi. I'm Emma Holmes. I'm a private detective employed by Cherry Underwood's parents.'

Linda's initially open expression had hardened to one of slight distrust but she said, 'You'd better come in then.'

'This must have been an awful shock for you,' said Emma.

Linda seemed to soften slightly. 'Awful. Poor Cherry. To think that it happened here. Her brother's coming later to pick up her things. I'm sure I won't know what to say to him.'

Emma was already wondering how she could meet Cherry's brother.

'I expect the police have been round,' she said.

'They were here all day yesterday. A nice young police-woman asking questions and then people photographing and cleaning the room where . . . where it happened.'

Edgar was very keen on photographing crime scenes, Emma knew. This was one of the reasons he was often described as 'eccentric'. All the same, it was a gruesome thought that, somewhere in this house, a woman had been stabbed to death.

'How well did you know Cherry?' asked Emma.

'Not very well,' said Linda. 'She only arrived on Saturday but she seemed a nice girl. Quite shy. I wondered how she'd got into this game. It's not for the faint-hearted.'

'Do you know Ted English too?'

'Has he been bitching about me?' asked Linda with a harsh laugh. 'Yeah, I know Ted. He's a sleazy so-and-so. Doesn't mean he's a murderer though.'

'When did you last see Cherry?' asked Emma. She knew what Linda had told Meg but wanted to hear it from the landlady herself.

'We had Sunday lunch and then Cherry said she had a headache and went to her room. I didn't see her again. Sounds awful but I thought she just wasn't feeling well. But I should have knocked or . . .' Without warning, Linda's face crumpled and she started to cry.

'Lind!' A woman came running down the stairs and got between Emma and the sobbing landlady. 'What have you been saying to her? Are you a reporter?'

'No,' said Emma. 'I'm a private investigator.'

'It's all right, Ida,' said Linda. 'She didn't mean any harm.'

'Are you Ida Lupin?' said Emma. 'It was you I came to see, really.'

Ida took Emma up to her room, which was large and comfortable with a sea view filling the two windows. 'Thank you for taking the time to see me,' said Emma.

'It's all right,' said Ida. 'I'm not exactly busy during the day.' Emma remembered Max saying once that pros found it hard to fill in the long days between their nightly performances. Even allowing for a late breakfast and the occasional rehearsal, their lifestyle left a lot of daylight hours unaccounted for. 'That's why a lot of pros play a lot of very bad golf,' said Max. Max used to fill his days with card games in Italian restaurants; Emma didn't know what he did now that he was a bona fide film star.

Ida said that she usually went for a walk in the morning and spent the afternoon practising with weights.

'It's not easy lifting a man over your head, you know.'

'I bet it isn't.'

Ida didn't look particularly muscular. She was a tall woman – though not as tall as Meg – casually but neatly dressed in slacks and a blue jumper. Her blonde hair was piled up in a bun but Emma imagined that she left it loose on stage to contribute to the Amazon/cave woman image. Hadn't Meg said something about a fur bikini?

'I understand that you also helped with Ted English's act on Tuesday night?' said Emma.

Ida seemed to stiffen slightly but answered easily enough, 'Yes, and last night too. He's got someone else for tonight. A proper magician's assistant.'

'And you're not a proper magician's assistant?'

'Oh, I did a bit of it in the old days,' said Ida. 'I did a bit of everything. But I'm too tall to be an assistant. You need to be little, able to get into small spaces, vulnerable enough to make the magician look dangerous. It didn't really work with me and Ted. He's a head shorter than me and about a stone lighter. And it was a hell of a tight squeeze in his cabinet.'

'Why did you do it then?' asked Emma. She remembered Ted saying that Ida had offered to help.

Ida paused for a beat before replying, 'I felt sorry for him. I know Ted of old. There's no real harm in him. Used to think he was a ladies' man.' She laughed. 'He even made a pass at me once but he didn't seem to take it too badly when I punched him. No hard feelings. I knew he'd be without an assistant so I offered. He couldn't afford not to perform.'

'Was it hard,' asked Emma curiously, 'to step in at the last minute?'

'The act wasn't hard but, like I say, it didn't look right. If we could have played it for laughs it might have worked – like that act Ruby Magic used to do with her dad – but Ted's too old-school. Twirl, smile up at the Royal Circle, go into the cabinet, abracadabra, disappear.'

'How did it work?' Emma couldn't help asking.

'I'm not meant to tell you but the cabinet has a false back. I was hiding behind it, clinging on for dear life when Ted spun the thing round. Good thing it was the last spot before the interval because I felt quite dizzy.'

'If you were prepared to help Ted, you can't think that he murdered Cherry.'

'Of course not,' said Ida. 'Ted wouldn't have the nerve to do something like that. I saw Cherry's body. It was horrible. Someone really laid into her.'

'Do you have any idea who that someone was?'

'Some sick bastard. Sorry. Someone not in their right mind.'

'Did you see anyone coming into the house on Sunday afternoon? A stranger?'

'No. I went to Worthing to see my ma. Got back around five. Rested in my room for a bit then went down for supper. Some of us stayed in the lounge to watch TV. Me, Linda, Geoffrey Bigg. Mario was there for a bit. I went to bed at ten.'

'And you didn't hear anything from Cherry's room?'

'No. I wear ear plugs to drown out the sound of Mario singing.'

Had Mario been singing at ten o'clock at night? wondered Emma. It did seem strange that no one had heard anything that night but maybe, in a boarding house, you became used to doors opening and closing, feet running up and down the stairs. Even so, Cherry's murderer had taken a huge risk. What if he'd met someone as he left the room, probably covered in blood? But maybe he'd been waiting until all the lights had been turned off. Watching the house and waiting.

'What did you do on Monday?' she asked Ida.

'There was no show that day but I went to the theatre at ten to do the band call.'

'Was Ted there?'

'Yes. He was one of the first. You get called in order of when you put your music on the stand. The stars don't get preferential treatment. Not that Ted was a star.'

'Wasn't he?'

'He was a good magician once but he's past it now. I saw

that when I worked with him. Bigg and Small were the stars – although they're not exactly young. The audiences like them, though, because they've been on TV.'

'Was everyone at the band call? Did you think it was odd that Cherry wasn't there?'

'Not really. She was just the assistant, after all. I saw Ted, Bigg and Small and Sonya, one of the gymnasts. Then I went into Brighton to have some lunch. Went back to the house and did some weights in the afternoon. Everyone keeps to themselves on a rest day. We were all there for supper, I think, except Cherry. But, again, I didn't think it was strange. Someone said something about her meeting a boyfriend.'

'Who said that?'

'I can't remember,' said Ida. Though Emma wasn't sure about that.

'What happened on Tuesday morning?'

'I came down to breakfast and there were a lot of people on the landing. Linda, Mario, I think Bigg and Small were there too. Linda asked if I could smell anything and I could. Linda thought it was coming from Cherry's room so, after we'd knocked, she went to get her key. Well, you know the rest.'

'Linda fainted, didn't she?' said Emma. She'd heard this from Meg and wondered if the swoon was genuine.

Ida seemed to catch some of the dubiousness in Emma's tone. She bridled slightly. 'Linda's very sensitive. I've known her for years.'

'Did you know Cherry well?'

'Hardly knew her at all. She arrived on Saturday. I'd already been here a week. Cherry seemed a nice little thing. Pretty too. I can't think why anyone would harm her.'

The strongwoman didn't seem to have much else to add. Emma asked if any of the other guests were in residence. 'I think Bigg and Small are at the flicks,' said Ida, 'but Mario's in. I heard him caterwauling earlier.'

When they left the room, Linda Knight was waiting outside.

'Got everything you need? We all spoke to the police, you know.'

'I know,' said Emma placatingly. 'It's just that Cherry's parents asked us to do some extra investigating.'

'Poor devils,' said Ida.

'I don't know how I can face Cherry's brother,' said Linda.

'When's he due to arrive?' said Emma.

'In about half an hour.'

'Don't worry, Linda,' said Ida. 'I'll be here. And Annie.' Linda said something that Emma didn't catch. She took the opportunity to head upstairs, where a tenor voice was massacring '*Cielo e mar*'.

Today Max was passing the time by having lunch with his agent, Joe Passolini. He'd had a different agent when he'd lived in Hollywood, a formidable bottle-blonde called

Gloria Goldman, but somehow Joe had hung on to his British affairs. It was thirteen years since they'd first met, in the stalls of the Theatre Royal Drury Lane, but Joe hadn't changed much. There were flecks of grey in his dark hair and he wore glasses to look at contracts, but Joe was still an Italian/Cockney/American wideboy in a pinstriped suit. He was in his late thirties now, married with two children, but he still looked as if he might be carrying a gun in his briefcase, an impression he took pains to foster.

They were in an Italian restaurant, in deference to their shared heritage, but the waiters were Sicilian, like Joe, and Max couldn't understand much of what was said. The food was excellent though, in contrast to the new 'pizzerias' springing up all over London, brightly lit cafés featuring candles in Chianti bottles and thick dough that had never seen a pizza oven. Sam would probably love them. Max ate tagliatelle al ragu, drank red wine and let Joe's talk of TV specials wash over him.

'TV is where the money is these days, Maxie boy. You should do a Christmas special. Maybe something with Ruby?'

'I'm not sure if she'll want to work so soon after having the baby.'

'She'll be desperate to get back in the limelight, if I know Ruby.' Joe was also Ruby's agent and Max was pretty sure that he'd been in love with her once. Nowadays, the relationship was one of warm friendship. Ruby was godmother to Joe's daughter, Francesca, and Joe had sent a whole hothouse of flowers to the maternity hospital.

'Pal would have you on his show like a shot,' Joe went on. 'Have you seen it? *Hug or Hit*?'

'I'll do a special appearance in hell first,' said Max.

'Pal's very big these days. Everyone loves Pal.'

'I don't.'

'Well, nor do I, to tell you the truth. Man's a creep of the first water. But those pop programmes are the key to young audiences. *Juke Box Jury*. *Top of the Pops*.'

'I'm too old for all that stuff, Joe. I'm fifty-six.' Max was on his second glass or he wouldn't have admitted this.

'Rubbish. Pal must be in his sixties and he's the king of the teenyboppers.'

'Let's stop talking about Pal, please.'

'You've got to do something, Max.'

'But that's the thing – I don't. I've got enough money. *The Prince of Darkness* is still doing well at the box office and I start shooting a new film in the summer. With Wilbur.'

Joe looked sour, as he always did at the mention of Max's film career.

'Films are all very well,' he said. 'But TV's the future.'

'I don't like TV.' Max was almost the last person he knew without a set. His children had one, at home in Somerset. Ruby had the latest model in her flat. Even high-minded Edgar was a fan of *Dr Who*.

'Aren't you going to watch the World Cup?' asked Joe. Max had temporarily forgotten that England were to host the football world cup in July, even though the papers were already trumpeting a home win.

'I'm not much of a football fan,' said Max. He'd always hated team sports, something that was often mentioned in his (almost entirely unfavourable) school reports.

'You've got to support Italy though,' said Joe. 'They're one of the best teams in the world. Mind you, Salvatore here,' he pointed at one of the waiters, 'tells me that the Azzurri will be playing in Middlesbrough. That's enough to put anyone off.'

'I did a summer season in Middlesbrough once,' said Max. 'I rather liked the place.'

Over espresso in tiny gold cups, Max asked Joe if he'd ever come across a magician called Ted English, also known as The Great Deceiver. 'I don't think so,' said Joe. 'Is he one of the old guard? All top hat and magic wand?'

'I suppose so,' said Max, who'd worn a few top hats in his time. 'He was quite friendly with Pal in his magician days. Also Tommy Horton, Rex King, Dazzling Dave Dunkley. That set.'

'Tommy Horton must be dead now. He was about a hundred when I last saw him. Think it was at the Apollo.'

'Maybe. He was a friend of Diablo's so he must be getting on a bit.' Max felt a sudden rush of melancholy, mourning Diablo and all the top-hatted magicians of the past.

'Why the interest in the Great Whatsit?' said Joe. 'Fancy a grappa?'

'No thanks. Oh, all right then. Ted English – the Great Deceiver – came to see me yesterday. His assistant was murdered. Shocking case. It'll be in the papers soon.'

'Are you turning detective again? I thought you'd stopped all that caper.'

'I'm no detective,' said Max, accepting a small glass of colourless liquid from Salvatore. 'I leave all that to Edgar. It's his job.'

'Hmm.' Joe looked sceptical and drained his grappa. 'So, Max, what do you want to do? Throw your old agent a bone here.'

'The only thing I'd like to do,' said Max, 'is a magic show. A proper old-fashioned magic show. At a number one theatre.'

'You might as well ask to play Hamlet on the moon. Variety's dead. Unless you do one of Larry Buxton's godawful nostalgia tours.'

'It was you who made me do *Those Were the Days*. Coronation night 1953, if I remember correctly.' Considering he'd defused a bomb live on stage, he wasn't likely to forget.

'That's different. That was TV. And it's a class show. Still going strong. I could get you a headline on it tomorrow.'

'No thanks. I want a real theatre with footlights and a live audience.'

'They're all bingo halls now,' said Joe. 'Another grappa?'

CHAPTER 9

The singing stopped as soon as Emma knocked on the door. 'Come in,' said a voice, considerably higher pitched than the tenor. Mario Fontana was standing by the window, which looked out onto a brick wall. Presumably only favoured guests got a sea view. Emma introduced herself and, as with Linda and Ida, the mention of Cherry's parents seemed to smooth her path.

'It's so awful,' said Mario. 'I should send them flowers but . . .'

He didn't say what his reservation was, but Emma got the feeling that the bouquet would never be sent. Mario Fontana (aka John Lomax) was a curiously nebulous presence. He had fair hair and pale blue eyes and, though tall, seemed somehow insubstantial. His Midlands accent was flat and expressionless. Emma wondered if John had invented the Italian persona just to give himself a character.

Lomax was quite open about the name change. 'It's

got to be Italian for opera. Of course, during the war, anything Italian was a no-no. German even worse. Bit of a challenge for classical musicians really. There's only so much Britten anyone can bear. But, now, Italy's fashionable again. Vespas, pizzerias, cappuccinos. *Roman Holiday*, Rossano Brazzi, three coins in the fountain. That's where I got "fontana" from.'

Emma asked if Lomax had ever been to Italy and he said he hadn't. She then asked him about his movements on the Sunday of Cherry's death.

'I went to Beachy Head,' said Lomax. 'It's a beautiful bus ride. I love buses. I just sit there letting the music play in my head. I got back to the house at about three.'

'Did you see or hear anything unusual?'

Lomax paused. 'I heard voices in Ida's room. It's next door to mine.'

'When was this?'

'At about four.'

Ida had claimed not to be back from Worthing until five. Emma asked if Lomax could hear what the voices were saying.

'I couldn't make out the words but they seemed to be arguing. I could tell by the tune.'

'Were they men or women's voices?'

'Women. One a mezzo, the other a soprano.'

'Have you any idea who killed Cherry?'

'It's usually the boyfriend, isn't it?'

'Did Cherry have a boyfriend?'

'I don't know,' said Lomax. 'But I'm sure she had her admirers. She was a pretty little thing.'

Meg hadn't expected much from the door-to-door. The houses on Marine Parade were large and somehow smug-looking. They also faced the sea, which ruled out any neighbours opposite. 'I don't know,' said Danny Black, when Meg shared this thought, 'what about a passing mermaid?' Meg ignored this but she was relieved to be working with Danny, for all his feeble humour, rather than DS Barker. They hadn't spoken since Tuesday night.

But, on the third house, Meg struck gold. Reginald Glover, aged fifty-eight, had been walking his dachshund, Trixie, late on Sunday evening. He'd seen a white-haired man going into number 84. 'He didn't knock. It seemed like he had a key. Or the door was open.'

'What time was this?'

'Just after eleven p.m. I always go out after the late news on the wireless.'

'Did you see him come out again?'

'Yes. I walked as far as Rock Gardens so Trixie could do her business on the grass. When I got back to my house, I saw the man walking away, towards the Aquarium.'

'What time would that have been?'

'About eleven-thirty.'

Solomon Carter thought that Cherry had been killed between nine p.m. and midnight. The white-haired man was their first real lead. Reginald's description wasn't very detailed ('It was dark and I wasn't wearing my specs'), but he said the man was of medium height and walking quickly. He was wearing a jacket 'like the Beatles wear'.

'A bit hip for an old man,' said Danny, as they walked back to the station.

'Who says he was old?'

'White hair.'

'It could have been platinum blond.'

This made Danny laugh a lot.

'Max Mephisto. Talk of the devil.'

Max, who had just parted with Joe outside the restaurant, paused in the act of lighting a cigarette.

'Gordon Palgrave,' he said slowly.

'No one calls me that now. I'm Pal.'

'I'm too old to call anyone Pal.'

Palgrave must be Max's age, or older, but, with his tanned skin and peroxide hair, he had a curiously ageless appearance. He could have been a thousand-year-old pixie or a preternaturally aged teenager.

'Which way are you going?' he said.

The opposite direction to you, Max wanted to answer. He had intended to pay a call on Ruby but didn't want to take Pal anywhere near his daughter or granddaughter. 'I'm just about to get a cab,' he said.

'I'll walk you to the rank.' To Max's horror, Pal slipped his arm through Max's. 'I've got a proposal for you.'

'I'm not the marrying sort.' Max disentangled himself.

'That's not what I've heard. I've heard that you're keeping company with a very tasty young journalist.'

Pal was the sort of person who always knew the latest gossip.

'I can't think what you mean,' said Max.

Pal laughed as if he'd made a joke and then instantly rearranged his face into solemn lines. 'Did you hear about Ted's girl? What a tragedy. Stabbed to death in her bed.'

This was an unnecessarily graphic detail and, to Max's knowledge, not one that was yet in the public domain.

'Did you know her?' he asked.

Pal didn't seem disconcerted by the question. 'Cherry? I worked with her once or twice. Good assistants are hard to find. I remember your Ethel.'

'I remember her too.' Max hated to hear Pal talk about Ethel almost as much as he'd hated him calling Sam 'tasty'.

'The thing is, Max. You know that Ted's on this nostalgia tour of Larry's?'

'I did hear that, yes.'

'I've just been having lunch with Larry. He thinks poor old Ted's past it. He wants to replace him with a real star.'

Max said nothing. Across the road someone shouted, 'It's Pal! Hug or hit, Pal?' Pal waved a jovial hand.

'Can you guess?' Pal squeezed Max's arm again.

'I'm sure I can't.'

'You, Max!' Pal laughed delightedly. 'He wants to replace Ted with you.'

CHAPTER 10

'Good work, WDC Connolly,' said Edgar.

He was pleased to be able to praise Meg. He thought he'd been a little harsh about the theatre visit and Bob had mentioned that Meg seemed quiet yesterday. Today, though, she was glowing with the knowledge of a job well done.

'The white-haired man has to be our main suspect,' said Bob. 'We'll get the witness in and do an identikit drawing.'

'They never really look like anyone human though, do they?' said Meg.

Edgar ignored this, though he knew what she meant.

'Could it have been Ted English?' he said. 'His hair was greyish.'

'Mr Glover definitely said "white",' said Meg. 'And he was going in the opposite direction to Ted's digs.'

'We'll show Mr Glover a picture of Ted when he comes in,' said Bob. 'There must be one outside the theatre.'

'If our man went towards the aquarium,' said Edgar,

'he could have caught a bus. We need to check with all the companies.'

'Unless he had a car,' said DC Black.

'If he had a car, you'd think he would have driven off in it,' said Edgar. 'But the witness described him walking away, moving quickly.'

'Unusual for an old man to move so quickly,' said Bob.

'I said to Danny . . . to DC Black,' said Meg, with a glance at her colleague, 'that he might not be old if he was moving fast. Maybe his hair was blond. Like Tommy Steele. Or dyed white. Like Harpo Marx.'

'That's a good point,' said Edgar. 'And wasn't there something about a Beatles jacket? That hardly sounds like the wardrobe of an elderly man. Though we have to be careful about stereotyping.' A picture came into his head of an elderly man in a white suit, moving quickly through the holidaymakers on the promenade. The man stopped and winked at him. Diablo.

Edgar realised that the others were looking at him. He hoped he hadn't winked back. He cleared his throat. 'DC Black, you keep on with the door-to-door. And ask around the Aquarium. There aren't many residential houses in the area but people might have been working on Sunday night. WDC Connolly, go back to number 84 and ask about the white-haired man. Bob, let's get an identikit done and hope it looks human. Good work, everyone.'

The younger officers left the room but Bob remained. Clearly had something on his mind.

'Just wondered . . . about Emma . . . Mrs Stephens. You know they're working on the case? Holmes and Collins?'

'I do,' said Edgar patiently.

'Should we share this with her? About the white-haired man?'

Edgar hesitated. The police investigation should remain confidential but, if anyone was likely to make a breakthrough, it was Emma.

'I'll tell her,' he said. 'But let's keep that to ourselves for now. Where's DS Barker today?'

'I sent him to talk to Cherry's parents.'

Edgar made a face. 'He's hardly the man for that sort of job.'

'I know,' said Bob. 'But I'm short-staffed and I think WDC Connolly is still too junior.'

'I think she'd be better than Barker,' said Edgar. 'But I'll try to get you some more manpower.'

Emma would say that phrase was 'sexist', one of her new words, but he could hardly say 'person power'. Not and retain any self-respect.

Emma was lucky. Not, she told herself sternly, that luck was the word to be used in connection with a grieving family. But Michael Underwood, Cherry's brother, was crossing the hallway just as Emma descended the stairs. She managed to attach herself to the party – Linda, Ida, Annie and Michael – that proceeded to Cherry's second-floor bedroom.

Emma had steeled herself but it was still horrible. The floorboards had been scrubbed but an ominous stain remained on the floor and on the flowered wallpaper. The air smelt suspiciously of bleach. Cherry's bed had been stripped and her suitcase lay on top of it. Next to the case was a red jacket with a fake-fur collar.

'I've packed everything away,' said Linda. 'Do you want some time on your own?' She glanced, rather accusingly, at Emma.

'No, that's all right,' said Michael. He had a northern accent, which made Emma wonder if Cherry had had one too. It seemed wrong that she had never heard her voice.

'I'm so sorry,' Linda was saying. 'Do tell your parents how sorry I am.'

'It's not your fault,' said Michael, looking rather helplessly at the suitcase and jacket.

'Michael,' said Emma, 'I'm a private detective employed by your parents.'

She knew that the women were all glaring at her, but Michael answered, mildly, 'I think they said something about that.'

'Is it OK to ask you a few questions?'

'Yes,' said Michael, 'if you like.'

Emma looked at Linda, who said, after a pause, 'We'll be right outside.'

'All right,' said Michael.

Emma sat on the bed and stroked the jacket's collar. 'This is lovely,' she said.

'She liked pretty things,' said Michael, as if speaking with difficulty.

'Cherry was younger than you, wasn't she?'

'Yes. Three years younger. My little sister.' That made Michael twenty-four. He looked older, perhaps because he was thickset, his fair hair already looking as if it was receding.

'I'm so sorry,' said Emma. 'This must be so awful for all of you.'

'We're broken,' said Michael. 'The whole family is broken.' It was a powerful image and Emma could see that it was an accurate one. The family might recover but the shape would never be the same again.

'Can I ask how Cherry seemed when you last spoke to her?' said Emma.

'I hadn't spoken to her for a while,' said Michael, 'but she rang Mum and Dad every Saturday. Last time she seemed in good spirits, excited to be in Brighton.' He looked towards the window but Cherry's room, like Mario's, had no sea view.

'Nothing bothering her?' said Emma.

'Not that I know of. And Cherry was never one to keep things to herself.'

'Did Cherry have a boyfriend? Anyone at home?'

'There was Harold. They walked out for a while. I think he was keen. But he married someone else last year.'

That made Harold a less likely suspect, thought Emma. Not an impossible one though.

'Someone said something about Cherry meeting a boy-friend on Sunday. Do you know anything about that?'

'No,' said Michael. He rubbed his hand through his hair, making it stand up in a crest. 'She didn't know anyone in Brighton. This was the first time she'd been here.'

That was the trouble with theatricals, thought Emma. They moved around so much it was hard to form relation-ships, except with each other. But the fact was that Cherry had arrived in Brighton on Saturday and on Sunday she was dead.

Meg arrived at the boarding house to be told, by Annie, that there was a private detective upstairs.

'A woman detective?'

'Yes. Emma, her name is.'

'I know her.'

'She's a pushy one. Managed to interrogate poor Cher-ry's brother when he was here. Now she's with Bigg and Small. They came in just as she was leaving so up the stairs she went again.'

Meg could just imagine it. She'd been with Emma when she travelled the breadth of England to follow a lead. A staircase wasn't going to put her off. Annie was looking decidedly flustered though.

'It was you I came to talk to you, actually,' said Meg.

'To me?' Annie sounded amazed and not unpleased.

'I wondered if you'd seen a man hanging about the place

on Sunday night. Medium height, white hair, wearing a dark blouson jacket.'

'A what jacket?'

'Like the Beatles wear. Or used to wear before they got all long-haired.'

'I didn't see anyone like that,' said Annie.

'Like what?' Linda appeared in the hallway. 'Oh, it's you,' she said to Meg. She sounded less friendly than she had on Tuesday. Meg explained about the white-haired man. To her surprise, Linda looked quite pale. 'Who told you this?'

'We've had a witness come forward,' said Meg, falling back on police-speak.

'I didn't see anyone strange in the house on Sunday night,' said Linda.

'Forgive me,' said Meg. 'But you look quite shocked.'

'You do, too.' Unexpectedly, Annie backed her up.

'It's just a silly story,' said Linda. She looked over her shoulder but the hall and staircase were deserted. A voice that could only be Mario's was warbling somewhere in the eaves.

Meg smiled encouragingly. No stories were silly as far as she was concerned.

'This house used to be owned by an old man,' said Linda. 'An old man with white hair. When he died, it was bought by a young couple. They used to wake up at night to find him sitting on the end of their bed. Sometimes his face was really close to theirs, as if he was short-sighted. Once he was rocking their child's cot. They sold up and I got the place cheaply.'

'Holy Mary, Mother of God,' said Annie, sounding comfortingly like Meg's own mother.

'Have you ever seen the man?' asked Meg.

'No,' said Linda. 'I don't believe in that sort of thing.'

Meg wasn't sure that she, in her turn, believed the landlady.

Emma descended the stairs to find Meg talking to Annie and Linda in the hall. Linda had one hand on her heart – Emma thought the day had been very hard on her – but Meg smiled as cheerily as ever.

'Hallo, Emma.'

'Do you know each other?' asked Linda, her manicured brows rising.

'We've met on previous cases,' said Emma. 'Thank you for your time today.'

'My pleasure,' said Linda. Rather acidly, Emma thought.

'Yes, thank you,' said Meg. 'I'll keep in touch.' And she followed Emma out into the street. A fine April rain was falling and the sea and sky had merged into one.

Emma suddenly felt the need to talk about something other than violent crime.

'I'm going to call on a friend,' she said to Meg. 'She lives a few doors down. Do you want to come?'

*

Emma first met Astarte Zabini when she investigated the death of her fortune-teller grandmother in 1953. Then she'd found the girl strange and rather unnerving but, over the years, they had become friends. Astarte took over her grandmother's gypsy caravan on the pier but was also now rather famous in Brighton for her readings and horoscopes. In some ways, thought Emma, as she waited on the black-and-white tiled doorstep, time had stood still for Astarte. She was just as beautiful as she had been at nineteen, still lived in the same house, had never married and had no children. Sometimes Emma felt sorry for her friend, at other times she felt something close to envy.

'Emma! How nice to see you.'

'Didn't you see me coming in your crystal ball?'

'I did, of course.'

'This is my friend Meg. Don't worry about the uniform. This is a purely social visit. To get out of the rain.'

'Welcome, Meg.' Astarte inclined her head, which was ringed with golden plaits like a crown.

Meg muttered something inaudible.

'I've got a cousin staying,' said Astarte, as she led the way up the stairs to the first-floor sitting room. Emma knew that Astarte had family everywhere and was expecting a middle-aged woman draped in fringed scarves. But sitting on the velvet sofa was a young man with long dark hair curling to below his shoulders and gold earrings in both ears.

'This is Logan,' said Astarte. 'Do you both want tea?'

When Astarte descended the stairs to the kitchen, silence fell. Logan showed no inclination to break it. He didn't seem at all perturbed by the appearance of two women, one of them in police uniform, but grinned at them amiably. His shirt was open almost to the waist and gold medallions gleamed amongst the black chest hair.

Finally, Meg said, 'Are you staying here long?'

'Just for a week or so. I don't like being in houses.' His voice was deep, with a hint of an Irish accent.

'Where do you normally live then?' Emma applauded Meg's savoir faire. Men like Logan made her nervous.

'In a caravan,' said Logan. 'I'm a proper gypsy. Not a didicoi.'

'What does that mean?'

'Someone with mixed blood. Not a real Romany. I'm pure Romany and, yes, I travel in a horse-drawn caravan.' He smiled at Meg. His eyes – like Astarte's – were a shifting mixture of blue and green.

Meg asked more questions and they learnt that Logan was related to Astarte through her Uncle Merlin. He had two brothers and a younger sister. He used to share a caravan with his family but now travelled with his brother Bartley. They liked to do something called 'sulky racing', which involved horses and carts. Logan and Bartley made their living fruit picking in the summer and selling scrap metal in the winter. But, since 1964, it had become illegal to do the latter without a permit. 'Everyone's got it in for us,' said Logan. 'There are no stopping places any more and, when we do stop, we get moved on. But we live a good life, a pure life, we do no harm. And there's nothing like seeing the road unfurl in front of you, the world seen through your horse's ears.'

Emma was quite sorry when Astarte reappeared with a tray containing her famous aromatic tea. Logan lapsed into silence again but he continued to smile at Meg, who pretended not to notice.

'Are you here because of the murder?' said Astarte. 'Poor Cherry. It's not second sight – I'm friends with Linda.'

'The landlady?' said Emma. 'I met her today. She seems nice.'

'Nice?' said Astarte. 'I don't know about nice. But Linda's a genuine soul.'

What was that meant to mean?

'It must be hard work running a boarding house.' Emma tried again.

'Very hard work,' said Astarte. 'I sometimes think I should rent out rooms. This house is too big for one person. But, when I think of all the fuss and bother, I can't face it.'

'And it means you have room for itinerant relatives,' said Logan.

'That's true,' said Astarte, giving him a warm smile. Emma was ashamed to find herself thinking that 'itinerant' was a sophisticated word for someone who had just told them, 'School and me – we didn't get on.'

'Were you at home on Sunday night?' Meg asked Astarte.

'Be careful,' said Logan. 'She's got her police hat on.' Meg blushed and looked down at her hard-brimmed hat, which she'd placed on the floor by her chair.

'I had a reading at six,' said Astarte, not seeming to resent the question. 'The client left at about seven-thirty. I was alone for the rest of the evening.'

'Did you see anything out of the window?' said Meg. The sitting room, like Linda's lounge, possessed French windows opening out onto a small balcony. There was a table in front of them and on it was a swathed item about the size and shape of a human head. Emma knew it was a crystal ball and she also knew that Astarte spent many hours in that spot, looking dreamily into its depths and then out to sea.

'I saw various people going past,' said Astarte. 'Mothers pushing prams, trying to get their babies to sleep, teenagers going out for the night, restaurant workers on their way into town.'

'Did you see a man with white hair?' said Meg. 'He would have passed by at about ten-thirty.'

'I went to bed at ten,' said Astarte. 'But I know the man you mean.'

'You do?' Emma and Meg both stared at her.

'Old Mr Henderson,' said Astarte. 'He haunts number 84. More tea?'

CHAPTER 11

'She said it in such a matter-of-fact voice,' said Emma. 'As if haunting was his day job.'

'That's Astarte for you,' said Edgar.

He was quite fond of the fortune teller, or at least he had grown used to her over the years, though he did wish that Emma wouldn't ask her to babysit. Already Marianne (aka Madame Mystica) had foretold that he would lose all his money and go bald at fifty. Unconsciously, he ran a hand through his hair.

'But she hadn't seen the white-haired man?' he said. 'The actual, living man?'

He hadn't been surprised to learn that Emma already knew about their best lead. Apparently, she'd met Meg at the boarding house, and they had called in on Astarte and her cousin 'who looks like a pop star'.

'She hadn't seen him,' said Emma. 'She goes to bed at ten. I'll have to ask at the boarding house again.'

'WDC Connolly will do that,' said Edgar. Then,

abandoning any attempt at confidentiality, 'What did you make of them? The other residents of number 84?'

Emma settled herself more comfortably on the sofa. The children were in bed and the television was off. The perfect time for a cosy marital chat about murder.

'I quite liked Ida,' she said. 'She knew Ted and said he'd once made a pass at her, which might give her a motive. Mind you, Ida said she'd turned Ted down. In fact, she punched him. But they were good enough friends for her to help him with the act. I can't see her killing Cherry in a fit of jealousy, although she'd definitely be strong enough. Ida mentioned something about Cherry meeting a boyfriend on Sunday but nobody else corroborated that. Her brother said that Cherry didn't know anyone in Brighton.'

Edgar had been slightly shocked that Emma had questioned Michael Underwood. But he supposed that she was employed by his parents and had a right to do so.

Emma was still considering the inhabitants of the boarding house. 'John Lomax – Mario Fontana – seems inoffensive enough but, then, so do plenty of murderers. His alibi is quite thin – riding on a bus thinking about music – but I can't think of a motive for him. On the other hand, he swears he heard voices in Ida's room when she claimed to be out. He said they were arguing.'

'How could he tell that?'

'It's all in the tune, apparently. Bigg and Small were

quite odd. They arrived back from the cinema just as I was leaving so I followed them upstairs for a chat.'

'Of course you did.'

'You know they share a room? Twin beds so I don't think they're lovers. It's an odd relationship though. Symbiotic.'

'Remind me what that means again.'

'I thought you went to Oxford.'

'Politics, Philosophy and Economics,' said Edgar. 'No long words. And I was only there for two terms.'

'I think it means inter-dependent,' said Emma. 'Reliant on each other. Like birds riding on hippos and getting rid of their ticks. I'm not sure Bigg and Small could survive without each other.'

'And did either of them see or hear anything on Sunday night?'

'Apparently not. They went out for a walk – together, of course – then came back for supper. Afterwards, Bigg watched TV with Ida, Linda and John while Small went to their room to listen to the wireless.'

'So Small could have killed Cherry? In theory.'

'I suppose so. But why?'

Edgar was unable to answer this. He looked at Emma, her blonde hair glowing in the lamplight, and felt a surge of love for her. There was no one with whom he'd rather discuss means and motive. He edged his arm along the back of the sofa.

His amorous intentions were thwarted by the telephone

ringing and Marianne galloping down two flights of stairs to pant, 'Brighton 28097.'

After a few seconds she shouted, 'It's Uncle Max.'

Edgar wondered what Max felt about being an honorary uncle. The children did this naturally for all family friends, except, oddly enough, Sam, to whom they were closest. Well, Max was not only an uncle but a grandfather now.

He took the receiver from Marianne. 'Hallo, Max.'

'Sorry to ring so late.'

'It's not that late.' *Go to bed*, he mouthed at Marianne.

'I've just been to see Ruby.'

'How is she?'

'Very well, all things considered, but finding life with a young baby rather hard. But that's not why I called.'

'I thought it wasn't.'

'I saw Pal today. Gordon Palgrave.'

'The creep from the TV show?'

'That's right. He told me that they're dropping Ted English from the bill. In fact, he offered me the gig. He must be well in with Larry Buxton. He's the producer.'

'Were you tempted?' asked Edgar. He sat on the stairs. Upstairs he could hear Emma and Marianne arguing: 'But I'm awake now.' A familiar tune, though not a very restful one.

Max laughed. 'You know me too well. I was. Slightly. The show's transferring to London next. Theatre Royal Drury Lane. A proper West End venue.'

'But you said no?'

'I don't want to do a variety show. Not at my age. It's so corny, all that nostalgia stuff. And I really don't want to be beholden to Pal. I bet he'll ask Dazzling Dave. One of that set.'

'Magicians do have amazing names.'

'There's nothing very dazzling about Dave Dunkley, believe me. But he and Pal go back years. That's why I'm ringing, really. Pal admitted that he knew Cherry and had worked with her a few times.'

'You really think he might be a suspect?'

'It's a leap, I admit. But he's such an unpleasant customer. He married one of his assistants, you know. She committed suicide a few years later. He never talks about her.'

'I'm not surprised.'

'It might be worth checking on Pal's movements. That's all I'm saying.'

After Max had rung off, Edgar remained sitting on the stairs. He remembered the TV show, the baying crowds, the giant hammer. And the man with gleaming white hair.

Ruby had never thought it would be so hard. She'd imagined herself pushing a pram in the park, surrounded, as usual, by admiring glances, but this time directed at the gurgling baby as much as the radiant mother. She'd seen herself singing lullabies, splashing in puddles, tenderly reading *Winnie-the-Pooh*. Perhaps she'd even do a few adverts, tasteful ones for rusks or fashionable baby clothes. No one told her that the baby would cry so much, that she would arch her back and refuse to be comforted, especially by Ruby singing lullabies. No one told her that she would feel tired all the time or that breastfeeding would hurt so much that her nipples bled. No one told her that she would be both bored and terrified or that, when she looked in the mirror, she would see a haggard creature with actual circles under her eyes. Ruby was thirty-six and she felt a hundred.

She hadn't wanted Max to leave. It wasn't as if he knew much about babies but he was a comforting presence. In fact, he was more comforting than Ruby's mother, who was full of advice and comments like, 'You're making a rod for your own back if you let her sleep in your bed.' Max just sat and listened to her. 'Give Poppy to me,' he'd said and, amazingly, the baby had settled to sleep on his starched shirt front. Max had suggested that Ruby have a bath and something to eat. Both had been wonderful. She'd nearly fallen asleep in the hot water and the toast and Marmite tasted better than any cordon bleu meal.

But, now, Max had gone home and Poppy had started crying again. Ruby warmed a bottle – she'd given up trying to breastfeed – but Poppy turned her head away from the teat. She wasn't hungry, she seemed to be saying, she was cross. 'There, there,' muttered Ruby, walking around the apartment where, only six months ago, she'd posed as 'Ruby Magic, Girl About Town'. Her pregnancy hadn't shown then and Ruby had lounged on her leopard print sofa in a short white dress and had felt marvellous. Now the sofa was covered with mysterious stains and Ruby knew that she wouldn't be able to do up the asymmetrical zip on the dress. She didn't think she could fit into any of her pre-baby clothes. Tears rolled down her cheeks as she patrolled the sitting room, bedroom, bathroom and modern galley-style kitchen. 'We should live together,' Dex had said. 'Babies take a lot of work.' But she'd laughed at him. She wanted to be on her own. 'Just me and the baby.' So, tonight, Dex was playing a gig in Manchester, probably even now chatting up dolly birds in short white dresses.

Briefly, Ruby wondered what her life would have been like if she'd married Edgar. She'd first met him in Brighton, when she was appearing at the Theatre Royal as Max's assistant. Neither Max nor Edgar had known then that Ruby was Max's daughter, which was probably why Edgar had allowed himself to flirt with her in a gentle, chivalrous way. Their courtship had been slow-moving, punctuated by Edgar's cases and Ruby's pursuit of fame as she travelled around the country performing in run-down theatres and church halls. Funnily enough it was when they finally got engaged that Ruby began to suspect that Edgar's real love was his sergeant, Emma Holmes. There followed an agonising period of hoping that Edgar would come to appreciate Ruby's superior charms – every other man did, after all – before Ruby found the courage to end the engagement. She'd become famous quite soon afterwards, when *Ruby Magic* appeared on TV. Ruby didn't regret anything. It would have been terrible to marry a man in love with someone else. But, deep down, there was still a niggling feeling of resentment. Why *couldn't* Edgar have chosen her? Ruby had genuinely been in love with him, although she prided herself that nobody knew quite how much.

Ruby presumed that babies would have featured somewhere in her fantasy life as Mrs Stephens. After all, Emma had three of them. Edgar wasn't well-off – Ruby was certain that she was now richer – but a police superintendent must earn a decent wage. Maybe, if Ruby had married him, she could have had a nanny who would whisk the child away and return it, cherubic and sweet-smelling, for a few Madonna-like hours. Why the hell didn't Emma have a nanny? Ruby would ask her next time they met. She'd always got on well with Emma's kids. In fact, she had thought she was good with children. But that was before she had one of her own.

Ruby paused by the window. She'd always loved watching the traffic pass by: the yellow eyes of the taxis, the lighted upper decks of buses, the steady stream of humanity. It seemed to her that London, like New York, was a city that never slept. 'Like you,' Ruby said to Poppy, still grizzling on her shoulder.

Ruby thought of her one trip to America, going on chat shows, being described as 'the next Lucille Ball' and asked if she had met the Beatles. She had. During the sleepless nights with Poppy, Ruby's past came back to her in glorious Technicolor, like a film she was watching at the cinema. Growing up in Hove, doing card tricks for her friends at school, dreaming her way through a secretarial course with fantasies of appearing on stage. The moment when she announced her intention of becoming a magician and her mother, instead or laughing or forbidding her, had winced and said, 'There's something I need to tell you . . .' All her life Ruby had known that she was different and now she knew she was. She was Max Mephisto's daughter. 'I'm still your dad,' Gavin had said but Ruby had been dazzled by the thought of her new father. Because Max wasn't just her real birth father, he was *famous*, a blazing star in the theatrical firmament. 'It's not something I'm proud of,' Emerald said, of that summer with Max, and the thought that her thoroughly respectable mother had such secrets gave Ruby the power to fly. She started getting *Variety* magazine and replied to an advertisement for 'a magician's assistant, no previous experience necessary, must be slim and attractive.' Well, Ruby knew she was pretty, even her austere mother told her that (they looked very similar). And how hard could the rest of it be? Ruby arranged to meet Raymond Fellows in a Hastings hotel.

The Great Raymondo had given Ruby the job on the spot. Her parents protested but what could they do, given that her mother had once had an act with a giant python and succumbed to the lures of a young magician with nothing to recommend him but good looks and a way with a pack of cards? 'I won't tell you how the tricks work,' Ray had said, 'that way you can sell them to the audience.' But Ruby soon worked them all out. The Great Raymondo's act was really very simple and his assistant's job was only to take the audience's attention away from the hat with a false bottom and the cards that were all jacks. 'I steer clear of knives,' Ray told her once, darkly. 'Ever heard of the Zig Zag Girl? Girl goes in the cupboard, magician puts the swords through and pulls out the middle bit so that it looks like a giant letter zed. Max Mephisto invented that trick.' Ruby twirled and smiled her way through that season in Hastings. She knew that her moment would come but even she was surprised when Ray told her that Max would be appearing in Brighton and was looking for a new assistant. 'I've put in a word for you.'

It had been in Hastings that Ruby first met Pal. He came to the show, which terrified Ray because he hated other magicians watching him work. Afterwards, Pal, who was still Gordon then, scattered faint praise: 'Always enjoy seeing that one, it certainly had some parts of the audience fooled.' They went for a drink and, when Ray was at the bar, Gordon slid an arm round Ruby's waist. 'You're too good for Ray. I could take you places. Come to my hotel room later and I'll put you through your paces.' 'No thank you,' Ruby had said, 'I'll make my own way to the top.'

And she had. *Ruby Magic* had propelled her into TV stardom and *Iris Investigates*, a detective show that Ruby also produced, had proved just as successful. She sometimes saw Pal wandering round the BBC, surrounded by sycophantic men and suspiciously young girls, and they exchanged insincere smiles. Ruby knew Pal hated her for turning him down and, especially, for being more successful than him, even though that ridiculous show of his was the flavour of the month.

Was it her imagination, or were the sobs diminishing? Ruby didn't dare to sit down. She stood at the window, rocking her baby to and fro, and remembering the time when she had been speared with a sword for the entertainment of the crowd.

PART 2

May

CHAPTER 12

Monday, 16 May 1966

Dazzling Dave Dunkley replaced Ted English in the show. The official story was that Ted was too upset to continue but, when Bob visited the magician in his new digs, he seemed more angry than grief-stricken.

'After all I've done for Larry Buxton. Kicked off the bill for Dave Dunkley and that lardy assistant of his. I'm going to sue.'

Bob had responded by reminding Ted not to leave town.

'Am I still a suspect then? Why haven't you found the real killer? You're useless, you lot.'

It was a question that Brighton CID were continuing to ask themselves. It was nearly five weeks since Cherry's body had been found. Meg's white-haired man seemed to have vanished like Astarte's ghost. Apart from the dog-walker, Reginald Glover, no one had seen the man entering or leaving 84 Marine Parade on Sunday, 10 April.

Edgar had used his extra man(person)power to check every bus route from the Aquarium to Worthing in one direction and Seaford in the other. But the elderly man in the Beatles jacket remained elusive.

Ted English was still their main suspect. He didn't have a complete alibi for the evening of Cherry's murder. He'd had supper at his digs in Charlotte Street at six o'clock and, afterwards, had gone to his room. But there were no confirmed sightings after nine p.m. Ted could easily have walked to Marine Parade, stabbed Cherry and returned to sleep in his bed, have breakfast and attend band call on Monday morning. But why? The pair didn't seem to be romantically involved. There was a thirty-year age gap between them and even Cherry's parents said that Ted had behaved 'like a gentleman' towards their daughter. 'In public anyway,' Iain Underwood told Emma darkly, which she reported to Edgar.

Several people at number 84 could have killed Cherry. Linda, Annie, Ida, Mario, Bigg and Small. None of them had complete alibis. But not even the imaginative Emma could come up with a motive for any of them. The fingerprints found at the scene did not match any on file. The murder weapon had never been found.

Edgar had even visited Gordon Palgrave in his Richmond home. Strictly speaking, as the superintendent, he shouldn't be conducting interviews but they were short-staffed and, besides, he was curious about the man he had last seen attacking a woman with a rubber hammer on his TV screen, the man Max had called 'an unpleasant customer'. It had been an unsettling encounter, for all sorts of reasons. Not that Palgrave had been unfriendly, far from it. He had welcomed Edgar with the utmost affability, a cheerful mine-host in a pastel-coloured jumper and checked trousers. The famous blond quiff was balanced on top of his head in a miracle of coiffure. It nodded along with its owner as Palgrave offered tea and coffee and led the way to the 'garden room', a hexagonal conservatory that looked out onto a vast, manicured garden. The striped lawn seemed to stretch into infinity, like an optical illusion.

Palgrave settled into a wicker chair with a sigh of contentment.

'I love this house. It's home. Cosy, you know. I've got bigger places in Spain and Scotland, but this is my retreat.'

He grinned at Edgar. His teeth were so white that Edgar had to resist the urge to shield his eyes. The weather had turned very warm and the sun beat relentlessly through the glass roof.

'Mr Palgrave—' Edgar began.

'Pal, please. Everyone calls me Pal. Besides, anyone who's a friend of my friend Max is a Pal of mine.'

Another grin but this time Edgar thought that it came with a hint of a threat. I know Max, the bobbing quiff seemed to say. I know your secrets.

'Mr . . . er . . . Pal . . . as you know, I'm investigating the murder of Cherry Underwood . . .'

'So tragic.' Palgrave sheathed his teeth. 'Poor girl.'

'I understand that you knew Cherry?'

'I knew her a little.' Palgrave's voice was still pleasant, but the quiff was now still. 'It's a close-knit world, the magic world. The magic circle, so to speak.'

Edgar knew that the Magic Circle was an exclusive society consisting of, in its own estimation, the best magicians in the country. Edgar remembered Ruby railing against it; women were not allowed to join. He wondered if Palgrave was making another veiled threat.

'You worked with Cherry in 1963,' said Edgar. It wasn't a question; he wanted Palgrave to know that he'd done his research.

'For one season only,' said Palgrave. 'She was a bright girl but not quite up to the standard I needed. Besides, I was already moving into television. You know I have a little show on the box?'

As *Hug or Hit* was currently the most popular show on BBC1, this was taking self-deprecation so far that it became blatant bragging.

'I don't watch much television,' said Edgar, untruthfully. 'Do you know how Cherry came to work with Ted English?'

'Oh, come now,' said Palgrave. 'You can't suspect Ted? He wouldn't hurt a fly.'

'I'm just trying to get some background information,' said Edgar. 'Did you introduce Cherry to Ted?'

'I might have done. Or it might have been Rex King.

Cherry worked with him too. We were quite a gang in those days. Me, Rex, Ted, Tommy Horton, Dave Dunkley. All for one and one for all, that was our motto.'

'Dave Dunkley has replaced Ted in the show on the Palace Pier.'

'I know. I spoke to Larry Buxton, the producer, about it. I've got some money in the show. I'm an angel, so to speak.'

Edgar seemed to remember that 'angel' was a name for someone who backed a theatrical enterprise. He couldn't see anything particularly angelic about Gordon Palgrave, despite the sun shining on his halo of hair.

Palgrave was growing expansive. 'We wanted Max Mephisto and he would have loved to do it, but he has film commitments. We had a good chat about it, Max and I. Dave was very much a second choice.'

'Do you know Dave Dunkley's assistant too?'

'Joanie? Yes, she's been around for a while. Think she worked with Tommy once and he's been retired for years.'

'Have you got addresses for all these people?'

'Telephone my assistant,' said Palgrave, handing over a business card. 'Maureen knows everything.'

'When you knew Cherry,' said Edgar. 'Did she have a boyfriend? Or did she ever mention anyone who was bothering her?'

'There was a boyfriend at home,' said Palgrave. 'Oop north.' He attempted an accent. 'I think he got a bit heavy at times.'

Emma had mentioned a Harold, who had wanted to marry Cherry. They had checked him out and he had an unimpeachable alibi for the night of her murder – he was waiting outside the hospital ward while his wife was having their first baby.

'When did you last see Cherry?'

'I really can't remember. But it was years ago. I've moved on from that set.'

What happened to 'all for one and one for all'? wondered Edgar. But Pal certainly seemed to have moved beyond seedy digs and early morning band calls. They parted amicably enough with Pal urging Edgar to call him any time. 'Or make an appointment with Maureen. I'm a busy man.'

PC Danny Black had attended the show on the pier and dutifully taken notes on Dazzling Dave Dunkley and assistant, whose real name was Joan Waters. Bob had suggested that Meg went with him but she had declined. Edgar wondered whether Danny had done something to upset Meg but the two of them still seemed to work together quite happily. Sometimes they reminded Edgar of Bob and Emma in the old days.

'It's quite a good show,' said Black. 'The magician saws the lady in half and you see splinters when the blade cuts through the box and everything. She had a red cape on and it looked like blood. I couldn't see how it was done. Maybe she curled up in one end of the box and there were fake feet at the other end. But it would have been hard. She wasn't small.'

'What do you mean?' said Edgar. He remembered Ted talking about Dave's 'lardy' assistant.

Black had blushed. 'She was big. Not fat. But strong-looking.'

'Like Ida Lupin?' said Meg. 'She's a strongwoman. That's her act. She lifts men over her head.'

'Yes, like her,' said Black. 'But not as good-looking.'

Edgar had never met Ida but now he rather wanted to. They were still keeping 84 Marine Parade under surveillance but, in a few weeks' time, most of the occupants would be moving on. Ida, Mario, Bigg and Small had all been retained for the London run of the show but the promised tour did not seem be happening. After June, Mario Fontana was singing on a cruise ship, Bigg and Small were having a rest before the panto season and Ida had a summer season in Blackpool. The variety circuit was still there, if you knew where to look.

Edgar and Emma were due to go on holiday in July. They were going abroad for the first time in their married life. Emma's parents had taken a villa in the south of France for the whole month. 'They want to escape the World Cup,' said Emma. 'They think there'll be football hooligans fighting in the streets.' His in-laws weren't far wrong, thought Edgar, all police forces had been warned to increase the numbers of bobbies on the beat. There were no matches in Brighton, but football meant drunkenness, which meant public disorder, assaults and sometimes even darker violence. Even so, Edgar felt a bit disappointed to be missing the final, although he doubted that England would go all the way. Edgar and family were going to France for the last two weeks in July. The children were already thoroughly overexcited. 'It's paradise,' said Marianne solemnly, looking up from the brochure showing the Villa Genevieve. 'This must be what paradise looks like.'

Bob could cope with the football hooligans, but Edgar prayed that they would have caught Cherry's killer before the holiday. He'd never relax otherwise.

CHAPTER 13

It wasn't the evenings that got to you, thought Joanie, it was the mornings. When you arrived at the theatre, even for a matinee, something about the very floorboards revived you. Dr Theatre, her dad used to call it. Even if you were shivering with flu and a fever, one look at the poster 'Appearing Tonight!' and your head would clear and your eyes start to sparkle. Joanie's mother had even performed on stage while in the first stages of labour. Her parents had a double act, Billy and Jilly Waters, juggling and comedy dancing. Joanie couldn't imagine what sort of comedy dancing Mum could have managed while doubled over with contractions. 'You were nearly born on stage,' Dad used to tell her. Joanie had made her first appearance in the dressing room of the Adelphi in Liverpool, Lou Lenny (of Lou Lenny and her Unrideable Mule) acting as midwife. It was no wonder, really, that she was in the business.

What would Mum and Dad think of this gig? Joanie

wondered, in the grim early minutes after waking in her boarding house and regarding the stained ceiling and swinging single light bulb. Magician's assistant wasn't exactly a starring role, especially when you were in your mid-forties. Of course, Ruby Magic had started off as an assistant and now she must be the most famous woman magician in the country. And, come to think of it, she must be coming up for forty soon. But Ruby had certain advantages, stunning beauty and a famous father being two of them. Joanie had always looked better with the light behind her.

It was Dad who first introduced her to Tommy Horton, who'd been looking for an assistant. That had been just before the war. Tommy had been OK; he'd seemed ancient then but was probably only in his fifties. Tommy was still alive, Dave had told her, but in a nursing home. 'He doesn't know what day it is now. Poor old Tom.' Tommy had always been forgetful, reflected Joanie. Not a great quality in a magician.

Joanie had joined the Wrens in the war and, barring the death of her parents in the London Blitz, thought of those years as the happiest in her life. She'd had vague ideas of staying in the navy but, before she knew it, she was out with a month's pay and her uniform jacket, which she dyed a smart forest green. She tried working in cafés and shops and had even completed a secretarial course before succumbing to the inevitable and contacting Tommy. He was retired by then but put her in touch with Pal. Joanie shivered. There was no heating in the upstairs room and, although it was May, the mornings were still cold.

After breakfast – Mrs O'Hara always put on a good spread – Joanie walked into town. She was staying in digs near the station. Dave's hotel was on the seafront but those places were out of her budget. Joanie's boarding house was in a grim terrace beside a singularly ill-named pub called the Bel Vue. The only view was of the glass roof of Brighton Station but the house certainly had a vantage point because it was at the top of a very steep hill. This made the walk into Brighton easy but the trip back a real slog. Today, Joanie made herself stride along. She needed to retain her fitness if she was going to squash herself into one side of the sawing box. 'It's part of the illusion,' Dave kept saying, 'people won't think that a big girl like you could get into such a small space.' He could be a real charmer sometimes. After the war, Joanie worked with Rex King – introduced by Pal, who else? – before settling into a partnership with Dave. They weren't friends exactly. Dave didn't care that Joanie was in freezing digs by the station. He never asked about her life (just as well, really) or enquired about her welfare. But they understood each other, and the routine was second nature now.

Joanie bought cold cream at Boots and some warm lisle tights at Woolworths. She had to wear nylons on stage but she felt the cold when away from the heat of Dr Theatre. Since she'd last been in Brighton, several new office blocks had shot up and there was a sign saying that work was about to start on an 'American-style shopping mall' called Churchill Square. Joanie was sure it would be very smart but she preferred the old shops on Western Road or in the Lanes. She had lunch in a Wimpy Bar and then caught the bus back to the station, walking the last and steepest part of the hill.

Mrs O'Hara always put on a high tea for the pros at four but Joanie was still full from her lunchtime hamburger. She walked back down the hill with Sonya, a gymnast who was appearing on the bill. Sonya was one of those tiny women who made Joanie feel elephantine, but she was pleasant enough and they had an enjoyable moan about the lodgings, Dazzling Dave and the rest of the cast.

Joanie shared a dressing room with Sonya, her partner Vanda, and Ida, the strongwoman. In fact, Joanie and Ida had briefly had a double act, The Stone Age Sisters. Ida was still wearing the fur bikini as her stage costume.

When Joanie arrived, Ida was lying on the floor with her legs above her head.

'Going in for contortions?' Joanie put her plastic bag down on the table.

'My varicose veins are killing me.'

'Mine too.' Varicose veins were the curse of every variety performer.

'Try standing on your head,' said Sonya. 'It helps.'

'I'll take your word for it, dear,' said Joanie.

She sat down to apply her make-up. There was only one

mirror and they took it in turns. Halfway through, Perry Small knocked on the door to ask for an aspirin.

'Time of the month?' said Joanie. She often made jokes that nobody else got.

'Headache,' said Perry. 'Not me but Geoff.'

Ida found him two dusty pills in the bottom of her bag. When he left, Sonya said, 'Those two. They're so weird. I bet if one has a headache, the other one does too.'

'Takes all sorts to make a world,' said Ida. 'You finished at the mirror, Joanie?'

The act went fairly well. Dave almost knocked the false feet off the end of the box but managed to conceal it with his cape. When Joanie emerged, spreading her red cloak like wings, she got a warm round of applause. There was nothing like it, the feeling that the crowd liked and appreciated you, the waves of sound breaking against the Circle and the Royal Box and rolling back towards you. Joanie felt the petty irritations of the day smoothed away as she bowed and smiled. This was love, or something very like it. Perhaps the most genuine love Joanie had ever experienced, apart from Mum and Dad, of course.

Being the last act before the interval meant that Joanie and Dave could relax a bit. They still had to appear in the finale but they could take off their shoes and drink bottled beer in Dave's dressing room.

'Next stop, the West End,' said Dave, raising his toothmug. 'We're on our way, Joanie.'

They'd been on their way before and never quite got

there but Joanie appreciated the sentiment. In fact, she felt a wave of affection for Dave, ridiculous black wig and all. She clinked glasses with him. 'Here's to us.'

Sonya was going out for a drink with the dancers so Joanie waited for the bus home on her own. If the applause was the highlight, this was definitely the lowest point of the day, waiting in the cold to go back to an empty room. Never mind, Joanie told herself, Mrs O'Hara might have made cocoa and she could go to bed with a Whiteoak book. The thought of red-haired Renny waiting for her cheered her up so much that she alighted from the bus with almost a spring in her step.

The last bit of the hill was hard work though, especially when you'd been twirling away on stage. The lights of the Bel Vue looked almost welcoming as Joanie rounded the corner. Nearly there. As she passed the alleyway by the pub, a man appeared from the shadows. She saw the glow of his cigarette. Joanie walked faster. Although Dave had told her recently that she was 'past the age of being hassled in the street', she was still nervous of strangers.

'Joanie! Stop!' said a voice.

Joanie turned. 'Oh, it's you.'

She wondered why she didn't feel more reassured.

CHAPTER 14

Edgar thought the telephone must be ringing in his dreams. By the time he had forced himself awake and stumbled out of bed, the ringing had stopped. Going out onto the landing, he heard Marianne saying brightly, 'Oh, hallo, Uncle Bob.'

'Marianne!' Edgar hurried downstairs. One thing he knew; a six a.m. call was not one that his ten-year-old daughter should be taking.

'Go back to bed,' said Edgar, taking the receiver.

'But it's morning,' said Marianne. And Edgar could see sunlight slanting through the stained-glass in the front door.

'Get dressed then.'

'I thought you should know,' said Bob, in his most emotionless voice. 'Another woman has been found dead. Stabbed. Buckingham Place. Up by the station.'

'Do we know anything about the dead woman?'

'Yes, sir,' said Bob. Sir. Things must be serious. 'She's

been identified as Joan Waters. A magician's assistant. From the show on the pier.'

'I'm on my way,' said Edgar.

Edgar's car was parked in a garage a few streets away. It would be almost as quick to walk. He set off at a pace. It was a particularly beautiful morning, the sky a pale sea-shell pink behind the crested battlements of the pier. By the time Edgar reached the station, he was out of breath and the foot with the missing toe, lost to frostbite in Norway in 1940, was beginning to ache. As he climbed the hill, he could see blue police lights flashing. Police tape surrounded a triangular-fronted pub that looked vaguely familiar. A uniformed PC was standing by the entrance to an alleyway. Bob was talking to a woman in curlers but he broke away when Edgar approached.

'That's Mrs O'Hara who runs the boarding house next door. The deceased, Miss Waters, was a resident there. Her body was found by a dog-walker at approximately five this morning. He knocked on the door of the nearest house and, as luck would have it, well, not luck exactly . . .'

'I know what you mean,' said Edgar. Dog-walkers again, he was thinking. Once Emma's life had been saved by a man called Arthur walking two pugs called Lancelot and Percival. It was Reginald Glover and his dachshund who had spotted the mysterious white-haired man leaving number 84 Marine Parade. If this was him again, the man would have some explaining to do. He asked Bob the name of the canine-loving citizen.

'Fred Prentice,' said Bob, consulting his notebook. 'He walks his dog early because he works at the station. I sent him home but said we might want to talk to him later.'

'What sort of dog did he have?'

Bob looked quizzical but answered, 'An Alsatian, I think. Big brute.' Bob and his family owned a small terrier called Scruffy.

'Were you first on the scene?'

'No. PC Dudeney was on the beat and he attended but the operator also telephoned me at home. I was here in half an hour. I called you as soon as I knew the victim's identity. I've left a message at the station for DS Barker, WDC Connolly and DC Black to join us as soon as they clock in. I know WDC Connolly doesn't have a telephone at home. Solomon Carter's also on his way. '

'Thanks, Bob. You've done well.'

Edgar approached the alleyway. PC Dudeney saluted him and stood to attention.

'Stand easy,' said Edgar, who was uncomfortable with anything that reminded him of his army days. 'I understand you were first at the scene?'

'Yes, sir.'

'Tell me what happened.'

'I was on duty at Trafalgar Street station and received intelligence that a member of the public had reported a . . . a deceased. I proceeded to Buckingham Place and found the gentleman in question, together with the owner of the boarding establishment. I took statements from them both and then waited for DI Willis. Sir.'

'Well done,' said Edgar. He wanted to tell the man to speak English but, even though it was couched in police language, the account had been lucid and easy to follow. He would mention Dudeney favourably to his superior officers.

Behind PC Dudeney was a human shape – a deceased – covered with a blanket, presumably from Mrs O'Hara's house. Edgar knew that he should wait for Solomon but he raised one corner and saw a face, white from loss of blood, with dyed blonde hair that was somehow touching in its doomed vanity. He replaced the covering and turned to Bob.

'You wait for Carter, Bob. I'll have a quick word with Mrs O'Hara indoors.'

'Righty-ho.' Bob liked to use phrases that he thought were RAF slang. He'd been too young to serve in the war but his brother had been a dashing flying officer.

Mrs O'Hara was only too happy to go back inside. 'I have to start breakfast soon,' she told Edgar. She led the way into the kitchen, a long room with a table running down the centre. 'You don't mind if I start buttering bread, do you?'

'Not at all.'

She cut it in a very dangerous way, angling the bread-knife towards her chest. Edgar averted his eyes from the blade. Cherry had been killed with a kitchen knife. Had the same weapon been used on Joan? He also realised that he was very hungry.

'How long had Miss Waters, Joan, been staying with you?'

'She'd been here just over two weeks. She was appearing in the show at the end of the pier. I got free tickets to go on the first Tuesday. It was quite entertaining.'

'Joan was a magician's assistant, wasn't she?'

'Yes. She got cut in half on stage. Quite an act.'

The serrated knife chewed through the bread.

'Do you know anything about Joan's private life? Are her parents still alive? Did she have a boyfriend?'

'She told me that her parents were both dead. They were in the business too. I've had quite a few showbiz types over the years.'

'And a boyfriend?'

Mrs O'Hara snorted. 'I wouldn't have thought so. Not at her age.'

'How old was she?'

'She wouldn't see forty-five again. A bit long in the tooth for all that climbing in and out of boxes.'

The landlady was now buttering the bread. Without warning, she put a piece in front of Edgar.

'You look like you need feeding up. Cup of tea?'

'Yes please.'

Mrs O'Hara put the kettle on the Aga. The kitchen was old-fashioned but cosy, with drying racks over the range and open-fronted cupboards. It reminded Edgar of the house in Willesden where he'd grown up. His mother now lived in Weybridge with her second husband and was the proud possessor of a fitted Formica kitchen.

Edgar bit into the bread. It was so thick and doughy that it glued his mouth together. While he was temporarily silenced, the door flew open and a woman in a dressing gown appeared.

'What's happening, Mrs O'Hara? There are policemen outside and Joanie's not in her room.'

She had a foreign accent and something about the way she moved made Edgar think she was an actress or a dancer.

'Sit down, Sonya,' said Mrs O'Hara. 'I've got bad news for you.'

Sonya turned to Edgar as if the news must be his fault.

'Joanie's dead,' said the landlady. And Sonya swayed and would have fallen if Edgar hadn't caught her.

Meg tried not to be excited when she got the DI's message.

'It might be another murder.'

'Cheery little thing, aren't you?' said Danny, who had arrived at the same time and was taking off his leather jacket.

Meg decided to ignore the 'little thing'. 'Put your coat back on,' she said, 'we can go up to Buckingham Place on your bike.' Danny, a part-time Mod, was the proud possessor of a red Vespa.

'Shouldn't we wait for DS Barker?'

'No,' said Meg. 'The DI would want us to get there as quickly as possible.'

Danny didn't need much persuading and soon the two of them were flying up North Street, past the office workers and shopkeepers opening up for the day. The time on the clock tower was eight-thirty. Meg didn't have a helmet and enjoyed the feeling of her hair whipping back into her face. Both her older brothers had motorbikes and this was like riding pillion with them. Except it wasn't, quite.

The DI blinked when he saw the Vespa approaching but he didn't say anything about disrespecting the uniform or not waiting for a superior officer. In fact, he seemed relieved to see them.

'Deceased is Miss Joan Waters, who appeared with Dave Dunkley in the end of the pier show.'

'I watched it!' interrupted Danny, then saw the DI's face. 'Sorry.'

Meg had had to stop herself gasping. Another magician's assistant. Surely this had to be linked to Cherry's death?

'Solomon Carter's examining the body now,' said DI Willis. And Meg could see a sinister crouching figure in the alleyway behind them. 'Cause of death was stab wounds and he thinks it happened around midnight last night. The super's been here and he's got an address for Dunkley. I want—' He stopped because a taxi drew up and DS Barker emerged.

'Thanks for waiting,' he said to Danny, who blushed. Meg, he ignored.

'You didn't need to get a cab,' said the DI. 'Plenty of buses go this way.'

DS Barker said nothing but his look of ill humour deepened. The DI repeated the information about the dead woman.

'The super is sending some reinforcements, but I want you, DC Black, to start door-to-door enquiries. DS Barker, you and WDC Connolly go to interview Dunkley.'

Meg wanted to object but didn't dare. Barker turned on his heel and headed down the hill, following the curve of the station wall. Meg followed.

CHAPTER 15

Edgar was not surprised to find Emma waiting for him in his office. She greeted him brightly, brandishing a tartan thermos.

'Hi, Ed! Just dropped the kids off at school and thought you might like a flask of soup. It's a cold day.'

'Emma,' said Edgar. 'When have you ever made me soup? And it's boiling out there.'

This was a slight exaggeration, but Edgar had taken his jacket off during the walk from the station. He opened the flask and the smell of Heinz tomato hit him like a blow.

'Spend long making this, did you?'

Emma grinned. 'OK. I want to know about the murder. Was she really another magician's assistant?'

'Yes,' said Edgar. 'Joan Waters, aged forty-five. Currently performing with Dazzling Dave Dunkley at the end of Palace Pier. Meg and DS Barker are interviewing him now.'

He was surprised at the expression of revulsion that briefly flitted over Emma's face.

'Why did you send Meg with that man?'

'It was Bob's decision but why not? DS Barker is an experienced officer. What have you got against him? Did he say something to annoy you the other day?'

Emma paused before replying. 'No. Well, he did make some crack about me being the boss's wife. It just, I don't think he's a very suitable companion for a young woman.'

'Meg's tough,' said Edgar. 'She can cope.'

'Have you asked her?' said Emma, quite sharply. 'Has Bob asked her?'

'I'll talk to Bob. I assume you'll want an update on the interview too.'

'It would be appreciated,' said Emma coolly. 'In return Sam could do some research on this Dazzling Dave.'

'David Dunkley,' said Edgar. 'Where is Sam these days? I haven't seen her for ages.'

'She's working on a story in London. But she could look in the newspaper archives. And in the births, marriages and deaths.'

Edgar knew that Sam was a good and thorough researcher.

'There were some other names Max mentioned,' said Edgar. He flicked through his notes. 'Tommy Horton and Rex King. Max said they were all part of the same set. Along with Gordon Palgrave. Pal. Could Sam do some research on them?'

'I'm sure she could. There must be acres of stuff on Pal.

We'll make some notes. In return for full police cooperation. Sharing information, like we agreed.'

Edgar couldn't remember making any such agreement; Emma probably bullied Bob into it.

David Dunkley was staying at a hotel called the Pelican. It wasn't one of the smartest on the seafront but the reception area looked clean and well-furnished. It was certainly a step up from Buckingham Place. It was strange, thought Meg, how just one letter separated the terraced street from the Queen's residence. It wasn't an observation she could make to DS Barker, who hadn't exchanged one word with her during the long walk down the hill and along the promenade.

Barker showed his warrant card and asked to speak to Mr Dunkley. In a few minutes they were knocking on the door of his first-floor room. Meg was grateful that they hadn't had to share a lift.

The man who opened the door was wearing a red dressing gown and there was something definitely wrong with his hair. It was jet black and the fringe was slightly off-centre, which gave his whole face a lopsided, asymmetrical appearance.

'Yes?' said Dunkley, holding the door half-shut behind him.

'Police,' said Barker. 'Can we come in?'

Dunkley backed away and Meg and Barker entered the room. It was small, with flowered curtains and a double bed that took up more than half the floor space. An open wardrobe showed a dress suit and a camel-hair coat. There was a brandy bottle on the bedside table.

'When did you last see Miss Joan Waters?' asked Barker.

'Joanie?' Dunkley's voice sounded distinctly quavery. Meg wondered how old he was – suspiciously black hair aside. 'I saw her after the show. She went to get the bus.'

'What time was that?'

'About ten-thirty.'

'And what did you do after the show?'

'A few of us went for a drink. At the Colonnade bar. By the Theatre Royal.'

'Who was there?'

'I don't know. Perry Small, Larry Buxton, a few of the chorus girls. That gymnast, Sonya. Look, what's all this about?'

'Joan was murdered last night,' said Barker. 'Knifed to death.'

Dunkley collapsed onto the bed. Meg thought of how differently she would have broken the news. She supposed Barker was trying shock tactics but it seemed a rather brutal way of extracting information and, in her admittedly limited experience, not the most effective. She also thought that Barker should not have given away the murder weapon.

Meg poured a glass of water from the sink in the corner of the room. 'Drink this,' she said to Dunkley. 'Take some deep breaths.'

Dunkley did look an awful colour, somewhere between green and grey. His hand shook as he took the glass.

'Joanie,' he said. 'I can't believe it.'

'Do you know anyone who could have done this?' said Barker, looming over the almost prostrate magician. 'Did she have any enemies?'

'Joanie didn't have an enemy in the world,' said Dunkley. 'I worked with her for almost twenty years. Everyone liked her.'

Meg sat next to Dunkley on the bed, ignoring Barker's dirty look. 'Did Joanie have any family?'

Dunkley shook his head. 'No. Her parents died in the war. She had no one. Rootless. Like me.'

And he started to weep. Whether for himself or Joan, Meg did not know.

'Why were you fussing him like that?' said Barker, as they walked back past the hotels on the seafront.

'I wasn't fussing,' said Meg. 'I was showing sympathy.'

'He's a possible killer.'

'And sympathy's often the best way of getting information,' said Meg. 'I've heard the super say so.'

'Oh, we all know you're the super's pet. I thought you were going to cuddle Dunkley at one point.'

'And you'd know all about cuddling people,' said Meg.

She almost thought that Barker was going to hit her but, after a murderous glare, he quickened his pace until he was walking ahead of her. That suited Meg just fine.

They were passing 84 Marine Parade. Meg wondered if, by some mysterious showbiz telegraph, the inhabitants already knew about Joan's death. As she looked up at the house, a voice, seemingly coming from the air, said, 'Meg!'

It was Logan, the man they had met at Emma's friend Astarte's house. He was standing on a balcony a few doors down from the guest house. Meg walked closer. Logan was wearing a white shirt, worn loose over very short shorts. She could see his gold medallions glinting in the sun.

'What are you doing this fine morning?' said Logan. 'That uniform is very sexy. Are you out on a case?'

'As a matter of fact,' said Meg, 'I am.'

'Murder?'

'I couldn't say.' Meg realised that she was almost flirting, standing in the street just after visiting a possible suspect. She'd never flirted with anyone before. It was surprisingly easy.

'I've got something to tell you,' said Logan. 'It's to do with the other girl that was killed. Perhaps we could have a drink tonight?'

'Can you tell me now?' said Meg. Barker had stopped and was looking back at her, tapping his watch meaningfully.

Logan laughed. 'Sure. Come on up. I'll throw down the key.'

'I'll be ten minutes,' Meg shouted at Barker. 'Don't wait.'

And, miraculously, she caught the key with one hand.

CHAPTER 16

Meg climbed the stairs to the sitting room, which somehow looked larger and grander than it had when she last visited. A crystal ball glittered on the table by the balcony doors but there was no sign of Astarte. Had Logan been consulting it? He glittered enough all by himself, what with his earrings and medallions and gleaming blue-green eyes.

Logan offered tea, coffee or 'something stronger'. Meg asked for tea. She wasn't quite used to the new craze for coffee. It was too scary, with its many permutations: whipped cream, chocolate sprinkles, the terrifying entity called a cappuccino. Tea was what they drank at home. Tea was safe.

While Logan was in the kitchen, Meg prowled round the room. On closer inspection, the red curtains and the pink sofas – even the grand piano – looked a little the worse for wear. A mirrored shawl thrown over one of the chairs had been dislodged to show a hole in the upholstery. The bookshelves contained several books in languages Meg didn't understand but, comfortingly, a whole row of Agatha Christies. The crystal ball sent tiny rainbows shimmering over the walls.

'Find anything you like?' Logan was suddenly standing behind Meg. 'There are books there written in blood and bound in human skin. There are books that would send you mad before you'd read a page.'

Meg turned to look at Logan. He was holding a tray and grinning at her, almost laughing. Was he doing what her brothers would call 'taking the mickey'? How could a book be written in blood? She only knew that her mother would be crossing herself by now and reaching for the holy water.

Meg tried for a light tone. 'I don't get much time for reading. My sister Aisling reads a book a day.'

'Sure and you're living life instead,' said Logan. He put the tray down on a glass table and began pouring the tea. There was no milk or sugar but maybe Logan was like Meg's father and unable to complete domestic tasks.

They sat on either side of the table. Logan's shorts were so short that you could hardly see them when he was sitting down. Meg was very conscious of his long legs covered, like his chest, in black hair. To distract herself she took a sip of tea and almost gagged. It tasted like warm grass cuttings. She looked up to find Logan grinning at her. 'It's made with stinging nettles. Very good for your eyesight, apparently.'

Meg put her cup down. She might be willing to believe that books could send you mad but not that you could make tea out of nettles.

'What did you want to tell me?' she said, trying to regain a professional tone. 'About Cherry, the girl who died.' The first girl, she said to herself.

'I arrived here on Sunday the tenth of April,' said Logan. 'I didn't mean to stay so long but one of our horses is lame and needs field rest. Bartley, my brother, has got some work in Ireland so it suits me to stay with Astarte. Besides, she's good company and . . .' He gestured towards the balcony doors and the sea. Meg knew what he meant.

'So I arrived at about four o'clock in the afternoon,' said Logan. 'Got a lift with a mate who's got a van. He dropped me off outside the Aquarium and I walked from there. When I got to Astarte's house, there was a girl standing on the pavement outside. A very pretty girl, blonde, though I prefer brunettes . . .' He grinned at Meg, who didn't react, although she could feel her colour rising.

'She was talking to a man, a young man, all done up like one of the Beatles. You know, tight trousers, zip-up jacket. I didn't think much of it except that I didn't like his style. But, last night, Astarte was talking about the murder. She'd been to see her friend, the girl's landlady, and I think it was preying on her mind. I realised that the girl must have been Cherry and that the day I saw her was the day she died.'

Many things rushed through Meg's mind. The first was

that Logan, legs spread wide in his shorts, was hardly one to sneer at tight trousers. But, more importantly, was the man talking to Cherry the boyfriend that Ida had mentioned to Emma (though not to the police)? Was he the white-haired man? After all, he had been described as wearing a Beatles jacket.

'What colour was the man's hair?' she asked.

'Blond, like the girl. In fact, I thought it might have been her brother. But there was something about the girl. Tension, fear . . . I don't know. Astarte thinks I picked up on Cherry's mental state but it's more that I notice body language. It's useful for telling fortunes.'

'Do you tell fortunes?' Meg couldn't help asking.

'Yes,' said Logan, 'you're going to meet a tall dark stranger who makes you disgusting tea.'

Now Meg knew she was blushing. She had no idea how to cope with this sort of remark. 'I'd better go,' she said. 'Thank you for the information.'

'We must have that drink sometime,' said Logan.

Meg arrived back at the station to find that the briefing meeting had already started. 'Superintendent Stephens said you were to go straight in,' said Rita, disapprovingly.

Meg was surprised to find the room so full of people. Not just the super, the DI, Danny and DS Barker but about ten other uniformed officers too. They must have been brought in from neighbouring stations. The DI was on his feet. On the chalkboard was written: Cherry Underwood and Joan Waters. Underneath, in smaller letters, 'Suspects: David Dunkley, Ted English, Persons Unknown.'

Meg tried to slide soundlessly into her chair but she tripped up on someone's discarded helmet and had to catch an unknown arm to steady herself. A few people laughed.

'Thank you for joining us, WDC Connolly,' said the DI. 'DS Barker has just been filling us in on your interview with David Dunkley. Have you anything to add?'

This was hard, without knowing what Barker had said, but Meg volunteered, 'He seemed genuinely upset about Joan.'

'You certainly fell for Dunkley's act,' said Barker. 'You were all over him.'

'I was establishing a rapport,' said Meg, with a glance at the DI.

'Quite right, WDC Connolly,' said DI Willis. 'That's why we send women officers on these interviews,' he said, to the room in general. 'It's to create a less threatening atmosphere.'

Meg thought she heard Barker mutter the word 'rapport' in disgusted accents.

'I didn't trust him,' said Barker out loud. 'And he was wearing a syrup.'

'Syrup?' said the DI in a pained voice.

'Syrup of figs. Wig.'

'So he could be the white-haired man,' said Danny.

Meg couldn't stand it any longer. 'I've got something,'

she said, adding 'sir' because the DI was looking rather boot-faced. 'That's why I was late. One of Cherry's neighbours had some new information. He saw her on Sunday the tenth of April, the day she died, at four p.m. She was talking to a young blond-haired man, dressed in a Beatles-type zip-up jacket.'

'Who told you this?' said Barker. 'Was it the half-naked man who was chatting you up?'

'It was Astarte Zabini's cousin,' said Meg with dignity. 'As I'm sure you know, Astarte is a friend of Superintendent Stephens.'

She had the satisfaction of seeing Barker look taken aback. The super said, sounding embarrassed, 'More a friend of my wife's really. But this is a good lead, WDC Connolly. Well done. This could well be the mysterious white-haired man. We need to show this witness our identikit picture.'

As Meg had foretold, the identikit looked like a child's drawing of a human, but she graciously volunteered to show it to Logan. She tried to conceal the fact that she didn't know his surname.

'Right,' said the DI. 'Let's summarise what we know about Dunkley's movements last night. After the show, he went for a drink at the Colonnade. We know that Perry Small was there too and Larry Buxton, the show's producer. Last orders are at eleven. That would have given Dunkley enough time to climb the hill to the station and murder Joan. Carter thought time of death was about midnight.'

'Colonnade's got a late licence,' said someone. 'Would have closed at midnight last night.'

'Let's establish exactly when Dunkley left,' said the DI. 'Still gives him just enough time. These timings are never that accurate. DC Black, did you get anything from the door-to-door?'

'No one heard anything,' said Danny. 'You'd have thought that Joan would cry out.'

'Not if she knew her attacker,' said the DI. 'We need to check Dunkley's alibi. And, talking of alibis, we need to know where Ted English was last night. Barker, can you check up on that? WDC Connolly, you talk to Perry Small, as you seem to have a rapport with the inhabitants of number 84.'

Was it Meg's imagination or did the DI give her the ghost of a wink?

Number 84 looked innocent in the sunshine. It was hard to believe that a girl had been brutally murdered there a few weeks ago. The reporters had even stopped hanging around outside. Meg wondered what it would be like to live in the house, where only recently there had been blood on the floor and the smell of death in the air. Maybe it was now haunted by Cherry's plaintive ghost as well as the white-haired man? She wondered why Ida and the other performers had stayed there. Were they hard-hearted or was it just very difficult to find suitable digs? Then she remembered Joan's boarding house in

Buckingham Place and Dave's depressing room at the Pelican. She might have stayed put herself, given that choice.

Annie opened the door.

'Oh, it's you again.'

'Hallo, Annie,' said Meg. 'I wondered if I could have a word with Perry Small.' Annie looked at her curiously but simply said, 'You'd best go up to his room. I think Geoff is out.'

Bigg and Small's room was on the top floor. Meg didn't know if she'd find them both there but, when the door opened, she saw that Perry Small was on his own. He was in shirtsleeves and holding an iron.

'Hallo,' said Meg. 'I'm WDC Meg Connolly. We've met before. Can I have a word?'

Wordlessly Perry stepped aside to let her into the room. There were two beds, neatly made, both with pyjamas folded under the pillows. One bedside table had a book on it, the other a bottle of pills. Two checked suits hung on the wardrobe door.

'I've just been steaming them,' Perry explained. 'Gets the creases out. Linda lent me a kettle.'

There was an ironing board by the wardrobe and the room smelt of damp cloth. Perry placed the iron on the board. It was the old-fashioned sort without an electrical lead.

Meg sat on one of the beds and, after a second's hesitation, Perry sat on the other. Meg remembered Bigg and Small when they had closed the show on the pier, wearing the brightly checked suits. Then they had seemed the ultimate professionals, every quip timed to perfection. Off-stage and on his own, Perry Small was far less impressive.

'I'm afraid I've got some news that will be a shock to you,' said Meg. 'Joan Waters has been killed.'

Perry put his hand to his mouth. His face seemed suddenly bleached of all colour.

'Killed?' he whispered from behind his fingers.

'Yes,' said Meg. 'I'm sorry. Did you know her well?'

'Everyone knew Joanie,' said Perry, echoing Dunkley. 'She was a real trouper. We've been on the bill with her a few times.'

'Did you see her last night? Talk to her?'

'Yes. I went to her dressing room to borrow some aspirin for Geoff.' Meg's eyes went to the pills on the bedside table. 'She was there with Ida, Sonya and Vanda. They were sharing. Joanie was putting her make-up on. She looked her usual self.'

'Did you see her after the show?'

'No. I went for a drink with Dave and some of the others. At the Colonnade.'

'Can you remember who else was there?'

'A couple of the chorus girls. One was Suzie something. Oh, and Ted English.'

'Ted English?'

'He'd been to see the show, apparently.'

'Wasn't that a bit odd?'

'Not really. Magicians often sneak in to see each other's shows. Sometimes they even go in disguise. Just to see if they can pick up some new tricks. I have to say, though, I thought there might be some unpleasantness between Ted and Dave – what with Dave taking his spot – but they seemed to be chatting quite pleasantly.'

'Did you notice what time Dave Dunkley left?'

Perry blinked but didn't question why she was asking. 'He left with me, just after midnight. We walked back to the coast road together.'

This gave Dunkley an alibi. It was still possible, thought Meg, for him to have doubled back and killed Joan – she knew that it wasn't possible to be completely accurate about time of death – but it looked increasingly unlikely.

Perry was rubbing his eyes. 'Poor old Joanie. We go back a long way. Geoff and I were just looking at some photos a few nights ago.'

Meg's ears pricked up. 'Photos?'

'We keep a scrapbook. It goes back years. Geoff's been on stage since he was a nipper. I wasn't much older, started as a ventriloquist. Want to see?'

'Yes please.'

Perry got a suitcase down from the top of the wardrobe. Inside was a leather-bound book. He flipped through the pages.

'Scarborough 1946, that was a tough house. There's Geoff judging the bathing beauty competition. Not that

I'd call them beauties. Blackpool 1947. That donkey was a vicious so-and-so. Oh, here's Joanie. The Adelphi, 1949.'

He showed Meg a picture of a girl in a spangled dress, gesturing towards a table that had been sawn in half. The photograph was black and white but the girl's hair shone in the stage lights.

'That's Joanie?'

'Yes. She was quite a looker in her day.'

And she looked very like Cherry Underwood.

As Meg descended the stairs, she saw Ida and Linda in the hall. They had obviously been waiting for her.

'Is it true?' said Ida, when Meg reached the bottom step. 'Is Joanie dead?'

'Where did you hear that?'

'Sonya just telephoned. She wasn't making much sense but I thought she said that Joanie had been killed, stabbed . . .'

Meg put a hand on Ida's arm. The strongwoman was shivering violently, though that could have been because she was only wearing a flimsy dressing gown.

'It's true,' she said. 'I'm very sorry.'

'Oh my God.' Ida covered her face with her hands. Linda put her arm round her. 'Let's go and sit down.'

Linda steered Ida towards a door at the back of the hallway. Uninvited, Meg followed. They were obviously in the private part of the house because the chequered tiles gave way to stone floors. Linda led the way into a large kitchen, where Annie was cooking something on the stove. She turned when they entered.

'Whatever's the matter?'

'Joanie's dead,' said Linda. 'Murdered. Just like Cherry.'

'Oh, heavens!' Annie put her arm round Ida. 'I'm so sorry, lovie. I'll make us all some tea.' It occurred to Meg that the three women seemed very close. She remembered Ida saying that she and Linda 'went way back'. She also hoped that she was included in the tea. And that it wasn't made of nettles.

'When did you last see Joanie?' she asked Ida, hoping that she sounded sympathetic rather than interrogatory.

'We said goodnight after the show,' said Ida. 'Joanie went to get her bus. Her digs were up by the station. I walked back here. Linda was still up and about and we had some cocoa.'

That gave Ida an alibi, at any rate.

'Was anyone else here?'

'Geoff. But he had a headache and went to bed. I think Perry and Mario went for drinks with some of the cast.'

Annie put mugs of tea in front of them all, including Meg.

'Who would do such an awful thing?' said Annie. She looked at Meg as if she might really know the answer.

'We will find whoever did this,' said Meg. 'I promise you.'

'Do you think it's the same person who killed Cherry?' said Linda.

'We're keeping an open mind,' said Meg, 'but there do seem to be similarities. One of your neighbours, Astarte's cousin in fact, said he saw Cherry talking to a young man outside his house on the day she died.'

'Is that the handsome gypsy cousin?' said Linda.

Meg tried to think of a professional police officer answer but ended up just saying, 'yes'.

'Ida,' Meg turned to the strongwoman, 'you said something to Emma Holmes about Cherry meeting a boyfriend that day.'

'Did I?' Ida looked genuinely surprised. 'Oh, I think it was something Perry Small mentioned. Just gossip really.'

Meg produced the identikit.

'Do you recognise this man?'

'He doesn't really look like anyone,' said Ida.

'What about the clothes? The blouson jacket?'

'So many people dress like that now.'

'Is that the man you mentioned before?' said Linda. 'The white-haired man?'

'Possibly,' said Meg.

'Astarte's seen the ghost too,' said Linda. 'The old man with white hair.'

That didn't surprise Meg. She thought of the leather-bound books in Astarte's sitting room. The books apparently written in blood.

'Do you think this man,' Ida pointed at the picture, 'might have killed Cherry? And Ida too?'

'Like I said, we're keeping an open mind.'

'That means you don't know,' said Linda.

'I wouldn't think Cherry and Joanie had much in common,' said Annie. 'They were both magician's assistants but that's it. I mean, there wasn't much similarity between Cherry and poor old Joanie.'

But Meg was thinking of the photograph in Perry's album. The girl with the shining hair.

Meg climbed back up the stairs and knocked on Perry Small's door. She heard the bedsprings squeak as he stood up. She had the feeling that Small hadn't moved since she left him. There was still no sign of Bigg.

'Sorry to interrupt you again. I've just got one more question.'

'What is it?' Was it Meg's imagination or was Perry's manner slightly more guarded now?

'Ida mentioned that you thought Cherry might have been meeting a boyfriend on the Sunday she died,' said Meg.

'Did I say that?' said Perry. 'Oh, I think I saw her talking to a young man and jumped to the usual conclusion.'

'And you didn't mention it to the police?'

'This wasn't in the house,' said Perry, as if this made all the difference. 'It was outside, by the street lamp.'

'Was this the man?' Meg produced the identikit.

'It's hard to tell,' said Perry. 'Maybe.'

'Can you remember what he was wearing?'

'A blue jacket, I think. Drainpipe trousers. I usually remember clothes.'

Meg made a note and told Small that she'd be in touch. It came out sounding slightly like a threat. Then she went back downstairs. The black-and-white tiled hallway was empty but she could hear voices coming from the kitchen. It sounded like an argument. 'She doesn't know . . .' Linda was saying. Her voice carried better than Ida's, whose reply was inaudible. 'It's not a crime,' Annie said, in a soothing tone. Meg had the impression that someone was crying.

She let herself out.

She was half dreading and half looking forward to calling on Logan again. As she waited in the porch of Astarte's house, she patted her hair into place and wished she had one of those little mirrors that women like Emma kept in their handbags. But, then, Meg never carried a handbag either.

To her surprise, the door was opened by Astarte, looking less mystic than usual in jeans and a white blouse.

'Oh, hallo,' she said. 'It's Meg, isn't it?'

'Yes. Is Logan in? I've got something to show him.'

'He's upstairs. Come on up.'

Logan was sitting at the table by the crystal ball. Again, Meg wondered if he'd been looking into its depths. Or maybe Astarte had been reading his future.

Logan stood up when Meg came in. 'Meg! You just can't get enough of me.'

Meg ignored him. 'I wanted to show you this.' She held out the picture. 'Could this be the man you saw with

Cherry?'

Logan gave the identikit more consideration than Ida had done. Astarte came to look over his shoulder.

'It's possible,' he said. 'But I thought he was younger.'

Reginald Glover hadn't seen the white-haired man's face but the artist had helpfully added some wrinkles.

'This isn't a true portrait,' said Astarte.

'Did you see the man too?' asked Meg.

'No,' said Astarte. 'I meant, this isn't a true portrait of anyone.'

'Of course not,' said Meg. 'It's an identikit facial reconstruction.' She thought that Astarte was being unhelpful.

'Sorry,' said Logan, sounding it. He accompanied Meg downstairs. 'What about that drink tonight?'

'I can't.'

'Why not?'

Meg wasn't expecting to be asked such a straight question. She ended up muttering something about not being allowed to drink in uniform.

'Couldn't you go home and change? When are you off duty?'

'Five o'clock,' said Meg.

'Where do you live?'

'Whitehawk.'

'I always think that's a beautiful name.'

Meg had never heard anyone say that the name 'Whitehawk' was beautiful, though she supposed it was when you thought of it as a white bird and not rows of small terraced houses.

'That's near Woodingdean, isn't it?' Logan was saying. 'Why don't I meet you at the Downs Hotel at seven? Just for a quick drink.'

There were many reasons why not. Meg was in the middle of a murder investigation. She should get a good night's sleep and be fresh for work tomorrow. She had never been inside a pub and the Downs was where her dad played darts. What would Aisling and her mum say if Meg arrived home, got changed, and rushed straight out again?

'Just one drink,' said Logan. 'What's the harm?'

And Meg heard herself agreeing.

CHAPTER 17

Right up until the last moment, Meg was sure she wouldn't go. It was fun to imagine that she would – all the way home on the bus she ran the scene in her head, pretending that she was the sort of girl who met handsome men for drinks – but she knew that, when she got back, she'd change into old clothes, help Mum cook supper and watch TV with Aisling and Collette. She was a serious woman with an important job, she hadn't time to waste on dates. Was this a *date*? The word seemed very daring and American. Meg imagined herself wearing one of those sticky-out skirts and a cardigan, talking about going to the prom. What was a prom anyway?

What would Logan think if she didn't turn up? He probably wouldn't care. It had been a casual invitation anyway. *Just one drink.* No, Meg would stay at home and devote herself to her aging parents, like one of the martyrs in the *Girl's Book of Saints* she got for her confirmation.

But, when Meg opened the door to the kitchen, there

was only Aisling, unenthusiastically pushing some sausages round the frying pan.

'Where's Mum?'

'Gone to parents' evening at Collette's school. Bet they'll say she's going to be expelled.'

Collette, who was sitting at the kitchen table, didn't look up from her comic. 'Miss Parsons said that my behaviour was exemplary. *Exemplary.*'

'Bet you can't spell it,' said Aisling.

Collette was at Meg's old school. Only Aisling had passed the eleven-plus and progressed to the grammar school. Meg remembered Miss Parsons, who had taught geography. She couldn't recall the old bag ever paying *her* a compliment.

'Shall we play cards later?' said Aisling. Their parents didn't like them to play cards but Aisling, Collette and Meg had recently discovered an addictive game called double rummy. Even Connor joined in sometimes, although he couldn't always tell the differences between spades and clubs. Aisling kept the playing cards in her school satchel.

'I can't,' said Meg. 'I'm going out.'

What could she wear? At least it wasn't like going to the theatre. She didn't have to be smart, just cool and trendy, which was far harder. Rifling through the wardrobe reminded Meg of the disastrous evening with DS Barker. This is different, she told herself. Logan was nearer her age; he wasn't an old man who thought that he could grope you because he'd bought you a drink and a programme. But maybe all men thought that? The idea of Logan kissing her made Meg feel quite dizzy, although not entirely in a bad way.

Eventually she put on slacks and a newish red jumper. Meg liked the colour and the shape but it was really too warm for May. Maybe they'd sit outside the pub. This was a comforting thought. Outside was less sinful.

Meg told Aisling that she was meeting a friend. She might give her the whole story later. It depended if there was a story to tell. She ran for the bus and missed it so arrived at the Downs at twenty past seven, rather hot and flustered.

'I thought you weren't coming,' said Logan.

He was sitting at one of the picnic tables at the front of the pub. Meg was relieved that he'd replaced his shorts with jeans, but his shirt was still open to the waist. Meg sat opposite him, feeling conspicuous in her red jumper. The Downs was at the top of the hill, looking down into the valley with the sea a blue glimmer in the distance. It was also at the main crossroads, so every passing car and bus got a good look at the drinkers outside. Maybe Meg's parents, returning from their session of Collette-praise, would see her there. Did it matter? Meg was twenty now, an adult; her parents couldn't object to her meeting a man. No, they couldn't object but they would talk about it, or her mother would, on and on with Padre Pio squawking in the background. Meg shuddered at the thought.

'Are you cold?' said Logan. 'Do you want to go inside?'

But the interior was of the pub was even scarier. Besides, Meg would get hot and her face would match her jumper.

'No, this is fine.'

'What would you like to drink?'

'Lemonade, please.'

'Coming up.'

Meg smoothed her hair down and tried to assume a dignified, sophisticated manner. Two teenage boys at the next table nudged each other and sniggered.

Logan emerged with a lemonade for Meg and a pint of beer for himself.

'Thank you very much,' said Meg.

'Glad you could make the time.' Logan was grinning at her again.

'I'm in the middle of a case,' said Meg, rather stiffly. 'I'm very busy.'

'What do your ma and da think about you being a policewoman?'

This seemed rather a personal question for a first date (it's not a date!) and 'ma and da' sounded so Irish that it reminded Meg of her grandparents.

'They're proud of me, I think,' she said, wondering if she had any evidence of this. 'My mum thinks I should be doing something more feminine and caring, being a nurse perhaps, but I think they're just relieved that I've got a steady job. I didn't leave school with many O Levels.'

'I didn't get any,' said Logan. 'But then I didn't really go to school. Ma would sign us up if we stayed at any place long enough but all the other kids laughed at us and called us gyppos. Me and Bartley just used to skive off.'

'Bartley's your brother?'

'Yes, there are five of us. Bartley's the oldest, then me, then three girls. What about you?'

'Seven. I'm in the middle.' Which meant that Meg's parents hardly ever got her name right on the first attempt.

'A proper Irish family,' said Logan. 'My dad was the seventh son of a seventh son.'

Meg couldn't remember what was so special about seventh sons. She betted it didn't apply to seventh daughters though. She noticed that Logan didn't even volunteer his sisters' names.

'Do you like your job?' asked Logan. Another rather personal question.

Meg thought about being called to Buckingham Place that morning, the body under the blanket, Dave Dunkley's face when they told him the news about Joan. She thought about riding on the back of Danny's moped and of Barker lunging towards her in the dark.

'I do enjoy it,' she said. 'Most of the time. Some of the cases are quite horrible but I like trying to work them out. It can be exciting. Last year I was on a case with Emma and we drove all the way to Whitby. You know, Dracula and all that.'

'I've read the book,' said Logan. 'Great stuff.' Meg must have looked surprised because he laughed and said,

'There's not a lot to do when you're on the road. I read a lot. I like horror stories.'

Meg could believe this, remembering his comments about books written in blood. She was embarrassed that she'd told him that she didn't have time for reading.

'Do you know Emma well?' asked Logan. 'I know Astarte likes her but she's seemed a bit stuck-up to me.'

'She's not like that at all,' said Meg. 'She used to be a detective sergeant. The first woman detective sergeant in Brighton. They still talk about her at the station. She's really brilliant. And very nice.'

'You're loyal,' said Logan. 'I like that.'

Now Meg knew that she was blushing. To change the subject she asked Logan how long he was staying in Brighton.

'Probably until the Appleby horse fair,' said Logan.

'What's that?'

'It's the biggest event of the year for gypsies. Hundreds of us get together in this little town in Cumbria. We buy and sell horses, have races, sell things. There are fortune tellers too. Astarte always has a crowd round her tent. But the main business is horse-trading. Every day of the fair, the horses are washed in the river and then trotted up and down the flashing lane . . .'

'The what?'

'Don't worry, PC Meg. It's not illegal. It's just where we show a horse's paces. Flashing just means fast trotting. I've got a horse called Grey Cloud who's a great flasher.'

'It's WDC,' said Meg. 'When is this fair?'

'June,' said Logan. 'Plenty of time.' Though he didn't say for what.

Emma and Edgar were also having a drink, although in their case it was cocoa at the kitchen table. Jonathan was in bed and the girls were watching television. Emma had a sheaf of notes in front of her and was talking Edgar through Sam's findings. Edgar, as ever, was enjoying seeing Emma at work. He had never met anyone who could summarise facts so succinctly.

'David Dunkley – that's his real name – was born in Sheffield in 1901.'

'So he's sixty-five.'

'You don't get any marks for that,' said Emma. 'He started as a magician quite young. Sam found a cutting from 1920, when he would only have been nineteen. He was called up in the second war but soon switched to ENSA, entertaining the troops.'

'Every Night Something Awful.'

'You got that from Max. After the war he went back on the stage. He seems to have been working with Joan Waters quite a long time. She's mentioned in this review from 1955. "His capable assistant, the statuesque Miss Waters."'

'Statuesque,' repeated Edgar. He thought of the body in the alleyway, the white face, the dyed blonde hair. A statuesque woman is no match for a murderous man.

'Was Dunkley married?' he asked.

'There's no record of a marriage,' said Emma. 'That doesn't mean he hasn't had mistresses.'

'That's true.'

Emma turned a page. 'Rex King. Also aged sixty-five. He's been married three times. To Belinda McGuire in 1939, Margaret Taylor in 1946 and Mavis Perth in 1960.'

'One wife at the beginning and one at the end of the war.'

'Yes. Makes you wonder what he did in between. But Rex definitely saw action in the war. He was in the navy and wounded in the siege of Malta. And, from 1947, there's a clipping of him at the Empire Theatre in Blackburn with his assistant, "Miss Joan Waters".'

Edgar whistled silently. 'So Joan worked for Rex King too. They certainly seem a tight-knit set.'

'Finally . . .' Emma shuffled her papers. She was enjoying this. 'Tommy Horton. He's older than the others. Born 1886. He's been on the stage since his teens. Fought in the First World War and was injured. Also involved with ENSA. Tommy's been married twice, to Grace Fanshaw in 1920 and to Greta Ableman in 1945. And, here's the interesting bit. Grace Fanshaw married Larry Buxton in 1925 and Gordon Palgrave in 1930.'

'Gordon Palgrave? Pal? Hang on, Max told me something about his wife . . . I think she committed suicide.'

'I'm sure we could check that,' said Emma. 'Larry Buxton's an impresario. The show on the pier is one of his. Might be worth talking to him.'

'I certainly will. Tommy Horton too. If he's still alive, that is. If he isn't, I'll have to get Astarte's help.'

'He's still alive,' said Emma. 'Living in an old people's home in Worthing. I was just thinking, maybe Sam and I should talk to him.'

Edgar had been expecting something like this. 'Why?' he asked mildly.

'Easier for two women to go into an old people's home. Less threatening. And we only want background information, after all.'

'I'll think about it,' said Edgar. He was sure Emma would visit Tommy whatever he said. Of course, Sam and Emma were still working for Cherry Underwood's parents. They were free to pursue that investigation any way they wanted.

'Do you think Joan's murder is linked to Cherry's?' he asked.

'I think it must be,' said Emma. 'Two magician's assistants killed in the space of a few weeks.'

'Meg saw a photograph of Joan when she was young,' said Edgar. 'She thought that she looked a bit like Cherry.'

'That's worth following up,' said Emma. 'But there are other links too. They were both involved with the same group. Ted English is another one of that set.'

'He was at the show last night,' said Edgar. 'Seen chatting to Dave Dunkley in the bar afterwards.'

'When did they leave?' asked Emma.

'At midnight, according to witnesses. Carter thought Joan was killed at around midnight.'

'Around,' said Emma. 'Either of them could have got a bus or a taxi to Buckingham Place and been there in minutes.'

'I know,' said Edgar. 'But why?'

'I was thinking of something Ruby once said.' Emma was putting the cuttings back in their envelope. 'We were talking about why magicians saw women in half or stick swords in them. She said, "It's because, deep down, men hate women."'

'Not all men,' protested Edgar.

'Sometimes you have to look very deep down,' said Emma.

'Another lemonade?' said Logan.

'I'd better not,' said Meg. 'I've got to be in work early tomorrow.'

It was half past eight. With any luck, Meg would be home before her parents.

'I'll see you home,' said Logan.

'No,' said Meg, too quickly. Then, trying for a lighter tone, 'It's not far. The bus stops at the end of my road. At the top of Queensway.'

'Then I'll walk you to the bus stop,' said Logan.

Meg was torn, as they crossed the road, the air smelling of grass and petrol, between wanting the walk to last for a long time and for it to be over quickly. As luck – or not – would have it, the green Southdown bus loomed into sight almost immediately.

'Goodbye, WDC Meg,' said Logan. 'I'll see you again soon.'

But he didn't say when. Meg took her seat on the lower deck feeling relieved that she'd got away with it (as she phrased it to herself) and also unaccountably depressed.

CHAPTER 18

Edgar did not have long to wait before seeing Larry Buxton. He arrived at Bartholomew Square at eight o'clock the next morning to find a maroon Rolls Royce parked outside and a man in a loud check jacket haranguing the receptionist.

'I demand to see Superintendent Stephens.'

'The superintendent isn't in yet.'

'Can I help?' said Edgar.

The man turned. He had a large ovoid face, made even larger by the complete absence of hair. His features – small nose, anxious eyes, surprisingly curly mouth – were clustered together, as if for safety, in the very centre of the egg.

'Are you Superintendent Edgar Stephens?'

'I am. And you are?'

'Buxton. Larry Buxton.' A fleshy hand was extended. 'Of Larry Buxton Enterprises. I'm producing the show on the pier.'

'You'd better follow me,' said Edgar. He led the way downstairs, past the cloakroom and the briefing room and the corridor that led to the cells. Edgar's office was lighter than some of the rooms, because it was only a semi-basement, but it still seemed oppressive, with the picture of Edgar's murdered predecessor, Henry Solomon, looking sorrowfully down from his portrait over the fireplace. Rita wasn't in yet and Edgar didn't feel like making Buxton a drink, so he gestured towards the visitor's chair.

'How can I help you?'

'Like I say, I'm in charge of the show on the pier. One of my girls was killed the other night.'

'Joan Waters.'

'Yes. Poor old Joanie. The thing is, the show's transferring to the West End next month.'

'I know.'

'That's why I came to see you. I don't want to sound heartless but . . .'

Edgar prepared to hear something heartless.

'. . . but how long will your investigation take? I don't want people to be put off from coming to the show.'

There it was.

'I can't say how long our investigation will take,' said Edgar. 'Can I ask you some questions, Mr Buxton?'

Buxton's eyes bulged. Edgar took this for assent.

'How long had you known Joan Waters?'

'Years. Everyone knew Joan. She'd worked with Dave since the war.'

'And with Rex King too, I believe?'

'I think so.' Buxton seemed wary now, passing a finger round the inside of his collar.

'Are Dave Dunkley and Rex King your clients?'

'Yes.'

'What were you doing after the show on Tuesday night?' There had been no show last night 'due to unforeseen circumstances'. Edgar had no doubt that it would open again tonight.

'I went for a drink with Dave and some of the other artistes. At the Colonnade. Next to the Theatre Royal.'

'What time did you leave?'

'I only stayed for one. Left about eleven.'

'What did you do then?'

'Went back to my hotel. The Grand.'

All the impresarios stayed at The Grand. It was a good thing; the posher the hotel, the more potential witnesses. Bob could send someone down to check what time Buxton had returned.

'Why do you want to know?' said Buxton, with a trace of his former belligerence.

'All part of the investigation,' said Edgar. 'Was Ted English at the Colonnade too?'

'Yes. Poor fellow. He's still very cut up about Cherry.'

'Did you know Cherry Underwood personally?' asked Edgar.

'Yes,' said Buxton. 'I was the one who discovered her, as

a matter of fact. She was working in a shop. Up Carlisle way.'

Edgar heard his wife's cut-glass accents, filling in Cherry's biography. She left school at sixteen to work in a draper's shop. There she met a man who offered her acting work. Edgar had assumed that the man who tempted Cherry to London had been Ted English. But it turned out to be the impresario himself.

'You offered Cherry a job? On stage?' He remembered Emma saying something about 'dodgy revues'.

'She was a pretty little thing. She did some shows for me but she was no great dancer. Not enough oomph for burlesque. So I introduced her to Pal. They did one season together and then Cherry teamed up with Ted English. Or maybe Rex King was first. At any rate, Ted and Cherry seemed to get on well.'

'Is Ted English one of your clients too?'

'Yes.'

'What about Tommy Horton?'

'Tommy? I haven't heard that name for years.'

'I understand your ex-wife, Grace, used to be married to Tommy.'

'You have been doing your research.' Another tug of the collar. 'In that case you'll know that Grace left me after only a year and married Pal.'

'And then died?'

'It was a tragic accident,' said Larry. 'I can't see how this is relevant. I just want to know if I can take my show to London. A lot of people will lose a lot of money if it doesn't happen.'

'It's not up to me what you do with your show,' said Edgar. 'Though I assume you'll have to find another magician.'

'You're right,' said Buxton, not seeming to notice any irony. 'Dave will never go on without Joanie and Ted has hit the bottle in a big way. What wouldn't I give for a really big name like Max Mephisto.'

The shadow of an idea, as unpleasant and insistent as the rats that lived in the basement cells, skittered across Edgar's brain.

Emma was driving to Worthing. Sam was sitting next to her, eating a bacon sandwich. There was a holiday feeling in the car, despite the seriousness of the investigation and the smell of the sandwich. The girls were at school and Jonathan was in playgroup. The sea sparkled on one side of them and, on the other, the buildings changed from the Regency hotels of Brighton to merge into the smooth cream apartment blocks of Hove and then the guest houses and factories of Shoreham. They passed the harbour, where cargo ships loomed alongside the fishing boats.

'I like Shoreham,' said Sam. 'It's a very real place.'

'Real usually means unpleasant,' said Emma.

'Spoken like someone who went to Roedean.'

Emma laughed. She never minded Sam teasing her

about her background although she sometimes got offended when Edgar did likewise. Emma and Sam were exactly the same age. Emma, the only child of rich parents, was sent to the famous girls' public school, which she had heartily disliked at the time. Sam was born in Southend, attended the local grammar school and then read English at University College, London, before going into journalism. She was actually far better educated than Emma, who had left school at eighteen, but the Roedean joke was never going to die.

'Ida Lupin said her mother lived in Worthing,' said Emma. 'Could there be a link?'

'I don't suppose so,' said Sam, crumpling up her greaseproof paper. Emma was willing to bet that she'd leave it in the car. 'It's the sort of place where people's mothers live. Do we really think that this old bloke is going to tell us anything about Cherry? If he remembers her at all, that is.'

'I don't know,' said Emma, 'but I think someone in that set knows something and Tommy Horton is the nearest to us. Rex King lives in London and I'm pretty sure we won't get close to Gordon Palgrave.'

'I'm going to London tonight,' said Sam. 'I'll see if I can find Rex.'

'Going to London again?'

'More stuff about Brady and Hindley,' said Sam.

Ian Brady and Myra Hindley had been convicted earlier that month of the murders of three children. Sam had covered the trial in Chester and Emma knew that it had affected her deeply. She didn't know why Sam was still reporting on the case or why it was taking her to London but decided not to ask.

Emma always thought that Worthing looked like a sanitised version of Brighton. The pier and the promenade – and even the people – were just that bit smaller and neater. The Cedars Care Home was a few streets from the seafront, a gabled building with a faintly Gothic appearance. The grounds were attractively landscaped, although the paths between the rockeries looked rather steep for elderly people to navigate. Emma and Sam were told that Tommy was walking in the Italian garden but, when they found him, they realised that 'walking' was a euphemism. Tommy was in a wheelchair, being pushed by a young man with a ring on every finger.

'He's a lovely old chap, Tommy,' said the manager, Elsie Raydon, who had greeted them at reception. 'But I'm afraid his mind does wander.'

'Does he have many visitors?' asked Emma.

'No. It's quite sad. His wife, Greta, and daughter, Heidi, used to visit but Tommy said he didn't want them to come any more. He thought it upset them to see him declining but I actually think it upsets them more to stay away.'

The young man, whose name was Craig, tactfully withdrew to allow Emma and Sam to talk to Tommy. He seemed delighted to have visitors, which made the exclusion of his family even more heartbreaking. The ex-magician was a shrunken figure but there was still a touch of showbiz swagger about him. He was wearing a blue blazer with brass buttons and his snowy locks were slicked back with hair oil. He grinned at Emma and Sam, showing rather startling false teeth.

'Do I know you?' he said. 'I used to know so many people. Lots of lovely young women.'

This gave Emma a chance to say, 'Did you know Cherry Underwood?'

'Cherry? What a pretty name. I don't think so.'

'What about Joan Waters. Joanie?'

'Joanie? Of course I knew Joanie. She was a wonder at the Selbit. What's Joanie doing these days?'

Emma and Sam looked at each other but neither felt up to replying. Emma asked if Tommy saw any friends from his theatrical days. 'Rex King? Ted English? Gordon Palgrave?'

Tommy shook his head. 'He's a bad man.'

'Gordon Palgrave?' said Emma.

'No. Ted English.'

'Ted English? Why?'

'He didn't treat her well.'

'Cherry?'

'No. Gracie.'

Emma felt as if the conversation was turning into some sort of nonsense rhyme. 'You remind me of a man.' 'What man?' 'The man with the power.' 'What power?' 'The power of whodo.' 'Whodo?' 'You do'. It was Sam who said, 'Your wife, Grace?'

Tommy was searching in the breast pocket of his blazer. He withdrew a black-and-white photograph, creased with age. It showed a woman standing on a beach with her hair blowing behind her. On the back was written one word.

Gracie.

'It was Palgrave who was married to Grace, though,' said Sam, as they drove back, the sea and the houses changing places.

'Larry Buxton, the producer, too,' said Emma. 'She left Tommy for Larry and Larry for Pal.'

'There's definitely a story there,' said Sam. 'There are all sorts of rumours about Pal but no one dares print them. He's got a lot of friends in high places.'

'Edgar thought that Grace committed suicide,' said Emma. 'Max told him.'

'I'll see if there's anything in the archives,' said Sam. 'I can go to Fleet Street when I'm in London.'

'It does make me think that we should look at Ted English again,' said Emma. 'He was the one who was closest to Cherry, Edgar says that he went to see the show on the night that Joan was killed. The group are so interlinked. Cherry worked with Pal, Rex and Ted. Joan worked with Rex King and Dave Dunkley. Tommy obviously knew her too. Larry Buxton probably knows all of them. Grace was married to Tommy, Larry and Pal.'

'Did you think Grace looked a bit like Cherry?' said Sam.

'A little,' said Emma. 'Meg thought that Joan looked like her too, when she was young.'

'She's sharp, Meg,' said Sam.

'She is.'

'We should talk to Cherry's parents again,' said Sam. 'Ask if they knew any of these people.'

'I'll do that,' said Emma. 'You see if you can track down Rex King.' They were nearing Brighton now; a group of musicians in white jackets were gathering on the bandstand. Emma wound down her window. Good old Sussex by the sea.

'I'll find Rex,' said Sam. 'Shall we stop for chips at Dr Brighton's?'

CHAPTER 19

'Ed! What are you doing here?'

Edgar had been expecting a slightly warmer greeting from Max. He'd caught the early train up from Brighton and thought that he might be offered coffee at the very least. His police rank had got him past the impressively bemedalled doorman but Max seemed disinclined even to let him into the flat.

'I wanted to talk to you,' said Edgar. 'It's about the Cherry Underwood case. You know another woman's been killed?'

'I heard,' said Max. 'Look, Ed. There's a nice café near Barkers. It's called Luigi's. I'll meet you there in twenty minutes. Tell Luigi you're a friend of mine.'

Edgar was beginning to get the picture. 'Is twenty minutes long enough?'

'She'll understand,' said Max.

The door closed and Edgar walked back down stairs, smiling blandly at the frankly interested doorman, and made his way out of the mansion block. At the corner of Kensington Square he looked back and thought he saw a curtain twitch in what might have been Max's flat. He didn't turn round again. It wasn't his business after all.

'That was close,' said Sam.

She was peering out of the window. Edgar was halfway round the square. If he just looked up, he would see her. Perhaps that was what Sam wanted?

'I've said before,' said Max, en route to the shower, 'I don't know why we need all this secrecy. Edgar and Emma would be surprised if they knew about us, but they wouldn't exactly be shocked.'

'They'd be interested, though,' said Sam. 'Or Emma would. She'd ask questions. I can't stand all that.'

Max understood. He didn't mind being talked about – he was a performer, after all – but he liked to keep his private life private. All the same, Edgar was his friend. He didn't like lying to him, even by omission.

When Max emerged from the bathroom, Sam was sitting up in bed, wearing one of his shirts.

'Max,' she said. 'What's the Selbit?'

'The Selbit? Why do you want to know?'

'I asked first.'

Max smiled. 'Selbit was the first magician to saw a woman in half. The cabinet trick is sometimes named after him. Actually, Selbit was the first person to use a woman assistant. Before him, they were always men.'

'I'd pay to see a man sawn in half.'

'You wouldn't have to pay. You'd get free tickets and a seat in the press box.'

'Tommy Horton said that Joanie was a wonder at the Selbit.'

'She was a good assistant,' said Max. 'I would have thought she'd be a bit big for cabinet work though.'

'Did you ever meet her?'

'A few times. She worked for Rex King just after the war.'

'I want to talk to Rex King. Do you know where I can find him?'

'I've got an address somewhere,' said Max. 'Just let me get dressed first.'

Anyone would know, thought Edgar, that Max was either an actor or a foreigner. His shirt was so white and his shoes were so shiny. He wore an immaculately fitting grey suit without a tie and carried a hat in one hand. His hair was still dark although there was now a grey streak running through the centre. Very useful for character parts, Max said.

Luigi greeted Max with a kiss on both cheeks and they spoke in Italian for a few minutes. Max claimed to have forgotten all his Italian but he sounded very fluent to Edgar. His body language changed too, lots of shrugs and despairing hand gestures.

'What were you talking about?' said Edgar, when Max finally sat opposite him.

'Football. Italy's chances in the World Cup.'

'Since when have you been interested in football?'

'I've always been interested in lost causes.'

Luigi brought two coffees over, significantly hotter and stronger than the one already offered to Edgar. There was a plate of pastries too. Edgar bit into one; he hadn't eaten anything since a piece of toast at the café on Brighton Station. Max got out his cigarette case but didn't light up. It occurred to Edgar that his friend was smoking less than he used to.

'So,' said Max. 'What's this about? Not that it's not good to see you.'

'I had a visit from Larry Buxton yesterday.'

Max grimaced. 'Lucky you.'

'Do you know him then?'

'Everyone in the business knows Larry. He's the biggest producer around now that Bert Billington's dead. Of course, Larry's father built the business up. I think he was Larry too. And a complete bastard.'

'Is this Larry Buxton a complete bastard?'

'Not quite complete. I think he's good to his wife and kids.'

'Larry was married to Grace Fanshaw, wasn't he? The woman who went on to marry Pal?'

'I believe he was. Poor woman.'

'I think you said that she killed herself?'

'Hanged herself not long after marrying Pal,' said Max, frowning into his espresso. 'What's all this about?'

'Larry Buxton's bringing his nostalgia show to London.'

'Still?'

'Yes, he says he'll lose too much money if it doesn't happen.'

'I told you he was a charmer.'

'He needs a new magician though.'

'I imagine he does.' Max looked up and saw Edgar's expression. 'No.'

'You said you missed the stage.'

'I said I didn't want to do a tinpot revue, if you remember.'

Edgar tried to put every ounce of persuasion into his voice, to conjure up the days when they were not just friends but comrades, creating tanks out of cardboard and warships out of scrap metal. Edgar and Max, together with Diablo and a conman called Tony Mulholland, had been part of an espionage group called the Magic Men. Their job had been to use the techniques of stage magic – camouflage, sleight of hand, misdirection – in the war effort. Edgar now saw their mission as a complete failure, but it didn't stop him sometimes having warm feelings about those times.

'Max,' said Edgar, 'someone has killed two women, two magician's assistants from the same show. I need someone in the cast that I can trust.'

'Do I have to have an assistant too?' said Max, sounding almost amused now. 'Just so that she can be killed?'

'I've got an idea about that,' said Edgar.

'No,' said Max, a second later. 'No, no, no.'

CHAPTER 20

Sam hadn't known what to expect from Rex King, the man whose first and second name both meant monarch. But King didn't seem like a megalomaniac. He was a trim figure in a golfing sweater, with a tanned face that spoke of many hours on the green and contrasted pleasingly with his greying hair.

'My name was originally Klinghoffer,' he told Sam, 'but my dad changed it during the first war. Didn't do to have a German name then. Or a Jewish one. Besides, King looks better on the billboards. Shorter and hence bigger.' He grinned.

'Are you still performing?' asked Sam.

'No, I'm a retired magician now,' he told Sam, 'but sadly I haven't been able to magic my handicap into single figures.'

King lived in Richmond, not far from Gordon Palgrave. He told Sam that they played golf together once a week.

'He's been a good friend to me, has Pal. A good pal. Ha ha.'

He laughed like it was written on the page but Sam didn't hold that against him. Rex had been very friendly, considering that she had turned up, unannounced, on his doorstep. He had offered coffee and now they were sitting in a room he called his 'snug', conveniently full of theatrical memorabilia.

'Mavis doesn't like this stuff hanging around the house. She's got very modern tastes.'

Rex was still married to wife number three, then. Mavis's interior decorating clearly ran on Swedish lines: wooden floors, open riser staircase, modular furniture, lots of beige and grey. In contrast, the snug was full of posters in red and blue, fairground fonts, signed photos of top-hatted men and bare-shouldered women. Pal grinned down from above the desk. 'To my old amigo, Rex. All for one . . .'

'Are you still in touch with other magicians?' asked Sam. 'Ted English? Dave Dunkley? Tommy Horton?'

'Poor old Tommy. I went to see him a few months ago. Didn't know who I was. So sad. And Ted and Dave have been in the wars recently.'

'Well, their assistants have.'

'Quite.' Rex looked sober for a moment. 'Poor old Joanie. I couldn't believe it when I heard.'

'When did you hear?'

'Pal rang me yesterday. He was very upset. Then Larry Buxton called. He offered me Dave's spot on the bill. Ha ha.'

'Did you accept?'

'No. Like I say, I'm retired now. Spend my days playing golf and driving Mavis to WI meetings. And, well, it doesn't seem like a very lucky production, does it?'

'It doesn't,' said Sam. 'As I said on the phone, my agency is acting for Cherry Underwood's parents. Did you ever meet Cherry?'

Rex took a sip of coffee. Sam wondered if he was playing for time. 'I worked with her a few years back. She'd been one of Pal's girls for a time. Nice little thing but not the brightest. You need to be quick to be a magician's assistant. Quick-witted as well as quick on your pins.'

'When did you last see Cherry?'

'I think it was three or four years ago. Summer season in Eastbourne. I had a bit of a turn on stage. Nothing serious but I thought it was time to retire. I introduced Cherry to Ted and they seemed to get on.'

'She managed Ted's act OK then?' asked Sam.

'She must have done. They stayed together.'

'Do you think Ted could have killed Cherry?'

Sam hoped to jolt Rex out of his complacency and it seemed to work. He choked on his coffee. 'Never. Not in a million years. Ted's a gentleman. I mean, he drinks a bit but he wouldn't hurt a fly.'

'You worked with Joan Waters too, didn't you?'

Rex gave Sam a rather hard look but answered easily enough, 'Yes. We worked together after the war. Pal introduced us, as a matter of fact. Joanie and I had both been in the navy – she was with the Wrens – and that created a bond. We got on well but my private life was in a bit of turmoil then . . . my first marriage ended badly . . . so did my second, ha ha . . . I had to give up the stage for a bit and Joanie took up with Dave. They had a good partnership.'

'Did you stay in touch?'

'Not really but I followed the business, read the *Variety* reviews, that sort of thing. I was in a bad way for a while but Pal got me a few charity gigs. I met Mavis at one of them. Wonderful woman. She's straightened me out.'

He grinned at Sam and, despite the protests of respectability, Sam thought she could still see the traces of the much-married ex-sailor.

'Did you know Grace Fanshaw?' she asked.

Rex sighed. His voice took on a reminiscent note. 'Lovely Gracie. She married Tommy when she was just twenty. Rumour was that she'd been married before that. To the mysterious Mr Fanshaw.'

'How did Tommy meet her?'

'She was his assistant,' said Rex. 'She'd been Pal's first. That's how Tommy met her. Grace had been a child star, had a tap-dancing act with her brother. She wasn't much of an assistant, truth be told, but you don't need talent when you look like that. God, I remember the outfit she had for the act she did with Pal. Some sort of French maid's uniform. Enough to raise your blood pressure to boiling point. And I was young then. It would probably kill me now. Ha ha. They were all mad about her. Pal, Ted, Dave, Larry.'

'And you?'

'I was only twenty myself. I think I was in love with her too but I hardly dared speak to her. She was so sweet, seemed devoted to Tommy, even though he was a lot older. We couldn't believe it when she left him for Larry. I mean, Larry was well off but Grace didn't seem like a girl who was interested in money. Then, a year later, she left Larry for Pal. Then . . .'

'Then?'

'Then she killed herself,' said Rex flatly. 'Such a tragedy.'

'Do you know why?'

'I don't blame Pal,' said Rex, although this wasn't what Sam had asked. 'He was devastated. He never married again. I think that Gracie must have had some sort of illness. Neurosis, or whatever they call it these days. Pal never talks about her.'

'What about Tommy?'

'He was heartbroken when Grace left him but he married again, a good few years later. Greta was German, did you know that? Like me. Ha ha. Tommy met her when he was with ENSA in Berlin after the war. Some people disapproved, said she only married him to get out of Germany – well, conditions were terrible for civilians – but they've made a go of it. She was a good looker though, Greta. Still is. Very like Grace when she was younger but a bit more solid, if you know what I mean.'

'They've got a daughter, haven't they?'

'Yes. Heidi. I said to Tommy, you couldn't have picked a more German name. Ha ha.'

Sam remembered the care home manager saying that Greta and Heidi had visited Tommy regularly until Tommy asked them not to. They certainly sounded devoted. She asked how old Heidi was.

'I haven't seen her for years. She must be about twenty now. Tommy would have been pushing sixty when she was born. The old dog. No wonder they only had one child. Ha ha.'

None of Rex's marriages had resulted in children, Sam knew. Pal was also childless, as were Ted English and Dave Dunkley. They certainly weren't breeding a new generation of magicians. Maybe that was a good thing.

'Tommy Horton said something about Ted treating Grace badly,' she said.

'Like I say, poor old Tommy's lost it. I don't think Ted ever even spoke to Grace. As a matter of fact, I mentioned Ted to Tommy when I last visited. I don't think the name registered at all. No, Ted worshipped Grace from afar, like the rest of us.'

Larry Buxton and Gordon Palgrave hadn't exactly worshipped from afar, thought Sam. She decided to go for another blunt question.

'We're working on the possibility that Cherry and Joan were killed by the same person,' said Sam. 'Do you have any idea who that could be?'

Rex's smile disappeared but he kept eye contact. 'You

always get funny types hanging around showgirls. A local nutter is my guess.'

He looked at her guilelessly, but Sam knew sleight of hand when she saw it.

Emma was collecting Jonathan from playgroup. He went there three mornings a week now. Emma always felt slightly guilty dropping him off, because he sometimes cried and clung to her, but he always looked very jolly at collecting time, waving daubs of colour that he called paintings and the girls called rubbish. Today he was brandishing a yogurt pot with seeds in it. An accompanying typed note explained that they were mustard and cress that would grow 'in a matter of days!' Emma looked at them dubiously – she was bad at growing things – and put the pot in her bag.

The play leader, a cheerful woman called Irene, came over to tell her that Jonathan had played very nicely today. Emma was relieved. There had been an unfortunate biting incident a few weeks back. The last thing Emma wanted was for Jonathan to get banned from playgroup. She relied on those three mornings for work. Also, she didn't want him to grow into a psychopath.

Sometimes Emma brought the pushchair but today she thought a walk would do them good. Jonathan wanted to see the sea so, encumbered by bags and artwork, they marched along by the blue railings. As they passed Marine Parade, Emma glanced across at Astarte's balcony. She wondered if the gypsy cousin was still staying. She'd found him a rather unsettling presence. Astarte's curtains were half-drawn but Emma thought that she could see the glint of a crystal ball. As she looked, she saw a woman carrying bags of shopping up the steps of number 84. Luckily, the coast road was clear. Emma grabbed Jonathan's hand and darted across.

'Can I help?'

The landlady, Linda Knight, looked at her and smiled. 'Looks like you've got your hands full, love.'

'Do you remember me? Emma Holmes? From the detective agency?'

'Yes,' said Linda. 'I remember you.'

'I was investigating Cherry's death.'

'So you were.' Linda had the door open. 'Made any headway?'

'Not really,' said Emma. 'And now another girl is dead.'

Linda sighed. 'You'd better come in.'

She led the way across the hall to a door that opened onto a stone passage and a large kitchen. Linda dumped her bags on the table and said. 'It's Annie's day off. Cup o' cha?'

'Yes please.'

Emma hoped that Jonathan wouldn't get bored and look for something to break. She rifled through her bag for a book or a game but Jonathan was looking past her. Linda had opened the window to let in a large ginger cat.

'Kitty,' breathed Jonathan. He loved all animals.

'He's called Pushkin,' said Linda. 'You can give him some kibble if you like.' She put some biscuits into Jonathan's hand.

While Jonathan began his stealthy pursuit of Pushkin, Emma said to Linda, 'I think we've got a mutual friend. Astarte Zabini, a few doors down.'

Linda looked up. 'Oh, Astarte's fabulous, isn't she? She did my horoscope the other day – I'm a Pisces – and it was so accurate.'

Emma never knew quite what to make of Astarte's horoscopes but she volunteered that she was Aries with Leo rising. 'My husband's a Pisces.'

'That's tricky,' said Linda. 'Fire and water. But Pisces can provide stability.'

'Ed is very stable,' agreed Emma.

'He's the chief of police, isn't he?'

'Superintendent. Yes.'

'That must be tricky too,' said Linda. 'What with you being a private investigator.'

'We make it work,' said Emma. 'I was a police officer once and I was really good at it. I didn't see why I should give it up just because I got married.'

'Astarte says marriage isn't in my cards,' said Linda, putting two cups of tea in front of them. 'How are you getting on with the investigation? Do you think the same person killed poor old Joanie?'

'Did you know Joanie then?' asked Emma, noting that several people had described her as poor and old.

'Not very well but she stayed here once or twice. Joanie was a good friend of Ida's. Ida Lupin. They even had a double act together once. A strongwoman act.'

Emma had interviewed Ida after Cherry's death. She remembered an intelligent, watchful face surrounded by long, blonde hair. She didn't look like a strongwoman. Did Joan? Emma had never seen a photograph of Joan, although she remembered the newspaper cutting describing her as 'statuesque'.

'Do you have any idea who could have killed Joanie?' she asked, deliberately using the diminutive that her friends used. 'You must have seen all sorts of people in your time.' She hoped that didn't sound as if the landlady was ancient. In fact, Linda was probably her own age, or younger.

She expected Linda to say no but, instead, the landlady said, 'I think it all comes back to the same man.'

'Who?' said Emma.

Linda looked around, as if she expected to be overheard, but the only living creatures present were Emma, Jonathan and the cat. Emma remembered the ghost of the white-haired man. Did Linda think that he was listening? It was an uncomfortable thought even if, like Emma, you didn't believe in ghosts.

'Pal,' Linda almost whispered.

'Gordon Palgrave?' said Emma. 'Do you think he killed Cherry and Joanie?' Edgar, she knew, had checked Palgrave's alibi for Cherry's death and he had been at some charity function. And, surely, if the famous Pal had been in Brighton on Tuesday night, someone would have seen him?

Linda looked down into her teacup. Was she reading the leaves, another of Astarte's specialities? Eventually she said, slowly, 'I don't mean that he killed them. I mean that it all comes back to him. Pal controls all that group – Ted, Dave, Rex, Tommy. There was a time when you couldn't get work as a magician without Pal's say-so. Oh, I don't mean a star like Max Mephisto. I mean the little people. The ones with plenty to lose. Pal knows people's secrets and he uses them to make you do what he wants.'

Something about the way Linda phrased this made Emma ask, 'Do you know Pal?'

'I've come across him a couple of times,' said Linda. 'And I know Ida has too. Pal never made a pass at me. I'm far too old for him. But he was notorious for chasing young girls. He'd tell them he could get work for them but only if they'd sleep with him. Someone told me that Pal used to work with Cherry. I wouldn't be surprised if that was the deal he offered her.'

'Who told you that?'

'I think it was Geoff. Geoff Bigg. Or Perry Small. I can't remember.'

The comedians were rather interchangeable, thought Emma. 'Pal sounds horrid,' she said. 'But how could he be responsible for the murders?'

'Pal has contacts,' said Linda. 'If he wanted someone dead, he'd know who to ask.'

Rex told Sam that Pal only lived a few streets away. Sam decided to pay him a visit. 'When you're not sure, knock on the door.' That's what Don at the *Evening Argus* always said. It was her duty as a journalist, Sam told herself, as she walked through the leafy streets. Pal's house was bigger than Rex's, set back in a verdant garden with monkey-puzzle trees and rhododendron bushes. Sam rang the doorbell with no expectation of it being answered but, after a few minutes, a familiar figure stood in front of her, quiff nodding a welcome.

'My dear young lady. Do come in.'

CHAPTER 21

Intrepid reporter that she was, Sam could not resist a quick look behind her. A gentle wind rustled the rhododendrons but there was not a soul to be seen. Should she have left a trail of breadcrumbs?

Pal led the way into a vast sitting room, so full of glittering objects that it looked like the Silver Falls on Palace Pier. Most of them were trophies, displayed in glass cabinets that ran the length of the room. There were also two white sofas facing each other across a chrome and glass coffee table. A large white TV loomed in one corner of the room with an armchair in front of it. Sam was willing to bet that was where Pal spent his evenings.

Pal sat on one of the sofas and gestured for Sam to join him. The carpet was so thick that she had trouble walking.

'So,' he said, 'to what do I owe this pleasure?'

Sam took out her visiting card. 'My name's Sam Collins. I'm investigating the death of Cherry Underwood.'

She'd expected the genial manner to disappear but Pal just leant back against the gleaming cushions and said, 'Well, well, well. Policewomen are getting younger and prettier.'

'I'm not a policewoman.'

'No, you're a private investigator.' He examined the card, giving the words a salivary relish.

'I've just been to see Rex King,' Sam ploughed on. 'He said that you used to work with Cherry.' Although what Rex had actually said was that Cherry 'was one of Pal's girls'.

'Good old Rex,' said Pal, his smile broadening. 'How was he?'

'He seemed fine.'

'He's had problems with drink, you know. Well, a lot of pros do. Not me. I've never touched a drop. Lemon barley is my only vice.'

Sam was not sure she believed this.

'When did you work with Cherry?' she asked.

'A few years back – 1963, I think. That was the last season I did. I concentrate on telly now. Have you seen my show, *Hug or Hit*?'

'No, I haven't.'

'You should. I could get you tickets for the live show. You and your boyfriend. Have you got a boyfriend?'

For a moment, Sam thought of Max grinning lazily at her. 'No,' she said.

'Shame. Lovely girl like you. I could set you up. I'm a great matchmaker. I introduced Rex to Mavis. She's a bit of a dragon but she's sorted him out.'

'What about Cherry?' she said. 'Did she have a boyfriend?'

'There was a boy up north,' said Pal. 'I think he was getting a bit heavy.'

'Do you remember his name?'

'Sorry. No. I hear so many names. It's essential on TV, to use somebody's name. Isn't that right, Sam? What's it short for, Samantha?'

'Sam is fine.'

'No boyfriend. Boy's name. Are you one of them? Not that I mind. I'm very broadminded.'

Resisting the temptation to ask, 'One of what?', Sam ignored the question and said, 'Did you know Joan Waters too?'

'Everyone knew Joanie. They don't make them like Joanie any more. More's the pity.'

'Did you ever work with Joan?'

'No, but, after the war, I introduced her to Rex and then Dave. Joanie and Dave hit it off immediately. That's matchmaking too, in a way. The right assistant and the right magician.'

'You were married to Tommy Horton's ex-wife, Grace, weren't you?'

The change was so immediate that it was terrifying. Pal stood up. His face was a mask of fury. Sam would not have been surprised to see cloven hooves appearing in his slip-on shoes.

'Interview's over. Get out.'

By the time Emma got home, Jonathan was cranky with hunger and tiredness. Emma made him a sandwich and ate a piece of bread herself. Then she settled Jonny on the sofa with his blanket, hoping he'd have a nap. He normally slept in front of *Watch With Mother* but that wasn't on until a quarter to four, by which time she would have collected the girls from school. Tiptoeing out, Emma went to the telephone. She'd promised Sam that she would talk to Cherry's parents. She knew she was putting it off, but she rang Edgar first. They chatted on the phone most days and it usually made Emma feel better. Maybe Linda was right when she said Pisces provided stability – he was a stabilising influence.

Edgar's secretary, Rita, answered the phone.

'Hallo, Mrs Stephens. I'm afraid the superintendent's in a meeting. He's only just got back from London, you know.'

'London?' This was the first Emma had heard of a London trip.

'Yes, he went to London first thing.' Rita sounded delighted to have this knowledge.

'Oh yes,' said Emma. 'I remember now. Well, tell him I called, will you?'

'Will do!' Rita rang off on a tinkling laugh.

To avoid thinking about Edgar and London, Emma dialled the Underwoods' number immediately.

'Mrs Underwood? Dolores? It's Emma here.'

'Have you got any news?' Emma hated to hear the hope in Dolores's voice.

'We've got a few leads. I don't know if you've heard but another young woman has been killed. A magician's assistant called Joan Waters.'

'I hadn't heard. We don't listen to the news any more. Iain doesn't even buy a paper. It's too upsetting. Magician's assistant? Do you think there's any link with Cherry?'

'It's definitely a line of investigation,' said Emma. 'Do you know if Cherry knew Joan?'

'I don't, I'm afraid. Cherry wasn't much of a one for writing letters.'

'Do you know if she knew Tommy Horton? Rex King? Gordon Palgrave?'

There was a silence. Then, Dolores said, 'I introduced her to Pal. I'll always blame myself.'

'You introduced her?'

'Yes, I knew him from when I was on the stage. I was on the bill with him a few times. When Cherry met that Larry Buxton, he lured her to London and got her involved in a very seedy show. Girls taking off their clothes in a nightclub, that sort of thing. So I thought that Pal might be able to get her work with a magician. Someone respectable. And he did. He introduced her to Rex and to Ted. He even worked with her himself once.

I thought it might be the start of great things. I thought she might even get on TV.'

Emma could hear the longing in Dolores's voice, even now. Marianne had recently told Emma that her ambition was 'to be on the telly'. Emma had had to force back the reply, 'over my dead body'. Well, now there were two dead bodies.

'What do you know about Gordon Palgrave?' she asked.

'He was always good to me,' said Dolores, 'but there were rumours about him back in the day. Seducing girls. Young girls. Verity couldn't bear him. I warned Cherry not to be alone with him . . .'

Her voice trailed off. In the static silence, Emma heard Linda's flat London tones, 'I think it all comes back to the same man . . . Pal.'

CHAPTER 22

'The super wants to see you in his office,' said Rita.

Meg looked at Danny, who raised one eyebrow, a trick he had recently perfected. When Meg tried, she looked, according to her sisters, like a deranged pirate. She tried to think if she'd done anything wrong recently. Riding on Danny's moped? But then, surely, Danny would get a summons too? Going out for a drink with Logan? But that had been in her own time. A chill went down her back. Had Emma told the super about Barker kissing her? If so, Meg would die of shame and then kill herself.

'He's waiting,' said Rita pointedly.

Meg got up, smoothed down her skirt and went out of the room. She knew that Danny and DS Barker were both watching her.

The super and the DI were waiting for her. Oh, hell's bells and buckets of blood, she must have messed up somewhere.

But the super smiled and asked her to sit down too. The

DI was looking worried, though, which didn't do anything to calm Meg's nerves.

'WDC Connolly,' said the super. 'DI Willis and I have been very impressed with your work. On this case and others.'

Meg breathed slightly more easily. 'Thank you,' she said.

'That's why we wanted to talk to you about a . . . about a special mission.'

Special mission. Was this one of those dreams where Meg was a secret agent and could fly? She saw the super glance at the DI as if expecting him to speak but the DI remained silent. He almost looked angry. But this was impossible. DI Willis was known in the station as 'the super's shadow'. He was Superintendent Stephens' protégé and never disagreed with him.

'As you know, two magician's assistants in the same show have been murdered. The show is moving to London in two weeks. It's essential for us to have someone keeping the cast under surveillance. Someone on the inside.'

He looked at Meg as if expecting her to know what he was getting at. Surveillance. It was another of those secret agent words.

'I've asked my friend Max Mephisto if he'll join the bill,' said the super. 'As you may know, we served together in the war and I trust him implicitly.'

Another pause. Meg felt a ridiculous urge to salute.

'Max is thinking about it.' Another glance at the DI. 'But, if he does do the show, he'll need an assistant. Another person we can trust. Someone with police training.'

'You don't have to do it if you don't want to,' said the DI.

'Me?' It was like one of those slot machines on the pier where you put your penny in and it took for ever to reach the bottom, making its way through all sorts of metal mazes and springs. Ping. The bell was ringing at last.

'You,' said the super.

'You want me to be Max Mephisto's assistant?' She thought of Ida appearing on stage in her fur bikini. A hysterical giggle was making its way to the surface and had to be suppressed. Meg coughed.

'Are you all right, WDC Connolly?' asked the super. 'Would you like a glass of water?'

'No. I'm OK.'

'You don't have to do it,' said the DI, again sounding almost angry. 'It's a lot to ask of you. Too much, some might say.'

'I'd love to do it,' said Meg.

Emma was presiding over a rather quarrelsome tea when Sam's feet appeared, descending the area steps.

'It's Sam,' said Marianne. 'I want shoes like that. Why doesn't Sam have to wear proper shoes?'

Sam was wearing tennis shoes, jeans and a cricket jumper. Emma had recently had a row with Marianne about having to wear lace-up brogues for school.

'Because she's a grown-up,' said Emma, going to open the door.

Sam didn't seem very much like a grown-up sometimes,

thought Emma. She sat down at the table to eat Sophie's pie crust and start a long conversation about football.

'England are sure to win the World Cup. A friend of mine says that Italy's got a better team, but we'll jinx them by making them play on some grotty old playing field full of potholes.'

'Very sporting,' said Emma. 'Why don't you kids go upstairs and watch TV?'

'We've missed *Crackerjack*,' said Sophie.

'It'll be *Hug or Hit* soon,' said Emma, with a quick glance at Sam.

'Don't want to miss that,' said Sam.

'Come and watch it with us,' said Marianne, pausing at the foot of the stairs.

'I will. Just need a word with Mum first.'

'Grown-up stuff,' said Marianne. 'I know.'

'Bribing them with Pal,' said Sam, when the children had clattered upstairs. 'Nice.'

'It worked,' said Emma. 'And what was all that "need a word with Mum" stuff? Don't call me mum.'

Sam laughed. 'Any chance of a beer, Mum?'

'I've got a bottle of wine somewhere.'

After Emma had poured them both a glass from a bottle of red that still had a raffle ticket on it, Sam said, 'I saw Pal today.'

'You didn't? I thought you were going to see Rex King.'

'Saw him too. They're neighbours. Both of them rich old men playing golf and hiding their secrets.'

'Do you think they have secrets?'

'I think there's something very dodgy in their past. Pal threw me out when I started asking about Grace.'

'Really?'

'Yes, he'd been quite friendly up until then. Creepily friendly.'

'I spoke to Dolores Underwood earlier,' said Emma. 'She knew Pal from her theatrical days. She says she actually introduced Cherry to him.'

Sam shivered. 'Ugh.'

'She said it was because Larry Buxton had her dancing in some seedy club. Honestly, I think they're all as bad as each other. I saw Linda Knight today. The landlady of number 84. She thinks it all goes back to Pal. She said that he controlled all the other magicians. Learnt their secrets and blackmailed them. She also said that he promised young girls work in return for sleeping with him.'

'Do you think that's what happened with Cherry?'

'I wouldn't be surprised. Linda also implied that Pal had contacts who would kill someone.'

She'd expected Sam to dismiss this, even to laugh. But, instead, her partner said, 'He is a very sinister man. He looked so angry when I asked about Grace. I think he would have had me killed if he could.'

'Do you really think a hitman could have killed Cherry and Joan?' Even the word 'hitman' sounded ridiculous when uttered in her kitchen, surrounded by the debris of a family meal.

'Well,' said Sam, 'whoever it was got into a crowded house and killed Cherry almost soundlessly. They lay in wait for Joan. That sounds quite professional to me. Why don't you ask Edgar if the police know of any criminal gangs in Brighton? Anyone who might murder for money.'

'I'll ask him when he gets in,' said Emma. 'He's been in London today.'

'What was he doing in London?' asked Sam.

'I've no idea.'

Sam looked at her curiously but didn't probe any further. She took a gulp of wine. 'What shall we do now? Can we find out what happened with Pal and Cherry?'

'I think we should talk to Ted English again,' said Emma. 'He might be able to tell us more about Cherry's private life.'

'Pal mentioned a boyfriend at home,' said Sam.

'I asked her brother Michael about that,' said Emma. 'I told you at the time. Michael said there had been someone but he was married now. I suppose that doesn't rule him out completely.'

'That's true,' said Sam. 'I feel that Cherry's still a bit of a hazy presence. We don't know enough about her. Joan seems much more solid.'

'Talking of which,' said Emma, 'Joan used to do a strongwoman act with Ida Lupin.'

'Ida Lupin? Oh, the woman who's living at number 84. Her and those two weird comedians.'

'Bigg and Small? They are a bit strange but they seem harmless.'

'I don't know,' said Sam. 'I'm beginning to think that no one in the theatre is harmless.'

'Hug!' shouted the children upstairs. 'Hug!' 'Hit!'

When Edgar got home, Emma had finished her second glass. She poured one for Edgar before presenting him with the rather blackened pie.

'You might need it.'

Edgar grinned and took a swig. Emma chose her moment to say, 'How was London?'

Edgar choked. 'I'm sorry I didn't tell you. It was rather a spur of the moment thing.'

'Tell me now.' Emma refilled her glass.

'I went to see Max.'

Whatever Emma had expected, it wasn't this. They saw Max fairly regularly, meals in London or day trips to Brighton. Emma had taken Max's children to the circus last year. She didn't quite know why Edgar had to see his old friend so urgently.

'He obviously had a woman with him,' Edgar was saying. 'Up to his old tricks. But I met him in a coffee bar. One of his Italian places. Anyway, I had this idea. It might be madness. I thought, what if Max took Dave Dunkley's place in the show.'

'In the nostalgia show? The one on the pier? That *is* madness.'

'They're transferring to London in two weeks. Larry Buxton came to see me yesterday, huffing and puffing in case he lost money. That's what gave me the idea. I'm sure the answer to these murders lies in the show. I need someone on the inside.'

Emma felt nonplussed. She was the one who came up with daring ideas, not Edgar. She had to fight the instinct to disagree with the plan on these grounds alone.

'You want Max to be the magician on the bill?'

'Max and his assistant.'

'His assistant?

'WDC Connolly. Meg.'

Emma put her glass down. 'Ed, you can't do that. You might be putting her in real danger.'

'That's what Bob said.'

'Bob is right.'

'I know it's a risk,' said Edgar. 'But Max would take care of Meg. He hasn't said yes yet but I'm hoping to work on him. He told me that he misses the stage.'

'I didn't realise you were this manipulative.'

'Guileless people can be very cunning,' said Edgar. 'Max said that to me once.'

'Bloody hell, Ed. What did Meg say?'

'She was all for it.'

'You don't surprise me.'

And that was the real reason that Emma was opposed to the plan. She was jealous.

CHAPTER 23

Marianne and Sophie always went horse-riding in Rottingdean on Saturday mornings. Usually Emma took Jonathan. He liked to watch the girls having their lessons with Emma's friend Vera and, afterwards, Vera often allowed him to sit on one of the horses. But, today, Emma asked Edgar if he'd take Jonathan to the park instead.

'He won't like it as much,' said Edgar, looking across the room to where Jonathan was pretending to ride Marianne's hockey stick.

'There's something I want to do while the girls are riding.'

'What?'

'I want to see Verity,' said Emma.

'Is this to do with the case?'

'Yes.'

Emma didn't offer any further explanation and Edgar, though he looked quizzical, didn't ask any more questions. There had been a constraint between them since

Edgar had told Emma his idea about Max and Meg. Emma only knew that she wanted to get on with her own investigation, ideally without having a child in tow.

Emma left the house to the tune of Jonathan wailing, 'Want to see the horses.' She felt a bit guilty, but only a bit. She drove to Rottingdean, dropped the girls at the stable, then parked on Steyning Road and walked, through the twitten, past the pond and the village green, to Tudor Close, the rambling mock-Tudor apartment complex where Verity Malone lived.

She hadn't telephoned ahead but she didn't think Verity got out much these days. Sure enough, Verity opened the door wearing a blonde wig and a red trouser suit.

'Well, if it isn't my favourite private detective.'

'Hi, Verity. I was just passing and I wondered how you were.'

'Rubbish,' said Verity. 'You're on a case. I can tell it in my water.'

What did that even mean? But Emma had to admit that Verity was as sharp as ever.

'I wondered how you were *and* I wanted to talk about a case.'

'You'd better come in then.'

Verity led the way into a comfortable, low-ceilinged sitting room that looked out onto communal grounds. A man mowing the lawn looked up and waved.

'You remember my son, Aaron? Such a devoted boy these days. He really looks after me.'

'That's great,' said Emma. 'I can't imagine my son ever looking after me.'

'How is your dear little boy? I remember him coming here and playing with my make-up case.'

'He's very sweet,' said Emma. 'And very hard work.'

'And how's your handsome husband? The dashing superintendent.'

'About the same.'

Verity laughed. 'So what did you want to talk to me about?'

'Cherry Underwood.'

Verity's smile faded. 'Poor Cherry. Poor Dolores. It means sorrow, you know, Dolores. I was the one who recommended you and Sam to her.'

'I know. Thank you.'

'No thanks necessary. I believe in women helping women. And I know how good you are. The police never put themselves out to solve the murders of young women.'

Emma knew she should defend the Brighton police but she didn't feel like it somehow.

'How do you know Dolores?' she asked.

'She was on the bill of one of Bert's shows,' said Verity. Her late husband, Bert Billington, was the leading theatrical impresario between the wars. 'Bert had his eye on her, of course. The randy sod. I warned Dolores about him and we got friendly.'

Emma was used to Verity's lack of sentimentality about

Bert but 'randy sod' still made her blink. Verity smiled graciously, a vision in red on the brocade sofa.

'I wanted to talk to you about some of the people in Cherry's background,' said Emma. 'I understand it was Larry Buxton who first discovered her.'

'Larry Buxton,' said Verity. 'His father, Larry Senior, was one of Bert's biggest competitors. Both as bad as each other.'

'Larry's producing the show on the pier. The one Cherry was in.'

'I haven't seen it. I can't bear all this nostalgia stuff. The past wasn't such a wonderful place, especially for women. I'm all for the future. Women's liberation, Betty Friedan calls it. The suffragettes fought for our right to vote, now we have to fight for equal pay and for our reproductive rights. I wouldn't have had three children if I'd had access to the pill.'

Outside, Aaron, the youngest of three sons, mowed the lawn in careful stripes.

Emma let this pass, unwilling to consider whether she herself had really wanted three children. 'What about Gordon Palgrave?' she said. 'Did you know him?'

To Emma's surprise – she didn't have Verity down as the religious type – the older woman crossed herself. 'He's a devil. Don't tell me Cherry was mixed up with him.'

'Dolores asked him to get her work as a magician's assistant.'

'If only she'd asked me,' said Verity, sounding genuinely

distressed. 'I'd have told her to steer clear. And magician's assistant! A half-naked woman being abused on stage by a man. I'd rather a daughter of mine was on the streets. At least that's an honourable profession.'

Verity didn't have a daughter so she would never be forced to test this rather controversial opinion. But Emma thought it was interesting that Dolores had known Verity's opinion of Pal ('Verity couldn't bear him') but she had still asked his advice.

'What's so awful about Gordon Palgrave?' she asked.

'I remember once,' said Verity, 'Pal was in one of Bert's shows. Bert went to see him backstage and there was a girl in his dressing room. They'd obviously been about to have sex. Bert sent the girl away – he said she looked scared out of her mind – and asked Pal how old she was. He said, laughing, "Definitely below the age of consent." Bert later found out that she was fourteen. Even he was shocked. He never booked Pal again.'

Emma thought of Marianne, only four years younger than this girl, and her desire 'to be on telly'. She said, 'I've heard that Pal bribed women to have sex with him in return for getting them stage work.'

'That's true,' said Verity. 'But they all do that. I've seen Rex King promising some poor deluded girl that he was going to make her a star. Dave Dunkley too.'

'What about Ted English?'

'I wouldn't put Ted in that category exactly,' said Verity.

'He's a bit of a sot but decent at heart. Even Dolores said that he'd treated Cherry well.'

'She suspected him of her murder, though,' said Emma. 'That's why she engaged us. She thought the police would go easy on him because he's a friend of Max Mephisto.'

'Max was never a friend of Ted's,' said Verity, who'd once been more than a friend to the young Max. 'He wouldn't go near Pal and his set. If you ask me, Pal kept tabs on all of them: Rex, Ted, even old Tommy Horton.'

'That's what Linda Knight said. Do you know her? She's the landlady of the house where Cherry was staying.'

'I don't, I'm afraid. I'm out of touch with that world now. But theatrical landladies, they know what's what. I'd listen to her if I was you.'

'Sam and I went to see Tommy Horton the other day.'

'Did you get any sense out of him?'

'Not really. He seemed quite senile. But he did say something about his ex-wife, Grace.'

'Ah, Gracie,' said Verity. 'She was a pretty girl but so stupid. Fancy falling for Larry's promises and then Pal's. You know why she killed herself? Because she found out about Pal and another teenager. Fancy killing yourself over a man. She should have killed him instead.'

And, despite the cosy setting and the smell of freshly cut grass, for a second Verity looked quite terrifying.

Sam was surprised to get a Saturday morning phone call from Don, the editor of the *Evening Argus*. Sam had once been a staff reporter on the paper and still did freelance work for them. Even so, it was rare for Don to ring her at home.

Sam lived in an attic flat in Kemp Town, not far from Emma and Edgar. She had recently moved from a shared house and she liked the freedom. She liked the view over the terraced houses towards the sea but she wasn't a home maker, so her tiny apartment was still full of boxes and piles of books. A friend who worked in M&S had given her an old clothes rack that served as a wardrobe. Sometimes, lying in bed, Sam imagined herself in Max's flat, moving through each room in turn: the tiled bathroom, the galley kitchen, the sitting room with its view over the treetops of Kensington Square, the bedroom with its king-sized bed . . . Don had disturbed one of those reveries.

'Hi, Don. This is a surprise.'

'Talking of surprises, guess who just rang me?'

'Bobby Moore.'

Don laughed. Sam didn't have him down as a football fan. 'Gordon Palgrave. Pal. You know, from *Hug or Hit*?'

'I know. What did he want?'

'He wanted to warn you off, my girl. He said that you'd turned up at his house asking impertinent questions. What was that about?'

'It's a case I'm working on with Emma.'

Don grunted. 'Well, be careful, Sam. Pal is an important man. Took care to remind me that he was good friends with our proprietor. Apparently, they play golf together.'

'What did you say?'

'I said that you were freelance and your own boss. Also, that he couldn't bully me. Though he probably could.'

'Thanks, Don.'

'No problem. And be careful. I don't want to find myself covering your murder. I haven't got a flattering photo of you, for one thing.'

Sam laughed. Black humour always made her feel better.

Emma drove home feeling thoughtful and hardly listening to the chatter about Toby's canter and whether strawberry roan was the best colour for a horse. It was as if Verity had lifted a curtain and revealed, not a lighted stage, but a murky backstage world full of exploitative men and vulnerable women. Verity had called Pal a devil. It struck Emma that a lot of magicians chose satanic stage names. The Great Deceiver. The Great Diablo. Even Mephisto was an abbreviation of Mephistopheles. And there was something diabolic about being able to dazzle the senses, to make people disappear, to mutilate them, all for the amusement of a paying audience. And by 'people' she meant 'women'. Emma thought of Verity's description of a magician's assistant. 'A half-naked woman being abused on stage by a man.' And this was what Edgar wanted Meg to do! She pressed her foot on the accelerator and ignored Marianne's question about whether she could have a pony of her own.

At home, she found Edgar preparing lunch and Jonathan

full of his adventures with the ducks. She softened slightly. Edgar wasn't the worst man in the world. That title currently seemed to belong to an entertainer called Pal. Despite Sam's encounter and Verity's description, Emma was very keen to talk to Gordon Palgrave.

But she'd have to make do with the next best thing. After lunch, she announced her intention of taking a walk. 'I might call in on Mum and Dad.'

'Shall we all come?' said Edgar, but he didn't protest when Emma said that it would be easier on her own. The girls had a friend round and were playing a game of schools with Jonathan as the sole pupil. Emma knew that Edgar was hoping for half an hour with the newspaper.

Instead of taking the coast road to Roedean, Emma headed north towards Freshfield Road, where Ted English was now renting a room. It was a part of Brighton that held many memories for Emma. In the cold winter of 1951, two children had gone missing from the streets around Queen's Park. They hadn't been able to save them – Emma walked faster at the thought – but they had been able to rescue a third. It had been Emma's first murder case and also the time when she realised that she was irrevocably in love with her boss.

Freshfield Road ran from Kemp Town to the Race Hill and the houses got shabbier the higher you climbed. Ted was living within sight of the stands.

'It's a dump,' he said, when he let Emma into the house. 'The police won't let me leave Brighton. I'm losing money every day. It's a disgrace. And it's still costing me four pounds a week.'

Ted seemed eager to pour his grievances into a sympathetic ear. Emma, sitting on the edge of the single bed to avoid the sloping eaves, only had to listen. She remembered when she first interviewed Ted in his Charlotte Street lodgings and he had cried into his handkerchief. Now he just seemed angry.

'I wouldn't have hurt Cherry. She was a lovely girl. Like a daughter to me. To think someone did that to her . . . I still can't believe it. I'm a wreck. Think I'm having a complete breakdown. And then for Larry Buxton to sack me like that. After all I've done for him. To replace me with Dave Dunkley, of all people . . .'

'Tell me more about Cherry,' said Emma. 'I'd like to talk to someone who actually knew her and cared for her.'

Ted, who had been pacing the tiny room, sat down. He suddenly looked rather old, with his grey hair and liver-spotted hands, one of which shook as he rubbed his chin. He hadn't shaved that morning and the stubble rasped.

'She was a nice girl from a nice family,' he said. 'Brothers and sisters. Close, you know. I didn't have that. I'm an only child. My mum died when I was twelve. I never knew my dad. I was on the boards by the time I was sixteen, juggling, tumbling, that sort of thing. I was fit back then. I met Pal at ENSA. He suggested I turn to magic. Even helped me out with my first act.'

'That was kind of him,' said Emma. It struck her as

suspiciously kind. Why would Pal want to help a potential rival?

'He was like that,' said Ted. 'He liked you to be in his debt. It was Pal who introduced me to Cherry. "Be good to her," he said, "she's not one of your floozies." But I never had any floozies.'

He sounded genuinely disappointed. Emma asked if he had ever been married.

'No wife, no kids,' said Ted. 'Not much to show for my life really.' Emma followed his gaze around the tiny room with its stained bedspread and threadbare carpet. She was momentarily lost for words.

'Cherry's mother had been on the stage, you know,' said Ted. 'So she knew you could get some unpleasant types. Well, she worked for Bert Billington. Say no more. Dolores asked Pal to introduce Cherry to some decent people. "I'm so glad Cherry's working with you," Dolores said, "You're a gentleman. Not like some of the others." Now, of course, they think I'm the devil incarnate . . .'

There he was again. The Great Deceiver. 'Mr and Mrs Underwood just want to find the person who killed their daughter,' said Emma. 'Did Cherry ever mention anyone bothering her? Following her?'

'No,' said Ted. 'When I saw her on the Sunday, she seemed in good spirits. We went through the act – she was shaping up very well – and I said I'd see her for the first house on Tuesday.'

But by Tuesday Cherry was dead. Emma remembered

asking Ted if he knew what Cherry had planned to do on Sunday afternoon and Monday and he said he didn't know. Ted had said she was in good spirits but, according to the police reports, Cherry had complained of a headache after lunch on Sunday. Had she been worried about something or someone?

'Someone said they saw Cherry talking to a young man on Sunday afternoon,' said Emma. She owed Meg for this nugget. 'Have you any idea who that could have been?'

'No.' Ted looked baffled, an expression that came easily to him. 'Cherry didn't know anyone in Brighton.'

'Do you know if Pal kept in touch with Cherry?'

'I wouldn't have thought so,' said Ted. 'Not now he's a big TV star.'

'What about Rex King?'

'Rex? He's retired now. Spends his time playing golf and being bossed about by his wife.'

'Do you know Tommy Horton?'

'Poor old Tommy. Good magician in his day. Haven't seen him for years though. Heard he was going a bit doolally.'

'Did you know Tommy's first wife, Grace?'

'I only met her a few times. Good-looking woman. His second was too.' Ted seemed genuine and Emma couldn't think why he'd lie about this. Why, then, did Tommy say that Ted had treated Grace badly? Did he just get the wrong name? If so, who was he really thinking of?

Emma asked Ted if he knew Joan Waters. As expected, he

answered that everyone knew Joanie. He'd never worked with her himself but he knew her from the circuit. No, he didn't think Joan had ever met Cherry.

'But, now Joan's dead,' said Ted, brightening up, 'they can't think it was me. I was drinking with Dave and all that lot. I'd been to see the show. Dave had quite a good act but he nearly muffed it a few times. He must be getting on a bit now.'

Emma thought that Ted and Dave Dunkley were probably a similar age.

'Who else was drinking with you?'

'Dave, Larry, Perry Small. Some of the dancers. Larry left early.'

Emma knew this from Edgar. The doorman at the Grand had seen Larry come in at eleven-thirty. That still left Ted and Dave, the two men whose assistants had been brutally killed, drinking together.

As Emma left, Ted asked her if she knew who would be taking the magician's slot for the London run.

'I don't, I'm afraid.' She wasn't about to mention Max, Ted's so-called close friend.

'Well, if you see Larry Buxton, tell him I'm available.'

Show-business people never ceased to surprise her.

CHAPTER 24

'Have you ever done anything like this before?'

'No,' said Meg.

She could not quite believe that she was having this conversation with Max Mephisto, sitting on his sofa in a room that looked out on one of those swanky London squares. She'd caught an early train and arrived at ten. Max was obviously expecting her. He ushered her into the sitting room and offered to make her coffee. Meg didn't dare ask for tea instead. Max left the room and Meg heard a tremendous grinding and clanking noise coming from somewhere in the flat but, when Max returned, he was holding the smallest cup she had ever seen. Meg raised it to her lips. The liquid tasted bitter and thick. Luckily it was gone in two gulps. Max said it was 'genuine Italian espresso'. Meg couldn't get the taste of it out of her mouth.

'Never been on stage? Even at school?'

'I was in a nativity play once. I was one of the kings because I was tall. I think that was the last time. And it wasn't a stage. It was on the altar at church. The kings had to process down the aisle.'

It had been magical, Meg remembered. The church lit by candles, Margaret Mary O'Hara and Patrick Delaney kneeling by the makeshift crib. Meg had been Frankincense, which meant carrying the thurible, the container that dispensed incense, something only altar boys were usually allowed to do. She remembered swinging it as she led the procession, the smoke drifting around her, cardboard crown over her nose. Sister Bernadette had said that she walked too slowly ('I know the kings took their time, girl, but the Baby Jesus would have been grown up by the time you got there') but Meg had wanted to savour every minute.

'I was brought up Catholic too,' said Max, greatly surprising Meg. 'I got to play Joseph once. Not a role with any great dramatic potential.'

'That must have been because you were tall too,' said Meg.

Max looked at her for a moment. He had very dark eyes, which made his stare particularly intense. Then he said, 'Stand up.'

Meg stood up, aware that her slacks didn't fit very well and that her jumper had ridden up. Max came to stand opposite her, still giving her The Stare. Meg knew that she was blushing.

'We're almost the same height,' said Max.

In fact, Max was a good few inches taller but Meg knew

what he meant. They were almost on eye level, if Meg could bring herself to look him in the face.

'Most magicians' assistants are small,' said Max.

'Joan Waters was quite tall,' said Meg. She'd noticed that on the coroner's report.

'That's unusual,' said Max. 'The height difference is usually part of the power play. The magician is in charge. The assistant rarely speaks. It's all part of the misdirection, of course. The assistant is often the one doing the trick but the audience doesn't suspect this because they're so passive. Of course, old-style magicians didn't speak much either, they relied a lot on mime, but I've always done a lot of talking. It helps to create a connection with the audience. The assistant has to manage that with smiles and eye contact.'

That must be why Max was so good at staring, thought Meg.

'You were great as Abanazar,' she said.

Max laughed, breaking the eye contact. 'I had a terrible assistant, then, as I remember. The girl playing Aladdin was never in the right place at the right time. But I wonder if we could do something with the fact that we're almost the same size.'

'Like what?' said Meg.

'Maybe we could dress alike, do the doubling thing. On stage, with the right lighting, the audience wouldn't be able to distinguish between us.'

'That would be better than wearing a spangled bikini,' said Meg.

Max laughed again. 'The sexualised costumes are all part of it, I'm afraid. The audience can't help following the glittery object. But we might be able to do something cleverer, where they won't know which one of us to look at.'

'Are you going to do it then?' said Meg. 'Superintendent Stephens said you hadn't decided.'

'Go and see Max,' the super had said on Friday. 'Go on Monday morning, when he's had the weekend to think about it.'

'Superintendent Stephens is a crafty sod sometimes,' said Max.

Meg decided not to answer that.

Emma disliked Mondays. Tempers were always rather frayed in the morning and there was no playgroup for Jonathan. At least she could still walk the girls to school. Emma dreaded next year when Marianne would take the eleven plus and move either to the grammar school in Hove or the secondary modern in Woodingdean. Of course, there was another option. Emma's parents had said several times that they would pay to send the girls to Roedean. Emma had always refused, saying that she didn't want them to grow up in a rarefied private school atmosphere. Would she feel differently if Marianne failed the eleven plus? But she wouldn't fail, would she? Marianne was a very bright girl. Emma tried to forget that Marianne's teacher had told her recently that imaginative 'unusual' children often did badly in the exam.

Emma and Jonathan waved goodbye to Marianne and Sophie as they disappeared into the entrance marked 'Girls'. Jonathan showed an inclination to whine, so Emma promised to take him to the Peter Pan playground on the seafront. To get there they passed the house where Sam had her flat. On impulse, Emma said, 'Do you want to see Sam?'

'Want to see Sam,' Jonathan agreed immediately.

Emma rang the bell that had 'Superman' written in Sam's characteristically sloping hand. Sam adored the comic book character because he was a journalist.

'Hi, Clark Kent. It's me and Jonny.'

'Coming down.'

Sam appeared, wearing jeans and a personalised T-shirt. It said 'Mark'.

'You've got a mark on your shirt,' said Emma, as they climbed the three flights of stairs.

'Cool, isn't it? Got it in Carnaby Street.'

In Sam's bed-sitting room, Emma took the only chair while Sam found the box of toys she kept for Jonathan. Then she sat on another box and grinned at her partner.

'Coffee?'

'No, thank you.'

Last time, Sam had heated up coffee she'd made the night before.

'Got a few things to update you on.' Emma got out her notebook. 'I saw Verity Malone and Ted English on Saturday. Oh, and Ed has had a mad idea.' She told Sam about the plan for Max to join the cast with Meg as his assistant.

'Gosh,' said Sam. 'I can just imagine Meg as the toast of Drury Lane. Do you think it will happen?'

'It depends on Max, I think. Meg is all for it.'

'Well, I suppose it's more exciting than her usual work.'

'I don't know,' said Emma. 'She's already been involved in two big murder cases.' She was aware that she was sounding sour, so changed the subject.

'Verity told me some pretty horrible things about Pal. Sleeping with fourteen-year-old girls, for one thing.'

Sam shuddered. 'You know, when I went into his house, I had the strangest feeling that I was never going to get out alive. I think he's really evil.'

'Verity said he was the devil.'

'Well, she did have a fundamentalist religious upbringing.'

'I'd forgotten that.' Emma remembered Verity crossing herself. Had Verity been a Catholic before being forced into her father's cult of one?

'Ted English seemed pretty fed up when I saw him,' said Emma. 'But he was more sorry for himself than for Cherry. I think he's still a suspect. He doesn't have much of an alibi for Cherry or Joan.'

'Did you ask him about Grace? Tommy's ex-wife?'

'He claimed only to have met her a few times.'

'Did you believe him?'

'I did. Made me wonder who Tommy was really talking about.'

'There's some mystery there,' said Sam. 'Pal looked

ready to kill me when I mentioned Grace. He's already been on to Don trying to get me sacked. Don told him that I was my own boss. He's not a bad sort, Don.'

There was definitely a mystery, thought Emma, as she and Jonathan made their way down the steps to the promenade. Another mystery was: how did Sam know that Max was appearing in Drury Lane?

Rather reluctantly, Meg said that she'd better be going. It was nearly midday and she thought the DI would expect her back by early afternoon.

She thought that Max would be only too glad to see the back of her but, instead, he said, 'Want to see the theatre first?'

'What theatre?' said Meg.

'The Theatre Royal Drury Lane. It's where we'll be performing.'

'Yes please,' said Meg. Did this mean that Max had agreed to the idea?

'Let me get my hat then.'

In the street outside, Max raised his hand and a London cab seemed to appear by magic. It was the first time that Meg had ever been in a black cab. She climbed in, glad she was wearing trousers, and Max took the pull-down seat opposite her. 'Drury Lane,' he said to the driver. Meg watched as picture postcard London unfolded in front of her: Hyde Park, the Albert Memorial, Buckingham Palace. She craned her head to see if the Queen was in residence.

'She's not at home,' said Max. 'The flag's not flying.'

'Have you ever met the Queen?'

'Just once. At a Royal Variety Performance. Princess Elizabeth, as she was then. Odd little thing. Wearing too much make-up.'

'Gosh.' Meg relapsed into awed silence. Were you allowed to say things like that about the royal family? Her mother had a photograph of the coronation on the kitchen wall even though her father said that they were no friends to Irish Catholics. People often asked if Meg were named after Princess Margaret and she felt embarrassed to admit that it was actually St Margaret of Antioch.

After her scenic tour, Meg was slightly disappointed with her first glimpse of the famous theatre. Max asked the taxi to stop in a side street that seemed full of dustbins.

'Is this it?'

'This is the stage door.'

Meg almost missed the scruffy door hidden between two boarded-up windows. Had Max conjured it out of nowhere, like the taxi? He knocked and a voice growled, 'Who is it?'

'Max Mephisto.'

Meg wanted to laugh at how quickly they were admitted after these magic words. A large man in shirtsleeves loomed in the entrance.

'Bloody hell. It really is you.'

'Hallo, Fred. Long time, no see.'

'Don't tell me you're appearing here.'

'Maybe. Just wanted to case the joint. This is Samantha, my new assistant.'

'Glad to meet you, Samantha. Well, you know the way, Max.'

Max pushed open a door and led the way along a narrow passage. In a strange way, it reminded Meg of the underground rooms in Bartholomew Square station: the same damp smell, the same pipes running overhead.

'Samantha?' said Meg to Max's back.

'I'm sorry,' said Max. 'It occurred to me that you'd need a stage name and that was the first thing that came into my head. You can change it if you like. Fred won't remember.'

'I like it,' said Meg.

The corridor led to stone stairs, streaked with what looked like soot.

'This is a really old theatre,' said Max. 'It was closed during the Great Plague of 1665 and nearly burned down a few years later. You can still see the fire damage on the lower floors.'

Now they were moving through a room that seemed full of painted boards. Meg couldn't see very much but she got the impression of castles and turrets. Eventually Max stepped through a small gap and said, 'Here we are.' Meg followed and gasped. She was actually standing on the stage, the wooden boards sloping slightly downwards, like a ship riding a wave. The only light was from a small red bulb in the distance but she knew that the seats – stalls, circle, Royal Box – were in front of her. She surprised herself by wanting to sing or dance, anything to fill this expectant void.

Max was smiling at her. 'Take a bow.'

Meg curtsied to the empty gallery.

'You see that,' Max pointed to the red light, 'that's the spirit lamp. Do you know why it's there?'

'No.'

'It's for the ghosts,' said Max. 'Every theatre is full of ghosts. Drury Lane is haunted by Grimaldi and Dan Leno, amongst others. The lamp is to keep them company.'

His eyes gleamed in the darkness and Meg suddenly remembered Abanazar advancing on the cowering Aladdin. *Give me the lamp, boy.* Then Max turned away and the stage was flooded with light. The wicked uncle disappeared and Meg saw a backdrop showing a castle wall and drawbridge.

'*Camelot,*' said Max. 'I took Ruby to see it at Christmas. Lots of sentimental stuff about the knights of the round table but there are some good tunes. I think there's going to be a film soon.'

'Are they stopping *Camelot* for us?'

Max laughed. 'No, it's come to the end of its run. I imagine we're a filler, until the next big show comes along. That must be why Larry Buxton got such a good venue.'

Meg looked up at the seats, now illuminated in all

their velvet glory. She imagined them full of people, like the theatregoers she'd seen on the Palace Pier, only even smarter, draped in fur coats and diamonds. She walked forward and peered down into the orchestra pit, surprised it was so small. The spirit lamp glowed in front of her.

'Well?' said Max. 'Can you imagine yourself performing here, Samantha?'

'Yes,' said Meg.

CHAPTER 25

Max offered to call a taxi to take Meg to Victoria Station but she said she'd prefer to go by tube. Max watched her disappearing into the crowds at Covent Garden underground station, an awkward figure in those terrible trousers but with something oddly compelling about her. He liked the way that she spoke, that unabashed Whitehawk accent, the way that she said what she thought, without artifice or flirtation. And she'd looked good on stage, suddenly more poised and confident. Max knew that she'd felt good too. He was never wrong about things like that.

Max went to the telephone box outside the Opera House and telephoned Ruby. He tried to ring her most days, knowing that she was struggling a bit with Baby Poppy, and talking about double acts had reminded him of the days when he and Ruby were Magician and Daughter. Max hadn't enjoyed their run at the Brighton Hippodrome for all sorts of reasons, the murder of the love of his life being one of them, but there was no doubt that Ruby had been his most accomplished stage partner.

Ruby answered immediately, which was unusual for her. Max could hear Poppy crying in the background.

'Can I take you out to lunch?' said Max.

'How can I?' said Ruby. 'Poppy's screaming blue murder and besides, I look horrible.'

'Sit tight,' said Max. 'I'm in Covent Garden. I'll be over in ten minutes with some food.'

In fact, it took him almost an hour to take a taxi to Luigi's, pick up some lasagne, and walk to Ruby's flat. Ruby opened the door with Poppy on her hip. Both of them had faces that were puffy from crying.

'Give me the baby,' said Max. 'Then go and wash your face and put the lasagne on some plates. It should still be hot enough.'

Max walked around the small sitting room with Poppy resting against his shoulder. When Rocco and Elena were born, he'd been surprised how much he liked babies. He'd been expecting not to be interested until they walked and talked. But he'd found that he was good at soothing crying infants, something that even his ex-wife Lydia had acknowledged. Maybe it was years of hypnotising audiences, even the Monday night crowd when landladies got their free tickets and sat on their hands rather than clap. Poppy was now hiccoughing gently.

'There, there,' said Max. 'Go to sleep and let your mother have a rest.'

When Ruby appeared, carrying the plates of pasta, Poppy was fast asleep.

'Typical,' said Ruby, but she looked better. Her hair was tied back and she'd even put on some lipstick. Max sat on the sofa, eating one-handed, with Poppy in the crook of the other arm. Ruby knelt at the coffee table, attacking her meal hungrily.

'What do you do for food usually?' said Max.

'Mostly toast,' said Ruby.

'I'll get Luigi to make a weekly delivery,' said Max. 'And, do you remember Madame Mitzi?'

'The mad Frenchwoman with the poodle act? Yes.'

'I ran into her in Barkers recently. Her daughter's a nursery nurse. Why don't I employ her to come in a few mornings a week, just so that you can have some rest and some proper food.'

Ruby's eyes filled with tears. 'You think I'm not coping.'

'I think you're coping brilliantly. I just think you need some help. Lydia had a nanny from the day the children were born.'

'Typical,' said Ruby, who wasn't a fan of her former stepmother.

'She was a good mother,' said Max. 'She just wasn't afraid to ask for help.'

'That's what Mum keeps saying,' said Ruby. 'Don't be too proud to ask for help. And, of course, that makes me say that everything is wonderful.'

'I think Emerald would be happy to help,' said Max.

'After all, she won't want Poppy preferring me.' He looked down at the sleeping baby. She had a faint version of his widow's peak.

Ruby laughed. 'It would be lovely to have someone to look after Poppy in the mornings. I could go back to bed, have a bath, feel more human.'

'That's settled then. I'll talk to Mitzi.' He'd ask Joe to find her. The showbiz network was still strong.

'What about Dex?' said Max, when they'd both finished eating.

'I don't want him to see me like this,' said Ruby, gesturing at her face, make-up free now that the lipstick had worn off.

'You look lovely,' said Max. 'And he'll want to spend time with his daughter.'

'That's what he says,' acknowledged Ruby.

'Well, then. Promise me you'll ring Emerald and Dex as soon as I'm gone.'

'All right,' said Ruby. She leant back against a chair and said, 'What were you doing in Covent Garden anyway?'

Max told her about Edgar's plan. 'Who knew that Ed could come up with something like that?'

'Ed's cleverer than you think,' said Ruby. She sometimes surprised Max by coming to her ex-fiancé's defence.

'I know he's clever,' said Max. 'But this is devious. And to involve one of his police officers too.'

'Why didn't you ask me to be your assistant?' said Ruby, looking lightly mutinous.

'One, because you've just had a baby. Two, because you're more famous than me now. Three, because I don't want you to get killed.'

Ruby, who had smiled at 'two', looked up at 'three'. 'Do you really think it's that dangerous?'

'Two women have been murdered.'

'What about Meg? Isn't she scared?'

'She's a policewoman. She's tough.'

'She's a bit tall for an assistant.'

'I thought we might make something of that. Use doubling maybe.'

'Maybe even some shadow play,' said Ruby. 'Me and My Shadow. That sort of thing.'

'That's a brilliant idea,' said Max. 'Have you got a pen and paper?'

They talked on, while Poppy slept peacefully in the magician's arms.

Edgar wasn't entirely surprised to get a call from Max saying that he was prepared to join the show. He'd known that the lure of the stage would be too strong.

'And with WDC Connolly as your assistant?'

Meg had returned to the station at three, saying nothing except that her meeting with Max had been 'interesting'.

'Yes,' said Max. 'I think we might be able to put together a decent act.'

Edgar wondered what Meg had done to convince Max. Even though it had been his idea, Edgar couldn't quite imagine her on stage. When Max had rung off, Edgar telephoned Larry Buxton.

'You're kidding! Max Mephisto is going to do my show? I could kiss you, Superintendent.'

'Please don't. And, remember, not a word about my undercover officer.'

'Mum's the word. Lucky you to have a dolly bird on hand.'

'She's an experienced officer,' said Edgar, thinking of Meg, with her blunt statements and laddered tights. 'Mind you treat her like one.'

'Of course,' said Larry. 'Thanks again. This feels like Christmas.'

Edgar was prepared for slightly less enthusiasm from Bob.

'I still don't like it,' he said. 'We're responsible for the safety of our officers. What if something happened to WDC Connolly? I could never face her parents again.'

'Have you met them?' asked Edgar curiously.

'Once,' said Bob. 'They seem a very nice family. Respectable.' Edgar knew this was one of Bob's highest terms of praise.

'WDC Connolly will be on her guard,' said Edgar. 'Those other poor girls weren't. Besides, it's a long shot that the killer is something to do with the show. It could just as easily be a random madman wandering round Brighton. Even a professional hitman.' Emma had mentioned this theory to him but, although Edgar had asked Bob to investigate Brighton's criminal fraternity, he couldn't quite bring himself to believe in a paid assassin.

Edgar's phone was ringing. He ignored it but, a few seconds later, Rita put her head round the door. 'Sorry to disturb you but it's Larry Buxton. He says it's urgent.'

What could Larry want now? Edgar wondered. Was he ringing to say that, after consideration, he didn't want Max Mephisto on the bill? It seemed unlikely.

'Hallo, Mr Buxton. What can I do for you?'

'It's Pal,' said Larry. 'He's dead.'

CHAPTER 26

'Dead?' said Edgar. 'Murdered?'

'Murdered?' said Larry. 'No. Heart attack. His housekeeper just telephoned. She found him about an hour ago. Sitting on his sofa. Stone dead. Bloody hell.'

'Was he dead when she found him?' asked Edgar, his detective brain clicking into gear.

'I think so. The poor woman was very distressed, naturally. She's worked for Pal for years. Said that he was just sitting there, staring, his eyes all glazed. She called an ambulance but there was nothing they could do. Pal had once given her a list of phone numbers in case of emergencies. I was top of the list. Makes you think, doesn't it?'

It certainly did. Gordon Palgrave, a man whose act, whose very name, involved being everyone's friend, had no one to call on in times of trouble. Except his agent, who seemed less grief-stricken than worried about the work involved.

'I suppose I'll have to arrange the funeral,' he was saying.

'Did Palgrave have any family?'

'I think there's a sister but they weren't in touch. Pal worshipped his old mum but she died a few years back. I'll have to come up with a statement for the press too.'

'Do the press know?'

'Not yet but it'll be out soon. Hospitals are the leakiest places on earth. Maybe I should do a tribute show . . .'

Larry's voice, which had become more thoughtful, died away. Edgar took the opportunity to say goodbye and hang up.

Bob was watching him. 'Pal's dead. I can't believe it. My boys are always watching him on TV.'

'My kids too,' said Edgar, remembering seeing his children transfixed by the figure capering on the screen. Hug! Hit! 'It is a surprise, though,' he said. 'When I interviewed Palgrave, he seemed in good health. He played golf regularly. He told me that he'd never smoked or drunk alcohol.'

'Why not?' said Bob who, although not a big drinker, enjoyed a pint of Harvey's.

'I don't know. I wonder if there was a religious background somewhere. How old was Pal, do you think?'

'Hard to tell with that hair but he's been around a long time. Sixty, possibly?'

Pal was sixty-nine. By the time that Edgar got home, his death was on the television and radio news. Emma was listening to the wireless as she cooked supper.

'The much-loved entertainer,' intoned the announcer, 'died at his Richmond home today. Cause of death has not been revealed.'

'Heart attack,' said Edgar. 'According to Larry Buxton.'

'Did Buxton ring you?' said Emma, turning off the transistor.

'Yes. He seemed very shocked.'

'It is a surprise,' said Emma. 'Sixty-nine's not old these days. Look at your mum.'

Edgar's mother, Rose, had recently taken up ballroom dancing at the age of seventy-three. She had been rejuvenated by a second marriage to a wealthy retired colonel. She dyed her hair and talked about 'having a snifter at the Con club'.

'And Pal seemed in good health when I saw him,' said Edgar, starting to lay the table. 'Did Sam say the same?'

'Yes, she thought he looked in good shape. Not overweight or red in the face. He told her that he didn't drink.'

'He told me that too.'

'Sam's going to ring Rex King,' said Emma. 'See if she can find anything out.'

'She's an incorrigible doorstepper,' said Edgar but he had to admit that he'd be interested in what Sam could discover.

He didn't have long to wait. The family were just finishing their rice and meatballs when the phone rang. Marianne jumped up but Emma was too quick for her.

'Hi, Sam. What did you . . . Really? . . . I can't believe it . . . Well, exactly . . . That's a good idea . . .'

Edgar and the children were all staring by the time Emma got off the phone. Even Jonathan had stopped playing table football with his meatball.

'What can't you believe?' asked Marianne.

Emma paused for effect. 'Sam rang Rex. There was no answer at first but, the second time, his cleaner picked up the phone. Rex is in hospital. He had a heart attack earlier today.'

'It must be suspicious, surely,' said Emma. They had tried not to talk too much in front of the children but now the kids were in bed. Emma and Edgar were drinking cocoa by the light of the television. The sound was turned down and the little figures capered silently on the screen.

'It's strange,' said Edgar. 'It's certainly a coincidence. But I don't see that it's suspicious exactly.'

Emma turned to face him, the glow from the TV turning her hair into a halo. 'Once you eliminate the impossible, whatever remains, however improbable, must be the truth.'

'Quoting Uncle Sherlock again?'

'Conan Doyle, actually. But there has to be a link, surely? Pal and Rex both knew Cherry and Joan. Sam said that she felt really uncomfortable with Pal and she doesn't scare easily.'

'I know what she means. He was very affable with me but there was still something chilling about him.'

'I told you what Verity said about Pal seducing a fourteen-year-old.'

'You did,' Edgar said grimly. 'I wish someone had reported him to the police at the time.'

'Would the police have done anything about it?' Emma favoured Edgar with one of her direct looks.

'I would have,' said Edgar. 'You know I would.'

'I know.' Some of the anger had gone from Emma's voice. Now she was musing in a way that reminded Edgar of the old days when she was his sergeant. He would rather she was his wife, of course, but he did miss those discussions.

'Something happened yesterday that gave those two old magicians heart attacks. What gives people heart attacks?'

'Congenital heart disease?'

'Or bad news,' said Emma. 'I wonder what news Pal and Rex had recently received.'

And Edgar remembered Larry's description of the dead man. *He was just sitting there, staring . . .*

CHAPTER 27

Though she said so herself, Sam was very good at getting into hospital wards. She dressed in her most conservative clothes – navy slacks, white shirt, a jacket of almost the same blue – and presented herself at the reception desk of St George's Hospital.

'Good morning. I'm here to see my uncle, Rex King. I think he came in last night.'

She'd decided on niece because it was harder to check than daughter. She assumed that Rex's wife would have been to see him and, if questioned, would remember that she didn't possess a grown-up child.

'Visiting hour doesn't start until two p.m.,' said the receptionist.

'I know,' said Sam, 'but this was the only time I could get away. I've got a little boy, you see, and my neighbour's minding him.'

She smiled a brave single-mother smile. It seemed to work. The receptionist checked her files.

'He's on Attlee Ward. On the third floor. It's not an intensive care ward so I'm sure that means he's doing well. Good luck.'

Sam had the grace to feel slightly guilty as she took the lift to the third floor. The doors of the ward were shut and, when she pushed them open, a voice barked, 'You can't come in. Visiting hour isn't until the afternoon.' A figure in a matron's uniform was blocking the way, no less formidable for being several inches shorter than Sam.

'I know,' said Sam. 'But I've got special permission to see Rex King. I'm his niece.' She brandished some wilting carnations.

'You can leave the flowers and go,' said the matron. Sam took this as authorisation to enter.

Rex was in the bed closest to the nurses' station. He was lying flat on his back, staring at the ceiling.

'Hallo, Rex,' said Sam. She wondered if she should have added 'uncle' for the benefit of Matron.

Rex's lips moved but he said nothing. His tanned face looked incongruous against the white hospital pillow.

Sam took the seat by the bed. 'It's Sam. Do you remember, I came to see you the other day?'

'Sam.' Rex frowned. 'The detective.'

'That's right.' Sam glanced round but Matron was busy berating a nurse for some misdemeanour or other.

'I bought you these.' Sam flourished the sad flowers.

'Thank you,' said Rex.

'How are you feeling? Can you remember what happened yesterday?'

'Bits of it,' said Rex. He tried to sit up and Sam leant forward to help.

'Does your bed tip up? Oh yes. Here we go.'

The bed lurched Rex into a sitting position and Sam helped him to arrange his pillows. Ever the caring niece.

'What do you remember?' she asked again.

'There was a knock on the door,' said Rex. 'I thought it was Pal. We were going to play golf and he was late. I opened the door and she was standing there, with the sun behind her. Grace.'

'Grace?' Whatever Sam had been expecting, it wasn't this.

'Gracie. Young. Beautiful. Just how I remembered her. Then . . . I don't remember anything else. I came to, here, in the hospital. They thought I'd had a heart attack but apparently I fell and hit my head. They're keeping me here to check if I've got brain damage. If they can find a brain, that is. Ha ha.'

Sam wondered who had called the ambulance. Was it the woman who had looked like Grace?

'Have you heard about Pal?' she said.

'Pal? No. I did wonder if he'd visit me.' Rex sounded rather disconsolate. Sam wondered if he would have many other visitors.

'I'm sorry,' said Sam. 'But Pal had a heart attack yesterday. A real one. He's dead.'

'Pal's dead?' Rex's tan suddenly looked a muddy colour. Sam poured some water from a jug by the bed and held it out to him.

'Thanks.' He took a sip.

'I know it must be a shock,' said Sam.

'It is,' said Rex. 'I expected him to live for ever. Well, he was always a good friend to me. Whatever other stories people will tell.'

The news that morning had been full of golden-hearted Pal, with his charity work and lovable TV persona. Clips from *Hug or Hit* had been played, Pal wrapping himself around overawed, or downright terrified, women. Sam wondered how long it would be before the 'other stories' got out. Only the radio news had mentioned 'the tragic death' of Pal's wife. Maybe the newspaper obituaries would be more comprehensive.

'Do you think he saw her too?' said Sam. 'The Grace woman?'

'If he did,' said Rex soberly, 'it would have killed him.' He started to cough, and Matron came over to tell Sam that she had to leave. 'You were only meant to hand over the flowers. Mr King must be kept quiet.'

Sam stood up.

'Will you come again?' said Rex.

Surprised, Sam said, 'If you want me to.'

'Of course I do,' said Rex. 'You're my favourite niece.' His faint 'ha ha' followed her out of the ward.

*

Outside, in the sunshine, Sam took off her jacket. She felt a sudden need to escape, not just from the hospital but from illness and death generally. It had been surprisingly sad to see Rex in his hospital bed, so starved of company that he welcomed the arrival of a private investigator pretending to be his niece. With a slightly heavy heart, Sam knew that she would visit again. And, although the case was interesting, it had a seedy backstory that made Sam feel angry and unhappy. All these girls – Grace, Cherry, Joanie – at the mercy of impresarios and so-called stars, living in grotty digs, dressing up every night for men to ogle at them. Men cutting women in half, men harming women.

Sam thought she'd had enough of cruelty for a while. She hadn't been lying to Emma about continuing to work on the Moors Murders; she was investigating the backgrounds of Brady and Hindley for a big piece in the *Argus*. After spending time in their darkness, she wanted to live in the light for a while. She took the bus to Kensington High Street.

Here was life: old men sitting outside cafés, a horse-drawn dray delivering to a pub, miniskirted girls waiting at zebra crossings, wolf-whistling errand boys whizzing by on bicycles. As Sam walked past Kensington Gardens, she saw a mother and two children opening the secret door in the hedge. The children had tennis rackets and the mother was carrying a small dog that yapped at Sam. Students were emerging from the entrance of Maria

Assumpta Teacher Training College, laughing in a distinctly non-religious way.

Alf, the doorman at Abbot's Court, greeted Sam with a mixture of deference and lasciviousness. Mr Mephisto was out, he told her, and he wasn't sure when he'd be back. Sam didn't want to wait in the lobby while Alf stared at her chest, so she stepped back into the street.

'Sam!' It was Max, like the Avenging Angel, in one of his Mod suits, hatless, dark hair lifting slightly in the breeze.

'Darling. This is a surprise.' He bent to kiss her.

'I know. I needed cheering up.'

'Well, I'm good at that.' He put an arm round her. 'It's very good to see you, Samantha.'

'Why are you calling me that? Only my mum calls me that.'

But Max just laughed and said, 'Samantha' again, in an entirely different voice. They made their way to the lift.

PART 3
June

CHAPTER 28

Monday, 6 June 1966

'Morning, Fred,' said Meg.

'Morning, Samantha.'

It hadn't occurred to Meg that she'd be Samantha to everyone at the Theatre Royal Drury Lane. She squared her shoulders and tried a bit of a hair flick. Having a pseudonym made her feel slightly braver. On the train that morning, she'd felt a fraud, sure that the cast would know immediately that she wasn't one of them. It hadn't helped that everyone at Bartholomew Square seemed to think that her being a magician's assistant was hilarious.

'I hear you're a can-can girl now,' Barker had said on Friday. 'Folies Bergère and all that. Are you wearing feathers on stage? They'll have to pluck a few birds.'

Meg had ignored him but she'd heard some of the others – even Danny – laughing.

'Appear on stage, wearing next to nothing? Over my dead body,' had been her mother's response.

'I'm sure that can be arranged,' Aisling had muttered.

'I'm undercover, Mum,' Meg had explained, for what felt like the hundredth time. 'It's all part of my job. I'm meant to be keeping an eye on everyone in the show. And I'll be wearing a man's suit.'

'Blessed Mary and all the saints preserve us.' Her mother sketched the sign of the cross with the hand that wasn't ironing.

Meg had a week to rehearse the show with Max. It seemed very little time to Meg but Max said that pros usually only had a day or two to get to know a new theatre. 'A week is luxury,' he said. But Meg thought that Max underestimated how long it would take to transform Meg from Whitehawk into Samantha, the magician's assistant.

Meg walked along the corridor. It gave onto a landing with three doors. Stone steps led down into the lower part of the theatre. Meg remembered that much but she couldn't remember which door to go through to get to the auditorium. Max had said to meet him in the stalls. There was no clue, just a fire bucket and a suit of armour, presumably left over from *Camelot*. Meg touched the gauntlet and was surprised to find that it was cardboard, not metal. A reminder that nothing was as it seemed. The brick walls were stained with what looked like soot. Hadn't Max said something about a fire?

As she stood on the landing, trying to make up her

mind, Meg heard someone walking quickly up the stairs. For some reason she felt scared, but she stood her ground. She was a police officer, after all.

A blonde head appeared. Ida Lupin. Meg relaxed.

'Oh, hallo,' said Ida. 'You're the policewoman aren't you? What are you doing here?'

Meg assumed that Max would have told everyone that she was going to be his assistant that week. She had not yet realised how little the pros communicated with each other.

'I'm in the show,' she said, feeling awkward. She explained, trying not to make it seem as if the cast were under suspicion.

'You're going to perform with *Max*?' Ida's large blue eyes became even bigger. 'With *Max Mephisto*?'

'He's a friend of the super's,' said Meg.

Ida whistled soundlessly. 'So that's why Max has condescended to be in our little show. He's working for the police.'

'Not exactly,' said Meg. 'I'm the one working for the police.'

'And you're going to be his assistant? It's not easy, you know, being a magician's assistant.'

'I'm sure it isn't,' said Meg. She remembered Ida on stage with Ted English, the way she had drawn the audience's attention to the cabinet, then danced her way in, emerging a few minutes later with her smile undimmed. Meg did not need to be told that this role was more difficult than it looked. She decided to concentrate on her current predicament.

'I'm lost,' she said. 'Max said to meet him in the stalls.'

Ida laughed, looking slightly friendlier. 'This way. Middle door.'

Back in Brighton, Edgar was already doubting the wisdom of sending Meg undercover. The news was still dominated by the death of Gordon Palgrave. His funeral last week, at Ebenezer Strict Baptist Chapel, was for close friends and family only but hundreds gathered in the road outside to see the hearse, crowned with flowers spelling the word 'Pal', being carried up the steps and through the austere-looking doors. They watched it come out again, thirty minutes later, and make its way to East Sheen Cemetery, where Pal would lie alongside his mother.

'It's what Pal wanted,' said Larry Buxton, who had taken it upon himself to keep Edgar informed. 'He left instructions.'

Larry had been a rather reluctant chief mourner, although Pal's sister Edna had turned up unexpectedly. 'She's thinking of the will,' said Larry, but Pal left the bulk of his estate to charity, with personal bequests to a few friends. Rex, who inherited Pal's golf clubs, had been too ill to attend the funeral but had sent a wreath. Ted English and Dave Dunkley had both been there though.

Edgar was interested in this background colour, but it didn't get the case any further forward. The killer of

Cherry Underwood and Joan Waters – if it even was the same person – remained maddeningly elusive. 'It's like a magic trick,' said Bob, in an unexpected flight of fancy. 'Now you see him, now you don't.'

Extensive door-to-door enquiries had yielded nothing of interest. Meg's card index was full but most entries simply read 'NSO', Nothing Suspicious Observed. The only potential lead was Meg's white-haired man but he too seemed to have performed a vanishing act. 'If he was ever there,' said DS Barker.

Edgar was still short-staffed but he couldn't justify the expense of extra officers any more. On top of all this, Meg would be absent for a week, rehearsing for her West End debut.

In his gloomier moments, Edgar wondered if they'd ever catch the man the local press were calling Houdini.

Max was sitting in the third row of the stalls, talking to a man Meg didn't recognise. Following Ida's directions, she emerged onto the stage, which was still full of castles and turrets. *Camelot* had closed that weekend but Ida said that they were still 'taking down the set'. Two men in overalls were dismantling what looked like a solid wall. They both ignored Meg, which was a relief.

'Hallo, Meg.' Max looked up. 'Come and join us. This is Tony, the musical director and conductor.'

Meg couldn't find the steps at first but, eventually, she clambered down, glad she was wearing slacks.

'Hallo, Meg.' Tony stood up to shake hands. He was youngish with what Meg thought of as a clever face, pale with glasses.

'You should call her Samantha,' said Max. 'That's her stage name.'

'Hallo, Samantha,' said Tony with a smile.

'I was thinking we'd perform to "Me and My Shadow",' said Max. 'Do you know that song?'

'Whispering Jack Smith?' said Meg. 'My mum's got the record.'

'It was written by Dave Dreyer, Billy Rose and Al Jolson,' said Tony. 'Great tune.'

Meg had always found the words rather sad.

Me and my shadow
Not a soul to tell our troubles to . . .
Just me and my shadow
All alone and oh so blue.

Max said, 'I've got a record so we can practise but it'll sound better when Tony and his orchestra play it.'

'I wouldn't bet on that,' said Tony. 'Well, I'd better be off. See you on the opening night.' He put on his hat and strolled out of the theatre, whistling.

'Shall we get started?' said Max.

Max and Meg made their way back onto the stage. The men in overalls were still working but Max took no notice of them. He showed Meg the record player, which was in an area by the stage that he called 'the wings'.

'It's simple really, what I've got in mind,' said Max. 'I'll come on first and do a few tricks, get the audience in the mood. Then the song will start and you'll enter stage right, which is actually left from where we're standing. You'll walk across the stage and then you'll start copying my movements. That'll take the most practice. The mirroring will have to be perfect. Then you'll disappear. That'll be easier.'

'It will?'

Max laughed. 'Trust me. We'll have a black curtain as a backdrop. Your suit will almost disappear into it.'

'So I am having a suit then?' Meg was glad that she hadn't lied to her mother.

'You are. Made by the best tailor in Soho. You've got a fitting this afternoon.'

Meg had never been to a clothes fitting in her life but then she'd never done any of this stuff before. By now she was in a daze, standing on stage with Max Mephisto while Camelot was falling about her ears. She had to resist a terrible urge to giggle.

'Let's just practise walking first,' said Max. 'Twice as slowly as seems natural. Don't rush anything. The audience will wait for you. Stop. Count to ten. Smile.'

Meg strode across the stage. 'Slower,' said Max. 'And you're slouching. Walk tall.'

But Meg had spent her whole life trying to disguise her

height. It was difficult, now, to put her shoulders back and look Max in the eye.

When Max suggested a break, Meg was surprised how tired she felt. They went to a café across the road, where Max drank black coffee and Meg had a sardine and tomato paste sandwich.

'How do you like the Theatre Royal?' Max asked.

Meg chewed quickly so that she wasn't speaking with her mouth full.

'It's a bit spooky,' she said, remembering her sudden fear when she'd heard the footsteps on the stairs.

'It's famously haunted,' said Max. 'The ghost of Grimaldi's meant to appear in the back row of the stalls if a show is going to have a long run.'

Meg knew she'd heard the name before.

'Who's Grimaldi?'

'Joseph Grimaldi,' said Max, 'the father of all clowns. He's why clowns are sometimes called Joeys. He was particularly associated with this theatre. People have reported seeing his disembodied head, in its white clown's make-up, floating in different parts of the building. He's also said to help young actresses sometimes, placing his hands on them to move them to the right part of the stage. But I take that one with a pinch of salt. Too many people think it's acceptable to place their hands on young actresses.'

'Not just actresses,' said Meg, without thinking. Max looked at her for a moment before continuing, 'Dan Leno haunts it too. He was a famous pantomime dame. The toast of Drury Lane. You know his ghost is near when you smell lavender. He wore it to cover up the stink of alcohol. Or urine, some say.'

'Yuck,' said Meg. 'Are there any other ghosts?' She remembered looking out over the empty seats from the stage and imagining them full of people. There was definitely something spooky about being in an empty building that was meant to be full of people.

'There's the man in grey,' said Max. 'He's another one who just sits in the audience, watching actors rehearse. Fred was telling me that, when they renovated the theatre in the 1800s, they found a skeleton dressed in grey rags, walled up in a forgotten room. He'd been murdered. Stabbed.'

'Stabbed,' repeated Meg, thinking of Cherry and Joan. But Max said, in the same light voice, 'And an actor was killed here in the 1700s. Accidentally stabbed in the eye.'

'How can you accidentally stab someone in the eye?'

'Another version says it was deliberate. A fight over a wig.'

Meg laughed but the word 'wig' reminded her of something. Then she remembered: Dave Dunkley opening the door of his hotel room, his hair awry.

'Come on,' said Max, draining his coffee. 'Let's practise the walk again.'

*

For a week, Meg commuted from Brighton to the Theatre Royal, Drury Lane. It was exciting to take the train to London with the men (and some women) in suits who apparently made the journey every day. Were they wondering about Meg, in her mufti clothes of slacks and jumpers, reading one of Aisling's film magazines? Meg hoped so and practised an enigmatic smile in front of the mirror. It felt good, too, to know her way about London. She caught the tube to Covent Garden and walked through the flower stalls and the vans delivering fruit and vegetables. Sometimes one of the stallholders gave her an apple and even, once, a strange fuzzy fruit that Max said was called a kiwi.

She knew the way to the stage door now. Fred was always there, wedged behind his desk, reading the *Racing Post*. 'Morning, Fred.'

'Morning, Samantha.'

She was starting to get to know the rest of the cast. Ida was always friendly but the others seemed slightly wary. Meg didn't know what they'd been told about her inclusion in the show. They were pleasant to her but she thought that was just because she came as a package with Max. It didn't take her long to realise that Max was treated with respect, almost bordering on fear, by everyone in the theatre. He was a famous variety performer. He was a *film star*. It was no wonder that even the assistant stage manager, a scarily fashionable woman called Barbara, addressed him as Mr Mephisto and blushed when he spoke to her.

Meg was surprised at how tiring it was to spend your days walking across a stage. She often slept on the train back to Brighton and, at home, yawned so much that her mother made her take an iron supplement. The super had said that she didn't have to come into the station but Meg found herself wondering what everyone was doing. Had they found the white-haired man yet? Was Barker still making the can-can jokes? Was Danny still keeping number 84 Marine Parade under surveillance? Occasionally, just before she went to sleep, she thought about Logan. It was June now, so presumably he'd left Brighton for the Appleby horse fair. *Hundreds of us get together in this little town in Cumbria. We buy and sell horses, have races, sell things. There are fortune tellers too. Astarte always has a crowd round her tent. But the main business is horse-trading. Every day of the fair, the horses are washed in the river and then trotted up and down the flashing lane . . .*

Maybe it was just as well that she'd never see Logan again. It meant she could dream about him and his horse, Grey Cloud, without reality getting in the way.

But Meg hadn't entirely forgotten that she was a policewoman on a case. She watched the cast closely and recorded her findings in a notebook with a picture of an owl on the front. Meg's mother said owls were unlucky but Meg liked its wise face. She was practising to be more owl-like and inscrutable and wondered if anyone would notice.

Ida Lupin – staying in Holloway with her sister (who's married with 2 children, IL not keen on bro-in-law). Eats steak sandwiches for lunch, reads mystery novels, looks sad sometimes.

John Lomax (aka Mario) – staying in digs in Covent Garden, gargles with honey and whisky ('for his voice'), also drinks a lot of whisky, you can smell it on his breath. Says he studied opera but Max says not true (NB: MM's mother was opera singer). JL sometimes drinks with GB and PS but doesn't seem particularly friendly with them.

Ben Beddow (unicyclist) – falls off a lot. Ida calls him the 'punicyclist' cos he's small and thin (NB she only said this to me). BB staying with mother in Streatham. Says he once had affair with Vanda (gymnast) but I doubt it.

Geoffrey Bigg – bad-tempered sometimes, PS calms him down. Takes a lot of aspirin. Sometimes smells of drink. Told me that he was a child star and looked like a cherub then (hard to believe). GB and PS staying in Covent Garden with JL.

Perry Small – 2 years older than GB but looks younger. Always taking care of GB, friendly with Sonya and Vanda but don't think he fancies them. Used to be ventrilacist (sp?). Can walk on his hands.

Sonya Covack (sp?) – gymnast. Hungarian but lived in England since war. Was friend of Joan Waters and cried when we talked about her. Has boyfriend in the army. Used to be a magician's assistant (only know cos she offered to help me but asked me to keep it secret – significant??).

Vanda Kiss (actual surname!) – Hungarian but only known SC a few years. They met during a show in Leeds (q: was SC a magician's assistant then?). Says she's had lots of boyfriends but no details. Hinted she'd had an affair with Max (he says no).

Suzie West – dancer. 'Head Girl', which means she's in charge. Seems friendly with SC and VK. Also once heard her chatting with GB and PS. They mentioned Brighton.

Doris (Dolly) Thornton – dancer. Knew Joan, says she wants to retire soon (arthuritis – sp?)

Patsy Green – dancer. Red hair.

Rose Blake – dancer. Says she once appeared on bill in Brighton with Max and Ruby French (he can't remember).

Freda O'Shea – dancer. Irish. Staying with family in Kensal Rise.

Susan Flanders – dancer. Says ballet trained and obvs thinks she's the best.

NB: all dancers except Freda staying in digs in Muswell Hill.

Although Max was always polite (something Meg liked about him), he kept his distance from the rest of the cast, preferring to play Patience in his dressing room rather than lounge around chatting in the green room. He told Meg that he'd been on the bill with Bigg and Small a few times. 'Once was in Hastings. I saw a dead woman in the audience. It was slightly disconcerting.' But Max claimed not to be able to tell the duo apart and didn't seem particularly friendly with either of them. He obviously liked Ida, who made him laugh, and Sonya, who had a nice line in sarcasm. Meg asked Max if he could remember Sonya being a magician's assistant and he said no but that gymnasts often did that sort of work. 'You need to be flexible to do some of the box tricks. I once worked with a Bulgarian contortionist. Sofija, her name was.'

The performers only got together once during the whole rehearsal time. It was Vanda's birthday and they all met for drinks in a pub called the Lemon Tree. It was a fun evening. That was when Meg learnt that Perry Small could walk on his hands. Even before that, everyone in the pub was staring at them. They were marked out as different by Max's height, Sonya and Vanda's glamour, Bigg and Small's matching suits, the dancers' habit of moving in unison. 'What's your party trick, Meg?' someone asked. 'I can sing a song in Gaelic,' said Meg. And did. 'That's beautiful,' said John Lomax. Admittedly, he was on his third whisky, but praise from a professional singer was very gratifying.

What would her family think, wondered Meg, if they

could see her now? Rather to her surprise, and alarm, her parents and Aisling were planning to come to London for the opening night. And, what was worse, there would be a delegation from Bartholomew Square police station.

CHAPTER 29

Monday, 13 June 1966 – Opening Night

Meg woke at six thinking, quite calmly, 'I can't do it. I'll telephone Max and tell him. He can find someone else to be his assistant.' Then reality reasserted itself: she had to appear on the London stage that night; there was no way Max could get a replacement and, besides, it was part of her job. Oh, and the Connollys didn't possess a telephone.

A few feet away, Aisling stirred. The small room contained two sets of bunk beds. Aisling and Meg had the higher berths as befitted their superior status. Down below, Collette was snuffling in her sleep.

'Are you nervous?' whispered Aisling.

'Yes,' said Meg. 'No. Totally terrified.'

Their laughter woke Collette, who remembered that she was cross about not being included in the theatre trip and refused to speak to them. Meg had initially been given only two 'comps', or free tickets, but Max had given her one of his. Even so, three train fares to London was a stretch on the family finances. Meg also wondered who was going to take Max's remaining ticket. His children lived in Somerset and, although they often came to London, Max said that he didn't want them coming to the show. That was a reminder that many people, including the super, thought that something might happen on opening night.

Meg swung her legs down. She could hear her father in the bathroom and wanted to get in before her sisters. Dad was a mechanic and needed to be at the garage early if he was going to leave early. Meg's mother was already up and frying bacon.

Usually Patrick Senior was the only one to be offered a cooked breakfast but, when she came downstairs, Meg was surprised to be presented with bacon on toast.

'To keep your strength up,' said her mother, Mary. Padre Pio, the budgerigar, squawked in surprise.

'Thanks, Mum.' Meg had thought she wouldn't be hungry but the sizzling pork fat had worked its magic. She looked at the clock over the stove. Still only seven-thirty. In exactly twelve hours she would be on the stage.

'You're not making a show of yourself, are you?' asked Meg's mother, for the hundredth time. 'No short skirts or any of that malarky.'

'I'm wearing a man's suit. I told you.'

'May all the saints preserve us,' breathed Mary.

*

Sam woke early and watched the pattern of the plane trees on the window. She could tell by the line of pastel-coloured sky that it was going to be a beautiful day.

Beside her, Max was sleeping soundly. Was he still nervous about first nights? He said he wasn't but Sam thought she'd noticed a slight abstraction yesterday, a tendency to drum his fingers on the table and lose the thread of conversations. But, then again, there were extra tensions in this performance, an inexperienced assistant and a potential murderer in the audience being two of them.

Damn, she needed to go to the loo. Now she'd thought about it, she could never get back to sleep. Sam got up and wrapped herself in Max's dressing down. Then she tiptoed to the bathroom, used the loo and washed her hands with Max's special green soap. She'd never met a man who washed as much as Max. Well, if Sam had a shower like his, instead of a cracked bath with a view of the mould on the ceiling, maybe she'd use it every day. Afterwards she thought she'd make coffee. Max had been teaching her how to use his Gaggia machine. Should she make him an espresso and present it to him, naked? Would that be too much? Probably.

Max's trilby hat was on the marble countertop in the kitchen. Sam picked it up to try on and spotted a piece of paper underneath. It was a flyer for the show.

Theatre Royal, Drury Lane
From Larry Buxton Enterprises
'Old-Fashioned Family Fun'
For two weeks only
The great MAX MEPHISTO and his assistant Samantha
Bigg and Small: laughter comes in all sizes
Mario Fontana: voice of Italy
Ida Lupin: strongwoman
Ben Beddow: one wheel, many tricks
The extraordinary Gymnastiques
The West End Dancing Girls

'Samantha,' said Sam to herself.

'I don't understand how going to the theatre is work,' said Marianne. They were walking to school, very slowly because Jonathan was on his tricycle.

Emma, her back aching from leaning over to push Jonny, or restrain him, said, 'It's complicated.'

'That's what you always say,' said Marianne.

'You'll have a lovely time,' said Emma. 'Grandma and Grandpa are coming to babysit.'

Sophie gave a little skip of happiness, but Marianne stopped in the middle of the pavement to say, 'If I'm going to be an actress, I need to go to the theatre all the time.'

'OK,' said Emma, 'but just not this time. You can make up your own play for Grandma and Grandpa.'

'Grandpa went to sleep last time.'

'Wake him up, then,' said Emma, silently apologising to her father. 'Look, there's the Lollipop Man!'

Ernie, who patrolled the road outside the school with a lollipop-shaped sign saying, 'Stop!', was a firm favourite with all the children. As Emma passed him, holding Jonathan firmly by one hand and the tricycle in the other, he asked her if she did juggling as well.

'And there's going to be a police presence?' said Bob.

It was the third time he had asked this. Edgar sighed. He knew Bob was worrying about his officer but it was only nine a.m. Edgar had the feeling that it was going be a very long day.

'The Met police will have officers at the theatre,' he said, with what he hoped was patience combined with authority. 'I've asked my friend Alan Deacon to give it his personal attention.'

'There'll be a few of us in the audience too,' said Bob. 'Me, Barker and Black.'

'Barker? Why's he going?'

'He asked,' said Bob. 'He saw the show before, on the pier.'

'Then he doesn't need to see it again.'

'I didn't see how I could say no,' said Bob, 'seeing as how I asked for volunteers. DC Black was quick to put his name down. I think he might be a bit sweet on Meg . . . WDC Connolly.'

'You're an old romantic, Bob.'

Bob's ears went red. 'Are you taking Emma?' he asked.

'I couldn't keep her away,' said Edgar. 'It's her case too.'

'I must say,' said Bob, looking more cheerful, 'I'm looking forward to seeing Max Mephisto on stage again. Remember when we saw him in *Aladdin* that time?'

'I'm not likely to forget,' said Edgar. The case that coincided with the pantomime was probably the most traumatic of his career.

'I asked WDC Connolly what's in the act,' said Bob, 'but she said it was a secret. Betty says that magicians are always like that.'

'They're a secretive bunch, all right,' said Edgar. He thought of the times when Max hadn't told him what he was planning, even when they were in the Magic Men together and he was nominally in charge. He prayed to all the gods of the theatre that Meg would be safe tonight.

When Bob had gone out, even managing to shut the door in a reproachful way, Edgar turned back to his notes on the case. In an attempt to follow Emma's methods, he'd written out the names of the magicians.

Gordon Palgrave (Pal)
Rex King
Ted English
Dave Dunkley
Tommy Horton

The first name was now firmly crossed out. Edgar remembered the curiously mesmerising figure in the golfing jumper, hair gleaming in the reflected sun of the conservatory. He didn't think that Pal had killed Cherry and Joan – he had alibis, for one thing – but Emma had told him what Linda Knight, the landlady of number 84, had said. *It all comes back to one man.* If Pal held the key to the murders, then Pal had taken the secret to his grave.

Edgar's phone rang and Rita was saying, in the disapproving voice she used for unsolicited calls, 'I've got a Mrs Edna Gee on the phone for you.'

'Who is she?'

'She says she's the landlady of a boarding house on Freshfield Road. Quite insistent that she talk to you.'

The address brought back instant memories: snow on the ground, a children's theatre in a garage, a trail of sweets. Edgar couldn't think of a connection to this case but, if he'd learnt one thing over the last few years, it was never to ignore a landlady.

'Put her through.'

Before Edgar had time to introduce himself, a rather rasping voice said, 'Are you Superintendent Stephens?'

'Yes I am.'

'Do you know a man called Ted English?'

'I know of him,' said Edgar cautiously.

'He's been staying here. I thought he was trouble from the beginning. A few weeks ago, he had a visitor. Blonde lady. Classy. Said she was a private detective.'

Edgar thought he recognised the description but he said nothing.

'I asked about. I've got contacts in the police.'

I bet you have, thought Edgar.

'I found out that this Ted had been involved in a murder. A poor young woman killed at Linda Knight's place on the seafront. So I told him he had to leave. I couldn't have a man like that in the house.'

'A man like what?'

'Involved in something like that. Oh, don't get me wrong. He was polite enough but you know what those quiet types are like. So, Ted left.'

'He did?' Edgar's team were meant to be keeping an eye on Ted English. Clearly the surveillance wasn't working.

'Yes. Ran off in the night without paying his bill, if you please.'

'I'm sorry to hear that.' Was Mrs Gee about to ask the police for recompense?

'Not as sorry as me. But it happens in this game. Never open a B and B, Superintendent Stephens.'

'I won't.'

'Anyway, why I'm ringing is . . .'

Now we're coming to it, thought Edgar.

'Yesterday, another woman came round asking for Ted. Younger than the first one. But another blonde. You have to ask yourself, what do all these women want with this old has-been? So I thought I should let you know, being a good citizen and all that.'

Edgar thanked Mrs Gee profusely and, before the call had ended, he had promised to send someone round to pay Ted's bill. After all, the landlady *had* been helpful. She had also given him a few more problems to solve.

Who was the young blonde woman?

And where was Ted English now?

CHAPTER 30

Max was surprised to get a call from Ruby when he was drinking coffee with Sam in companionable post-coital silence. Max hadn't spoken to Ruby for a few days because he knew that Dex was staying and had assumed that the couple would want time to themselves. Mitzi's daughter, Camille, had proved a real godsend, coming for two hours every morning and allowing Ruby to reclaim some of her life. Max also thought that Emerald was visiting more often.

Certainly, Ruby sounded cheerful this morning.

'We're coming to see you,' she announced.

'When?' said Max, stupidly, suddenly imagining Ruby descending on him and Sam, lying in his disarranged bed.

'Tonight, silly. The show.'

'The Drury Lane show?'

'What else? It's sold out but I rang Larry Buxton and he's letting us have the Royal Box. Me and Dex. Dex says it'll be the first time a black man's ever sat there.'

Max was silent for a moment. He hadn't told Ruby that it was his opening night for the simple reason that he didn't want her there. If there really was a murderer hanging around the production, he didn't want any of his children anywhere near the Theatre Royal, Drury Lane.

'What about Poppy?' he said.

'Mummy's babysitting,' said Ruby. 'Isn't that a turn-up for the books? See you later. Break a leg.'

Max turned to Sam. 'Ruby's coming tonight.'

'So I gathered. You didn't sound overjoyed.'

Max had given his complimentary ticket to Sam. He wondered why he hadn't tried to stop Sam coming to the show. He supposed it was because he knew that she would come, whether he liked it or not. At least this way he knew where she was sitting.

'I was surprised,' said Max. 'That's all.'

'Will she be with Dex?'

'Apparently so.'

'There you are,' said Sam, stretching. She was wearing one of his pinstriped shirts and the sun, slanting through the bedroom blinds, shone on her face and conker-brown hair. You're beautiful, Max wanted to say but didn't.

'You don't have to worry about Ruby,' said Sam.

'I wasn't exactly.' He didn't know how to explain his complicated feelings of guilt and protectiveness, so he stayed silent. Sam got up.

'I'm going to have a shower,' she said. 'Make the most of your bathroom.'

Max reached for his cigarette case, took out a cigarette, looked at it and put it back.

'What are you going to do this afternoon?' he asked. 'I've got to leave for the theatre at two-thirty. For the run-through.'

'I might go and see Rex King,' said Sam. 'He's still in hospital.'

'Rex King? Why are you still visiting him?'

'He's an important witness,' said Sam. 'What if seeing this Grace lookalike person was what killed Pal? If we find her, we might be getting close to solving the mystery.'

'But why would Grace appear to Rex?' said Max. 'He's almost the only one of that set who didn't marry her.'

Sam was on her way to the door but now she stopped and looked back at him.

'Did you know her, Grace?'

'I met her a few times. She was Pal's assistant for a while. Tommy's too. And I think she'd had another act before. She always seemed a sad figure to me, a bit lost.'

'So you didn't have an affair with her too?'

'No,' said Max. 'I'm not attracted to sad women.'

He thought of Florence, who had been so full of life and ambition. Of Lydia, who'd had a tragic past but had risen like a glorious phoenix. Sam was looking at him rather quizzically.

'Rex isn't the worst of that lot,' said Max, 'but be careful.'

'The worst one is dead,' said Sam. 'If there aren't any more murders, does that make him the prime suspect?'

'I hope to God there aren't any more murders,' said Max.

'Don't worry,' said Sam. 'Emma says the place will be swarming with police tonight.'

'What an audience,' said Max. 'Worse than landladies.'

Meg was staying in a women's hostel for the two-week run of the show. The DI had been apologetic. 'We can't really stretch to a hotel, I'm afraid.' But for Meg, who'd hardly ever spent a night away from home – apart from holidays with her grandparents in Ireland – it was another adventure. The address was Tottenham Court Road and, as Meg emerged from the tube, carrying her dad's Gladstone bag, she saw a huge building towering above her, its hundreds of windows glinting in the sun. This must be what New York is like, she thought. What were they called? Skyscrapers. Meg looked up. The sky was palest blue with a few wispy white clouds. The top of the monstrous tower really did seem to be lost amongst them. There was still scaffolding on the highest floors. A notice said that the building was called 'Centrepoint' and would consist of thirty-four storeys of shops, offices, something called 'retail units' and flats. Imagine living up there, thought Meg, so high above the city that you could almost see the sea. Her parents had friends who had been moved from council houses to tower blocks in Brighton. They missed the community, Meg's mum said, but Meg thought that she might prefer the company of birds and low-flying planes.

The hostel was only a few hundred yards away, sandwiched between the Dominion Theatre and a pub. Meg was keen to see what was showing at the theatre – she was almost a professional now – and was disappointed to see that it had been turned into a cinema. People said that this was what would happen to the Hippodrome in Brighton, which had closed two years ago. 'Live theatre's dead,' Max often said. He could be very gloomy sometimes.

'Young Women's Christian Association', read the notice over the door of the hostel. Meg's mum would be relieved by the 'Christian', although this probably meant Protestants too. Meg rang the bell and, seconds later, she was being greeted by a tall woman in a black suit.

'I've got a room booked. My name's Margaret Connolly.' Meg wasn't sure why she gave her full name. Maybe it was the suit.

'Let me see.' The woman led the way to the reception desk and scanned her ledger.

'Connolly. Yes, here it is. Staying for two weeks?'

'That's right.'

'Here for work or study?'

'Work,' said Meg. 'I'm a police officer.' She didn't think the woman, who gave her name as Miss Marsh, would appreciate the detail about being a magician's assistant.

'Well, we've never had one of *those* before,' said Miss Marsh. 'You're sharing a room with two other girls.' She pronounced it 'gels'. 'They're both trainee nurses. There wasn't room for them at the hospital, apparently.'

Mum would approve of the nurses even more. Meg decided not to tell her. Miss Marsh led her up a staircase covered in green linoleum. The room was on the first floor and consisted of three beds, three chests of drawers and a large portrait of the Queen.

'Here you are,' said Miss Marsh. 'The facilities are next door. No baths after ten p.m. Evening meal is at six.'

'I won't be here for it, I'm afraid,' said Meg. 'I have to work every evening. It's sort of surveillance.'

Miss Marsh looked very dubious. 'Meals are included. There's no reduction.'

'That's OK.'

Meg went to the window. If she craned her head forward she could see Centrepoint. She mentioned it to Miss Marsh. 'I've never seen such a tall building.'

'It was built on the site of a gallows,' the woman replied. 'No good will come of it.'

With that, she made her exit. Meg sat on her bed – the furthest from the window – and wondered what to do with the rest of her day. It was only midday. Maybe she could go to the cinema or walk to Hyde Park. Anything to take her mind off the fact that, in seven and a half hours' time, she would be on stage in front of hundreds of people who had paid for the privilege of watching her disappear.

Sam knew that she hadn't been entirely truthful with Max about her reasons for visiting Rex King. It was true that Rex was a useful source of information about the Pal set of magicians, but he wasn't a witness in any real sense. Rex hadn't been in Brighton when Cherry or Joan were murdered. When they had first met, Sam had suspected that Rex knew more about the case than he was telling her, but now she thought that he had just been reluctant to discuss Grace's suicide. Maybe Pal had warned his friends never to mention his ex-wife.

But Sam knew that investigation was not all that was on her mind as she walked through Hyde Park to St George's Hospital. This would be her third visit to the retired magician and, the second time, they had developed quite a crosstalk around their mythical family bond as uncle and niece. 'Give my love to Babs and the twins,' Rex had called out when she left. Sam smiled to herself as she walked through Kensington Gardens, looking its best in the spring sunshine. This time she might introduce Janice and the triplets. She'd enjoyed Rex's company, that was the truth, and she also felt slightly sorry for him. Rex had said that his wife, Mavis, was too busy to visit him more than once a week, on Sundays. At least this meant that Sam wouldn't run into her 'aunt' today.

And it was good to show Max she had other things to do besides waiting for him to appear on stage. She was worried that she was getting a bit too dependent on Max. When she had visited him, unannounced, after seeing Rex in hospital the first time, that had been a shift in their relationship. Sam had needed Max – to cheer her up, to remind her that another life existed – and she didn't like the feeling of vulnerability. Since that day, she had spent more time at Max's flat. It was beginning, worryingly, to feel like home.

At the Albert Memorial, Sam passed a woman pushing a pram, one of the new sorts with high wheels like a tractor. Sam had never wanted to get married or have children. Well, she was thirty-six now. It was almost too late. 'The clock's ticking,' her mother had told her when she went home for Christmas. Part of the Max Mephisto legend was the time he defused a ticking bomb live on stage. Back to Max again. Sam thrust her hands in her pockets and walked faster.

Rex had been moved to Bevan Ward, for recuperating patients. The doctors still thought that he might have sustained a bleed on the brain when he fell, so he was being kept under observation. When Sam arrived, Rex was reading *Film Frolics*. One of the nurses brought the magazines in for him.

'Lydia Lamont's getting married again,' he said, as Sam approached. 'To Seth Billington.'

Sam knew all about the second marriage of Max's ex-wife. Or was it the third? No one seemed to know, not even Max. 'Lydia was sparing with autobiographical detail,' he once said. Rex showed Sam a double page spread in glossy colour. Lydia and Seth were staring into each other's eyes in the grounds of the stately home that Max had inherited from his father. They were often described as the most beautiful couple on earth but Sam thought they both looked rather gormless. She also thought that Lydia should move out of Max's house.

'Cousin Janice and the triplets send their love,' said Sam, sitting by the bed. The ward was full of anxious-looking families looking for extra chairs and vases for flowers.

'Poor old Jan,' said Rex, joining in at once. 'She's had it hard.'

'That husband of hers will be the death of her.'

'The things I've heard about him.'

'And that so-called sister of his.'

They grinned at each other. Sam produced the book she had brought. *The Clocks* by Agatha Christie. Tick, tock.

'Thank you,' said Rex. 'I love a good murder.'

So did Sam but she wasn't sure she would have put it quite like that, under the circumstances.

'I might be getting out of here next week,' said Rex. 'I'm almost going to miss the place. And your visits.'

'You'll be able to have a drink though.' Rex regularly bemoaned the lack of alcohol in hospital. Sam had been tempted to smuggle in whisky disguised as Lucozade.

'Mavis will have me on a strict regime,' said Rex gloomily.

'Shows she cares, I suppose,' said Sam. To cheer him up, she produced the flyer for tonight's show.

'Thought you might like to see this.'

'A number one venue,' said Rex. 'Wish I could be there. I'd love to see Max perform again. And Bigg and Small.

Can't believe they're still going. Did you know he was Grace's brother?'

'Who?' said Sam. She was still fixated on the name 'Samantha'.

'Geoffrey Bigg. They had a double act when they were children. The Little Biggs. Didn't I tell you that?'

'I think you said something about Grace being a child star,' said Sam. Or was that Max? At any rate, this was something new. A link they hadn't known.

'It was a very saccharine act,' said Rex. 'A tisket, a tasket. Lots of skipping around the stage in matching outfits. I think that's where she caught Pal's eye though. He always liked them young.'

Suddenly Rex could say something like that and he seemed less like a lovable character and more like one of the seedy men skulking around Soho clubs advertising 'Schoolgirls! French maids! Nudity!'

Sam decided to go but, before she could stand up, Rex uttered a strangled cry that made two nurses hurry over to the bed. His mouth dropped open and his eyes stared, in what seemed like horror, at the double doors of the ward.

Sam swung round. A young woman stood framed in the doorway. She had long blonde hair and was wearing a waitress's uniform.

'Gracie?' croaked Rex. 'Is that you?'

CHAPTER 31

'I'm not Grace,' said the woman. 'I'm Heidi.'

For a moment the name meant nothing to Sam, then she remembered. *You couldn't have picked a more German name, ha ha.*

Heidi's voice was very English though. Pure Home Counties.

'I'm sorry,' she said, as the nurses fluttered around Rex, taking his pulse and pulling the curtains round him. 'I didn't mean to startle anyone.'

Sam had stood up. 'You're Tommy Horton's daughter, aren't you?'

'Yes. How did you . . .'

'I recognised the name. I'm Sam Collins, by the way. I was visiting Rex.'

'Heidi Horton. I came because . . . well, because I think I'm the reason Rex is in here.'

'Did you call on him a couple of weeks ago?'

'Yes. He took one look at me and fell to the floor. I used

his telephone to call an ambulance but I was too scared to go to the hospital with him. I rang and they said he was all right. I've been getting up the courage to visit. I don't get a lot of time off.' She gestured at the uniform.

'Are you a waitress?'

'Only part time. I'm at teacher training college. Maria Assumpta. This is just to earn pocket money. Things are tough at home with Dad . . . well, with Dad away.'

Tommy's nursing home fees must be expensive, thought Sam. She remembered Rex describing the dodgy-sounding act Pal and Grace had performed together. *God, I remember the outfit she had . . . Some sort of French maid's uniform. Enough to raise your blood pressure to boiling point. And I was young then. It would probably kill me now.* She also remembered that Tommy's second wife had supposedly looked very like his first.

The nurses had pulled the curtains back, apparently satisfied that Rex wasn't about to die. Heidi approached.

'I'm Tommy's daughter. I'm sorry. I think I gave you a shock the other day.'

'I thought you were Grace,' said Rex, with a faint attempt at 'ha ha'.

'Dad's first wife? Someone else told me I looked like her. There's a photo at home somewhere but I can't see it myself.'

'The uniform,' said Rex. 'She wore a uniform like that on stage.'

'It's Lyons' Corner House,' said Heidi, tweaking the apron. 'Too hot in this weather.'

'Did you call on Pal that day too?' Sam asked Heidi. 'Gordon Palgrave?'

'How did you know?' Heidi looked rather scared now. In truth, she didn't look much like the only photograph Sam had ever seen of Grace Fanshaw, a glamour shot in black and white: black lips, white face, whiter hair. Heidi was fresh-faced and her hair was more golden than silver. There really was something of the Alpine goatherd about her.

'Did you call on Pal?' Sam asked again.

'I was going to,' said Heidi. 'I walked round his house to see if he was in and I saw him sitting on the sofa. Just the back of his head. But I didn't go in. I lost my nerve.'

But Pal had seen her somehow, thought Sam. But then she remembered the glass-fronted cabinet. Pal would have seen a blonde woman reflected there, amongst his trophies and humanitarian awards. Had he thought that Grace had returned, to drag him to the underworld, to the prizes that he really deserved? *Verity told me some pretty horrible things about Pal. Sleeping with fourteen-year-old girls, for one thing.*

Sam found a chair for Heidi ('only two per bed', Matron reminded her), and poured Rex some water. His colour was almost back to normal.

'Why did you call on Rex and Pal that day?' she asked Heidi.

'Sam's a reporter,' Rex (half) explained.

'I don't want anything in the papers,' said Heidi, sounding scared again.

'Don't worry,' said Sam. 'I'm not working on a story.'

'Pal came to see Mum and me about five years ago,' said Heidi. 'I would have been about fifteen. Dad had just had his first stroke and Pal said he wanted to see how we were, if we needed money, that sort of thing. Mum thought it was kind but I thought he was creepy. When Mum was out of the room, Pal sat too close to me and put his arm round me. I jumped away and he said, "Don't worry, I won't kiss you, I could be your father." I said he couldn't be and he said, "You don't think old Tommy's your dad, do you?" Then he said it was either Ted English, him or you.'

Rex made an angry exclamation, but Heidi continued. 'I didn't think about it for years. I loved Dad and I knew he loved me. Even when I visited him in the home, we went for walks, looked at flowers. It was lovely. But, then, a few months ago, Dad asked Mum and me to stop visiting him. I thought: maybe it's true then. I went to see Pal but lost my nerve. I called on you and, well, that was a disaster. Yesterday, I went down to Brighton to see if I could find Ted. I found his lodgings but he had left. Just as well really.'

Heidi wiped her eyes on her sleeve. Rex leant forward. 'Heidi, my dear, listen. Pal couldn't be your father. He was impotent. No, that's not the word. Infertile. He always joked that it gave him a free pass with women. And I'm not your dad either, honoured though I'd be. I only met your mother once and that was when you were a baby. I'm pretty sure Ted's never met her. Tommy's your dad, all right.'

'Thank you,' said Heidi, wiping away more tears. 'I feel so stupid. It's just I miss seeing Dad. Everyone at the home is very nice, especially Elsie, the manager, and Ringo, one of the orderlies. We call him that because of the rings. Ringo says that Dad misses us too, but I just started to think, maybe he's not my dad . . .'

'He is,' said Rex. 'It was a wicked thing for Pal to imply.'

Finally, thought Sam, Rex was beginning to realise the truth about his golfing partner.

Meg spent a pleasant hour and a half watching *Born Free*, a film about a woman who raises three lion cubs in Africa. It made Meg want to travel and/or devote herself to animals. She wished they could have a cat at home but maybe it would eat Padre Pio. At any rate, the tale of Elsa the lioness distracted Meg from her impending doom. It was only afterwards, when she was finishing her cheese on toast in Lyons, that she thought about 'Me and My Shadow' and the long walk across the stage. Then she felt such a jolt of fear that she almost doubled over. Meg had never known a feeling like it. She'd been nervous before her eleven plus, which she'd failed, and her driving test, which she'd passed. But that had been an inner dread, a gnawing doubt in her own abilities. This was physical, making her pulse quicken and her heart pump. Breathe, she told herself. Her hands and feet were freezing as if blood were no longer flowing to the extremities. Perhaps this was why it was called getting cold feet?

After a few minutes' strenuous breathing, Meg felt a bit better, although the waitresses were looking at her oddly. She stood up on her frozen feet, paid her bill and went back to the hostel. There was no sign of the two nurses or of Miss Marsh. Meg was admitted by a man in a boiler suit who looked at her with undisguised interest. She swapped her jumper for a smarter blouse and brushed her hair. In a few hours, she'd be wearing a man's suit, starched white shirt and a bow tie. Meg loved her suit. It made her feel tall and thin and, for the first time in her life, she liked being those things. She looked at her watch. Three o'clock. She might as well head to the theatre.

Of course she was far too early. 'Curtain up', as Max called it, was at seven-thirty and the artistes were meant to arrive at four for the musical rehearsal. Fred looked up from the *Racing Post*.

'You're keen, Samantha.'

'Nervous, more likely.'

'Nothing to be nervous about. I used to be on the boards myself. Lion-taming act.'

'Really?' Meg thought about Elsa and her cubs. The film had convinced her that wild animals should be free. She looked at Fred and he seemed to feel the reproach in her gaze.

'Never hurt an animal in my life,' he said. 'But one of them attacked my partner, Beryl. Took her arm off. Thought it was time to quit.'

'What happened to Beryl?'

'I married her. As if she hadn't suffered enough, eh?' He went back to his paper and Meg made her way along the corridor, which now smelt comfortingly familiar. Should she go to her dressing room, which was tiny and windowless but, to Meg, the height of glamour, not least because it had the name 'Samantha' on the door? But she knew that, as soon as she sat in front of the mirror, which was surrounded by lights (just like the movies!), the Fear would return.

Maybe if she stood on the stage she'd feel better. She remembered the first time that she'd entered the enchanted space with Max, the sudden feeling of wanting to entertain. At the moment all she felt like doing was curling up in a ball, which wasn't quite the spectacle a paying audience expected. Meg made her way through the painted flats – as she now called them – past the prompt corner and the lighting rig and stepped out, stage left.

The spirit lamp glowed in front of her, the light that kept the ghosts company when the theatre was empty. Meg walked across the boards, trying to remember how to put one foot in front of the other. Then she stopped. The theatre wasn't completely empty. A man was sitting in the back row of the stalls; she could just make out a white face and a grey jacket. Meg heard Max's voice, the upper-class drawl that she could never quite imitate. *There's the man in grey, he's another one who just sits in the audience, watching actors rehearse . . .*

'Who's there?' said Meg, her voice echoing shakily around the empty auditorium.

'It's me. Geoff.' Geoffrey Bigg stood up. He was wearing the grey check suit that he wore on stage. 'Sorry. Did I scare you?'

'No,' said Meg. 'I'm fine.' It was only afterwards that she wondered why the comic had been sitting there, one half of a double act, watching the empty stage.

Emma was prepared to enjoy the train journey. While Edgar was buying the tickets, she went into the station shop to buy sweets and magazines. She was looking longingly at *Film Frolics* (one of her weaknesses) when the top copy was picked up by a tall girl with long hair that almost reached the hem of her orange miniskirt. The girl scanned the pages and then put the magazine down with obvious reluctance. Her eyes met Emma's and she smiled. The face and smile suddenly looked very familiar.

'Excuse me,' said Emma. 'Are you Meg Connolly's sister?'

The girl blushed in a way that was very reminiscent of Meg. 'Yes. I'm Aisling.'

'I'm Emma Holmes. I went to Liverpool with Meg last year.'

'Oh my goodness,' said Aisling. 'Ma!' She turned to a

woman weighing sweets at the pick and mix. 'Ma. This is Emma. The private detective.'

A woman with Meg's brown hair, threaded with grey, came over. She looked very like her daughters, but her face was sharper, less trusting. A tall man hovered beside her, looking too big for the small shop.

'I'm Mary, Meg's mother. And this is Pat, her dad. Are you going to London for the show?'

'Yes,' said Emma. 'Isn't it exciting?'

By the time they left the shop, Emma was fast friends with the whole family. She introduced them to Edgar, who was waiting by the platform.

'Will you sit with us?' asked Aisling.

Emma knew that Edgar would have bought first class tickets but she loved the alacrity with which he said, 'We'd be delighted to,' and followed the Connollys into the second class compartment.

Emma tried to remember what Meg had told her about her family. She'd said Aisling was the clever one and the girl certainly seemed articulate and confident, her accent far more middle class than Meg's. But Emma thought that Meg was brighter than she knew. She had something of her mother's quick wit ('The super, are you? Well that's a bold claim to make.') combined with her father's sweetness.

'I can't believe Meg will be performing on stage,' said Aisling. 'I've never even seen her in a school play.'

'She was one of the three kings once,' said Mary. 'At

St John the Baptist. It was a beautiful nativity. Maybe you were too young to be in it. Patrick was in the choir.'

Her husband and daughter both laughed.

'Patrick had a beautiful singing voice as a boy,' Mary protested. 'He's my third eldest and second boy,' she explained to Emma and Edgar. Emma had the family sorted in her head now (Marie, Declan, Patrick, Meg, Aisling, Collette and Connor) but she thought Edgar looked rather confused.

'Who's babysitting Collette and Connor tonight?' she asked, partly to show off her specialist knowledge.

'Declan,' said Mary. 'He's so fond of the little ones.'

Emma had met Declan once, she'd even ridden behind him on his Lambretta. It had been a rather traumatic day but, from the little she'd seen of Meg's oldest brother, he didn't exactly strike her as the babysitting type.

'Mum,' said Aisling. 'Dec just wanted to bring his girlfriend. That Sandra.'

'Sandra's a nice girl,' said Mary. 'They won't be getting up to anything.'

Aisling exchanged a look with her father but said nothing. Mary had turned to Edgar. 'You're a friend of this magician's, aren't you? This Max Mephisto.' She said the name with suspicion, as if it wasn't real. Which it wasn't.

'Yes,' said Edgar. 'We served together in the war.'

This seemed to satisfy the Connollys and Pat vouchsafed that, as a trained mechanic, he'd been seconded to an armoured division.

'Didn't see much action but I suppose we had our uses.'

'I saw action in Norway,' said Edgar, 'and that was enough for me. I was seconded to a . . . to an espionage group . . . and that's when I met Max.'

'Golly,' said Aisling. 'Like Dick Barton.'

'Not quite,' said Edgar with a smile.

'Is he a respectable man, this Max?' asked Mary. 'Aisling tells me that he's getting divorced. That I can't like.'

'It was his wife's fault,' said Aisling. 'She ran off with Seth Billington.'

'Marriage is for life,' said Mary.

'Max is very respectable,' said Edgar. 'In fact, although he doesn't like to mention it, he's actually a lord.'

This kept the conversation going until the train pulled into Victoria.

CHAPTER 32

It was better when Max arrived. He'd even brought Meg a sandwich from one of his favourite cafés. It had brown bread, gherkins and spiced meat that Max said was 'pastrami'. It was delicious. Max had a paper cup of coffee. Meg didn't think she'd ever seen him eat.

It was the first time Meg had rehearsed with an orchestra. She was surprised how ordinary they looked, men and women in jeans and T-shirts, carrying battered instrument cases and dry-cleaning bags containing evening clothes. Tony, the conductor, grinned at Meg and said, 'Hallo again, Samantha.' This made her feel more confident and having the real music helped too. Max came on to his signature tune of the 'Danse Macabre', which segued into 'Me and My Shadow' for the routine with Meg. The orchestra played quietly for the build-up, 'underscoring' Max said it was called, and then crashed into life for the reveal. At the end, someone said 'Bravo', which cheered Meg a good deal.

Meg and Max were last on the bill but they rehearsed first. Max then retreated to his dressing room ('Patience doesn't play itself') but Meg stayed on to watch the other acts. Most just walked through their routines, but the dancers and gymnasts went through all the movements, although often stopping in the middle to ask for changes to what they called the 'tempo'. Ida Lupin performed to 'A Hard Day's Night', which got a few laughs. At his request, she also lifted Billy, one of the stage hands, up over her head. Mario Fontana announced that he was going to sing 'half voice', which was still loud enough for Meg. Ben Beddow fell off his unicycle several times. Bigg and Small were professional, almost curt. 'We say something funny here,' they'd announce, straight-faced. Or, 'Here's our famous soft-shoe shuffle.' Their music was 'Happy Days Are Here Again', which sounded almost sinister played 'adagio' by the yawning orchestra.

After the rehearsal, the theatre started to wake up. The stage was swept and the fire curtain fell into place. The musicians wandered away to get changed, and front of house started to open up the box office, bar and gift shop. The stage manager, a man called Dick Branstone, appeared wearing a dinner jacket, slightly green with age. Meg took refuge in her dressing room, where she changed into trousers, shirt and tailcoat. The top hat had a concealed veil that would drop to cover her face and allow Meg to melt into the black curtain for her disappearance. She looked at herself in the mirror. Her dad used to talk about a woman called Vesta Tilley who had an act where she dressed as a man and sang songs like 'Burlington Bertie'. Did Meg look a bit Burlington Bertie? Well, if she did, it was too late to do anything about it now.

Meg's next problem was that she couldn't do up her white bow tie. After straining to see her reflection and getting her right and left hands mixed up, she thought she should ask for assistance. The white satin already looked a bit the worse for wear. She was too embarrassed to ask Max but maybe one of the dancers or gymnasts could help. Meg stepped out into the corridor. It was empty, all the doors shut. The silence felt almost expectant. Meg remembered the first time she'd seen the theatre, when she'd stared out at the deserted auditorium and imagined she heard the noise of the crowd. She thought of all the performers who had walked up and down this passageway, returning from triumphs and disasters. Suddenly, Meg needed to speak to someone very badly. She knocked on the door that said, 'Sonya and Vanda'.

Sonya was wearing a fur coat over her costume.

'Hallo, Meg,' she said. 'You're looking very smart. Like a city gent.'

'Can you help me with my tie please?' said Meg.

'I am expert at ties,' said Vanda. 'I have had many lovers.'

Meg was used to this sort of thing by now. 'Tell me some of them,' she said as Vanda leant forward to tie the bow.

Meg could see the top of her head, which had a few grey hairs amongst the black.

'Your hair would curl,' said Vanda. 'Some of them are royalty. Crowned heads of Europe.'

'Come off it, dear,' said Sonya.

Meg's tie was now a perfect white butterfly. She looked at herself in the mirror and saw the gymnasts exchanging glances.

'Do you still get nervous before performances?' she asked. She wanted to talk about The Fear.

'Not really,' said Vanda. 'If I fall, I know she will catch me.'

'I'm worried about him,' said Sonya. 'The killer.'

This was the first time any of the cast had mentioned the real reason why Meg was taking the part of Max's assistant.

'I keep thinking about Joanie,' said Sonya. 'I didn't see her body but the landlady, Mrs O'Hara, said she was hacked to death. Who would do something like that? To Joanie, too, who was such a good soul.'

'Sonya!' Vanda made the sign of the cross. 'Do not talk about such things.'

'Aren't you frightened?' Sonya turned to Meg. She should have looked odd in her leotard and rather mangy fur coat but, to Meg, she suddenly looked like a seer, a mystic, a relation of the Zabinis perhaps. *You're going to meet a tall dark stranger who makes you disgusting tea.*

'I'm not scared,' said Meg. Not of a murderer anyway,

she said to herself. 'There are police outside and in the audience.'

'I don't trust the police,' said Vanda, who was putting resin on her feet.

'I liked the young one,' said Sonya. 'Danny something. And Superintendent Stephens is quite attractive for an older man.'

How old was Sonya? Meg wondered. As with a lot of theatricals, you couldn't tell. She was small and dark-haired, with a body that seemed almost jointless in its suppleness. As Meg watched, Sonya raised a leg casually until it was parallel with her head. Joanie had been forty-five but Meg thought that Sonya was at least ten years younger. Ida Lupin was forty-three though, despite her golden hair.

'The super's coming tonight,' said Meg. 'Danny too.' And Barker, but she didn't want to give him the compliment of saying his name.

'Good,' said Sonya. 'Maybe I can seduce him.'

'He's got a lovely wife,' said Meg, unaccountably irritated. 'They're very happily married.'

She prayed that she wouldn't make a fool of herself in front of Emma.

Emma was impressed by her first sight of the Theatre Royal. It was much bigger than its namesake in Brighton, with a grand portico and rows of pillars. 'Max Mephisto', screamed the billboard and, in smaller letters, 'Courtesy of Larry Buxton Enterprises'. None of the other performers got a mention. The audience were already filing in. Aisling nudged her mother, 'Look at all the people.' Mrs Connolly was now looking distinctly nervous. Emma wondered how Meg was feeling, somewhere in the mysterious world of backstage.

Emma and Edgar were sitting just behind the Connolly family. As they edged along the row, Emma looked up at the Royal Circle above them. She caught a glimpse of grey hair, a tweed jacket.

'Ed!' Emma turned to her husband. 'Isn't that Ted English? Up there. Look. Near the pillar.'

Edgar looked. 'I think it is. I think I'll go and have a word.'

He had to perform a difficult three-hundred-and-sixty-degree turn and force his way back along the row. Emma wanted to follow him but couldn't. She took her seat, trying not to feel resentful. She was the one who'd spotted Ted, after all. Emma tried to concentrate on chatting to the Connollys about the theatre and Meg's possible state of mind. 'Sometimes she's sick when she's nervous,' said Aisling. 'Hope it doesn't happen on stage.'

After about ten minutes Emma heard a familiar voice apologising. People were getting to their feet to let Edgar past. He sat down next to Emma, looking embarrassed.

'Did you talk to him?'

'Yes. Claimed he was just here to see the show. Said he was an old friend of Max's. Well, Max said they weren't close but they do know each other. And they're both magicians. Ted might just want to see his act. I suppose it's plausible.'

'Did you ask Ted about the blonde woman and about paying his bill?' Edgar had told Emma about the telephone call from the landlady.

'Yes. He was quite shameless. Said he must pay me back one day.'

'And the woman?'

'Said he didn't know any young blondes. "I should be so lucky" were his actual words.'

Emma craned her head round but Ted was now hidden from her sight.

'It's very frustrating,' she said.

'I managed to have a word with Bob,' said Edgar. 'He's going to tell DS Barker to keep an eye on Ted.'

Emma did not like to think of the loathsome Barker being anywhere near the theatre but she knew she couldn't say any more without giving Meg away. Aisling turned and started chatting again. Emma composed her face into pleasant lines. She had an empty seat on the other side of her. Probably a comp for one of the other acts. She hoped nobody claimed it.

Aisling told them about her hopes of studying at university and Edgar offered to read her application form. 'I was only at university for less than a year,' he told her, 'but it was a wonderful experience.' Emma suddenly felt slightly left out. She'd never wanted to go to university, or finishing school, which was where most of her contemporaries had been headed. But Ed's voice was suddenly alight with such warmth and remembrance. Usually he only looked like that when he was talking about her or the children.

'I don't know about university,' said Mary, sounding half-proud and half-exasperated. 'I don't understand why you can't be a nurse or a teacher. Those are nice jobs for girls.'

'I'd be a terrible nurse,' said Aisling. 'Remember when Meg cut her head open and I fainted.'

'Meg tried to stick the cut together with Sellotape,' Mary told Edgar and Emma. 'You can imagine the mess. And Aisling just lying on the floor. Luckily Collette had the sense to call me in. I was only hanging out clothes in the garden.'

'I can imagine Meg doing that,' said Edgar. 'She's full of initiative.'

For a second they all glanced at the stage, where Meg and her initiative would soon be performing. It was five minutes to curtain up. The theatre was almost full now. Emma was annoyed to see people standing up again at the end of the row. Someone must be coming to take the empty seat next to her.

'Hallo, Emma.'

'Sam! What are you doing here?'

'Max gave me a ticket.'

'Max?' said Emma.

In answer, Sam grinned and opened Emma's programme,

pointing to the words, 'The great MAX MEPHISTO and his assistant Samantha.'

Emma looked at her friend. 'After you?'

Sam shrugged, still grinning. 'Good seats, aren't they? Of course, Ruby went one better. She's in the Royal Box.'

Emma looked up and saw Ruby outlined against the velvet and gilt of the box at the very edge of the Royal Circle, closest to the stage. Ruby was looking beautiful in red satin, her glossy dark hair piled on top of her head. Next to her, Dex was elegant in a midnight blue velvet jacket. The couple were attracting a considerable amount of attention.

'Dex says that it's the first time a black man has ever been in the Royal Box,' said Sam.

Emma's antennae were already on alert and they twitched at the casual way Sam mentioned Ruby's boyfriend. She was also slightly shocked to hear Sam say 'black' instead of 'coloured'. Ruby had once said that this was what Dex called himself but it still sounded wrong. But, before Emma could say anything more, the lights dimmed and the conductor appeared at his rostrum.

Aisling looked round. 'It's starting!'

'Can we watch backstage?' Meg had asked Max.

'No,' he said. 'We'll wait in our dressing rooms until called. We'd only be in the way standing in the wings. Besides, I don't want anyone stealing my act.'

'Our act,' said Meg.

She'd been disappointed. She remembered watching the show at the Palace Pier Theatre, sitting next to DS Barker and trying to forget the taste of the horrible tomato drink. It would have been exciting to watch from the sidelines, seeing things with an insider's eye. Were the performers standing on their marks? Would John Lomax hit the high note that he often missed in rehearsals? Had Bigg and Small remembered their patter, particularly the so-called funny bits? Would Ben fall off his bike? Would Vanda fall and Sonya catch her?

The show on the pier had started with all the artistes on stage, singing the opening song and waving to the audience. But Max had refused to do this. 'It'll ruin the mystique if I march around grinning like a baboon.' Meg was amused to see the show's director, a mild-mannered man called Tim Williamson, give in to Max's every whim. All the same, she wondered what Max would be like if he'd grown up in a family of seven children. There wasn't so much opportunity for whims then.

So Meg had to sit in her dressing room, listening to the signature tunes of the other acts, until Barbara, the ASM, knocked on her door. After hearing the dancers' snowflake music and '*O Sole Mio*', she couldn't take it any more. She opened her door, looking for distraction. Ida's dressing room was opposite. She wasn't on until the second half and was always good for a gossip. As Meg approached, she was suddenly taken aback by her shadow on the brick wall. Her hair was pinned up and secured with a hairnet and this, combined with the tailcoat, made her look like someone completely different. Meg raised her hand to knock on Ida's door when she heard voices from inside. Nothing wrong with that; Ida was probably chatting to one of the other pros, maybe Sonya, who was an old friend. But something made Meg hesitate. She remembered Mario describing voices coming from Ida's room on the night that Cherry had been killed.

Meg retreated back to her room. She was just inside when Ida's door opened and a woman came out. She had white-blonde hair, so it wasn't until she passed close by that Meg recognised Linda Knight, the landlady of number 84 Marine Parade.

Emma and Edgar went to the bar in the interval. They had invited the Connollys to join them but they had seemed rather scared at the thought. Sam had disappeared. Had she gone to see Max in his dressing room? They must be very close if Sam dared interrupt his pre-performance rituals.

'Do you think Sam and Max are having an affair?' Emma asked Edgar, when he'd fought his way back with two gins and two tiny bottles of tonic.

'Sam and Max?' said Edgar. Then, as Emma watched, something in his face seemed to change.

'I think it's possible,' he said slowly.

'Do you? Why?'

'Remember that morning when I went to call on Max unexpectedly? I told you he had a woman there. Sam's boots were in the hallway. I've only just realised. I'd make a pretty poor witness.'

'All those trips to London,' said Emma. 'Do you think she was with Max?'

'Maybe. Funny, I wouldn't have thought she was his type. I mean,' he said quickly, 'she's very . . .'

'I know what you mean,' said Emma. 'But Max and Sam have always got on well. She makes him laugh. I don't suppose Lydia was much of a joker.'

'No, I think she took everything very seriously. Especially herself.'

Edgar looked round and Emma guessed that he was thinking about security. There were uniformed officers at the door and Emma knew that there were plain-clothes men and women in the audience. There was no sign of Ruby and Dex. They were probably being served champagne in their box.

'I've checked outside.' Bob materialised at their side. 'Nothing suspicious reported.'

'And friend Ted?'

'Barker's sticking close.'

For a second, Emma felt almost sorry for Ted English.

'Good work, Bob,' said Edgar. 'Want a drink?'

'Not while I'm on duty.' Edgar looked rather guiltily at his glass with its fast-dissolving ice cubes. He wasn't officially on duty – and nor was Bob – but Emma knew that he still felt responsible for Meg's safety, and everyone's safety really.

'Are you enjoying the show?' Emma asked Bob.

'Yes,' he said, ears reddening. 'That strongwoman was quite something.'

Emma had also enjoyed Ida's act. She had a genuine rapport with the audience and there was something uplifting – literally – about a woman displaying her superior muscle power.

'Are you looking forward to seeing Meg on stage?' she asked.

Bob grinned. 'I'll believe it when I see it.'

'Never believe what you see,' said Edgar. 'That's what Max always says.'

A bell rang.

'Ladies and gentlemen, please resume your seats.'

Meg spent the second half trying not to be sick. The nerves had now reached her stomach and the pastrami and gherkins were churning like clothes in her mum's new twin tub. Meg took a sip of water that tasted odd and sulphuric.

'It's going to be OK,' she told herself. 'You're with Max. He'll look after you. All you have to do is walk across the stage.'

But Meg had never been good at walking. In a sickening lurch of memory she remembered every time she'd tripped over in public: taking up the offertory at mass, getting a prize in assembly, entering the church as Marie's bridesmaid. She would fall on stage and everyone would laugh. Max would be furious. Me and my shadow. The lyrics, which she hummed under her breath to keep in time, now seemed less sad and more sinister.

Me and my shadow
Strolling down the avenue
Me and my shadow . . .
And when it's twelve o'clock
We climb the stair
We never knock, for nobody's there
Just me and my shadow . . .

'Miss Connolly!' Barbara's call was a relief. Meg put on her top hat and went to the door, only to have it knocked off by the frame. Idiot. How was she ever going to make it through the act at this rate?

Max was waiting outside his dressing room.

'All right?'

'Yes,' said Meg hollowly.

'You'll be great.'

They made their way to the wings. The dancers were finishing their second spot, their feet thudding on the floorboards. Max walked a slow circle, counter-clockwise, then grinned at Meg.

'It'll be fine.'

And suddenly it was.

CHAPTER 33

Emma had never expected Meg to be so good. She knew that Max was able to cast a spell on the audience, making them see what he wanted them to, so she was always on the alert when she watched him perform. But, somehow, he always won her over. She always looked at the fluttering dove in the rafters when she should have been watching Max's hands. She always believed that the cabinet was made of solid wood and that the blades were real. Sometimes she deeply resented Max for making her feel so gullible.

Today's act was rather different. Apart from the beginning, when Max was alone on stage, chatting to the audience and causing a startled gentleman's wallet to explode only to have it return, unharmed, to his hand, it was more like a dance or a mime. The audience gasped when Max's shadow appeared. Here we go again, thought Emma; it wasn't Max's shadow, it was Meg. But the lighting, the music and the sheer brilliance of the mirroring made it seem as if Max were replicated on the stage. Sometimes it seemed as if the shadow were mocking its owner, sometimes it seemed almost malign, tricking Max into performing his famous double-take. By the time Meg and Max had both appeared and disappeared several times, Emma felt quite dizzy. The final trick, when they both vanished in a puff of smoke and clash of cymbals, turned laughter into tumultuous applause. Then Meg and Max were both on stage, bowing in unison. No curtsying for Meg. Max ushered her forward for her own ovation and she beamed out into the audience. Emma saw Mary and Aisling both wiping their eyes. Pat called, 'Bravo' and he wasn't the only one.

'Wasn't she good?' Emma whispered to Edgar as they stood for the anthem.

'Splendid,' said Edgar. 'I'll never trust her again.'

'Well done.' As the curtain fell, Max hugged Meg. He smelt of aftershave and sweat. Meg knew that she, too, was wet with perspiration. Who knew that acting was so exhausting? The applause was still continuing. It sounded like the sea crashing against the cliffs at Ovingdean Gap.

'Want to take another bow?' Billy asked Max.

'No,' he said, 'leave 'em wanting more.'

The whole cast now gathered for the final curtain call. For Meg, this was the best moment of the night, perhaps of her entire life. Everyone was laughing and congratulating each other. She found herself hugging both Bigg and Small before taking her place beside Max in the line. The heavy curtain swept upwards and the audience cheered. Meg wished she could see her parents in the crowd. Surely even her mother would be applauding? She saw Max blowing a kiss to Ruby in the Royal Box. The curtain went down and came up again. More cheering, some people standing.

'Another one?' said someone.

'No,' said Max again and led the way offstage. Slightly disappointed, Meg followed Max back to the dressing rooms. The atmosphere in the corridor was now completely different. People were in and out of each other's rooms, laughing and joking. 'Did you see me mess up that pirouette?' 'No one noticed, darling. You were wonderful.'

'You were great.' Ida patted Meg's shoulder. 'I was watching backstage.'

Meg tried to give Max a reproachful look (other people got to watch from the wings) but he was in his room, opening the tiny fridge under the table. 'Come in,' he said to Meg, but it seemed that half the cast followed. Max produced a bottle of champagne and the sound of the cork popping was like every fantasy Meg had ever had, dreams where she was beautiful and rich, courted by men and envied by women.

Typically, the bubbles went up Meg's nose and she started to cough. Mid-splutter, she saw Billy ushering her parents and Aisling into the room.

'Is this all right?' said her mother, sounding

uncharacteristically nervous. 'Emma told us to ask if we could come backstage.'

'It's fine,' said Meg. 'Did you enjoy the show?'

'It was very clever,' said Mary, accepting a glass of champagne from Max.

Aisling was more forthcoming. 'You're a star,' she said, hugging Meg. 'The toast of Drury Lane.'

Meg laughed but she couldn't forget what Max had said about Dan Leno. He was a famous pantomime dame. The toast of Drury Lane. Had Max's aftershave smelt, very slightly, of lavender?

The champagne, or maybe the applause, went to Meg's head. By the time she got back to her own dressing room, she felt so light-headed that she had to sit down. Her parents had left, anxious about missing their train. Most of the cast were planning to meet in the Lemon Tree and, by the sound of it, lots had already left. She could hear Sonya and Vanda talking in Hungarian as they made their way along the corridor. Mario was singing, 'I've Got a Lovely Bunch of Coconuts' in a completely different voice from the one he used on stage. Bigg and Small seemed to be arguing in their dressing room. Gradually, the voices faded.

Meg looked at herself in the mirror, surrounded by its showbiz lights. Her eyes were huge in a face whitened with greasepaint. Joseph Grimaldi. *People have reported seeing his disembodied head, in its white clown's make-up, floating in different parts of the building.* Meg swung round but the room was empty. No floating head, no grey man, no pantomime dame. Meg knew she should hurry up and get changed but she felt a strange reluctance to swap her well-fitting suit for her slacks and blouse. When she unpinned her hair, it hung down in greasy strands. Hell, she'd have to wash it tomorrow morning. *No baths after ten p.m.* Miss Marsh wasn't going be happy if Meg started running water at midnight. *And when it's twelve o'clock, We climb the stair, We never knock, for nobody's there.*

Meg took off her tailcoat and hung it up. She was just starting on the buttons of her shirt when a sound made her freeze. The door was opening, very slowly. Meg wanted to scream but her voice seemed to have deserted her. 'The assistant rarely speaks,' Max had told her. She was struck dumb, stuck in a ghastly mime show.

'Caught you,' said a voice.

CHAPTER 34

'Shall we stay for a drink?' Emma asked Edgar.

'If you like.' Edgar glanced at his watch. 'It's only half past ten. The last train's at midnight.'

Emma knew that she wanted to drink with the cast in the pub. She wanted to congratulate Meg and watch Sam and Max's body language. She didn't want to miss the last act. But, when they got to the Lemon Tree, the only people at the bar were the gymnasts and the fake Italian singer. There was a noisy table of women who looked like they could be the dancers. Bob was standing nearby, looking anxious. No Max. No Meg. Emma had seen Ruby and Dex getting into a taxi outside the theatre. She supposed Ruby now had a baby to get back to. It was an odd thought. Sam had vanished as soon as the curtain had fallen. Really, thought Emma, rather sourly, she was the one who should be doing the disappearing act.

'Gin and tonic?' said Edgar.

'Could I have a glass of champagne?'

She might as well try for all the decadence she could get.

Emma went to stand with Bob. 'Did you enjoy the show?'

'Very much,' said Bob. 'I couldn't believe WDC Connolly was so good. A very slick performance.'

Slick was a horrible word, thought Emma, but it was the right one. Meg and Max had been smooth, seamless, moving almost as one. Although Emma liked Meg, and had a high opinion of her, 'smooth' was not a word you would associate with her. She was a somewhat chaotic force, moving too fast and knocking things over, her tights laddering, her hair escaping from its ponytail. The on-stage Meg, in her black-and-white suit, had been monochrome, like an image on the TV screen. Emma preferred the colour version.

'Do you remember when we went to the Hippodrome together?' said Bob suddenly. 'When we were investigating the murders at Lansdowne Road?'

'I remember,' said Emma. Thinking of Meg and Barker, she suddenly felt very fond of Bob, who had treated her so politely that night.

'We had fun, didn't we?' she said.

But Bob was wandering down a different memory lane. 'Betty was in that show,' he said. 'I think that was when I first fell in love with her.'

Edgar appeared with the drinks. 'Have we still got officers outside?' he asked Bob.

Bob immediately took on a professional stance. 'Yes. Two at the front and one by the stage door. I've told Black and Barker to patrol the building. Barker reported that Ted English left about twenty minutes ago and was last seen waiting at a nearby bus stop. Do you really think something will happen tonight?'

'I don't know,' said Edgar, 'but I'll be happy when all the female performers have left.' He looked at the group by the bar. 'Who's not here?'

'Bigg and Small,' said Emma. 'The unicyclist, whatever his name is. Ida Lupin. Max. And Meg. I think those are the dancers over at that table. There were six of them.'

'One of them offered me a drink,' said Bob, as if that proved it.

Barker advanced into the room.

'Look at you,' he said, 'all dressed up like a fella.'

'Go away,' said Meg, aware how childish she sounded.

Barker obviously thought so too. 'You don't mean that.'

'I do.'

'You know,' said Barker, examining the good luck cards stuck to the side of the mirror, 'you were good on stage. Made me see you in a different light. Not a silly little girl any more.'

'If you thought I was a silly little girl,' said Meg, 'why did you try to kiss me that time?'

'Now, don't be like that. I've forgiven you.'

'*You've* forgiven *me*?'

'Let's have a kiss and make up.'

'No!'

Barker had hold of her arm now.

'Just a little kiss.'

'She said no,' said a voice. Meg couldn't see who it belonged to until the door swung open and revealed Ida Lupin, still in her fur bikini.

'What's it got to do with you?' Barker let go of Meg. 'Who are you anyway? Tarzan's Jane?'

'She said no,' repeated Ida and, with one neatly aimed punch, knocked Barker to the floor.

Emma was enjoying herself, even though her only company was her husband and her ex-colleague. The gymnasts were still at the bar, talking in what sounded like Hungarian. Mario Fontana had finally been joined by some other performers, recognisable by their clothes and loud theatrical voices. There was no one Emma recognised. Where were Bigg and Small, Ida and the rest of the cast? Where were Max and Sam?

Emma drained her glass. That was the trouble with expensive drinks, they came in such small quantities. Edgar and Bob were still only halfway through their pints. Emma was about to suggest another round all the same when a voice hissed, 'Emma!'

It was Meg, standing in the doorway, wearing a coat over her stage outfit. Emma was about to exclaim, 'Here's the star!' when she realised Meg's manner was secretive, almost furtive. She didn't look worried though. Her eyes were shining and her skin glowed. Emma remembered Max saying once that being on stage makes a woman twice as good-looking. She'd thought that he'd meant the make-up and costume but now she realised he had been describing something entirely different.

Emma hurried over to Meg. 'What is it?'

'It's Barker—'

'I'm going to tell Edgar.'

'No, wait. It was great. He made a pass at me and Ida knocked him out. He went down like a stone. He's still lying on my dressing room floor.'

'Golly,' said Emma. 'Is he OK?'

'Who cares? You know,' Meg took hold of Emma's arm, 'I was scared at first. I thought it might be him. The murderer. Houdini. But he wouldn't come after me. After all, I'm not blonde.'

Emma looked at Meg. She saw a stage and, walking across it, as real as on a TV screen, a procession of women: Cherry, Joan, Grace, Ida . . .

'Ida,' she said. 'She's blonde.'

'And she's there on her own,' said Meg. 'Let's go back.'

'Hang on,' said Emma. 'We'll take Edgar and Bob with us.'

'Oh,' said Meg. 'I'd forgotten about them.'

It wasn't until they were hurrying through the narrow streets that Emma realised that she was still carrying her champagne glass. She placed it carefully on a window ledge. Meg led the way to a doorway between two boarded-up windows.

'Is this the stage door?' said Edgar. 'I thought we had an officer here.'

'I thought so too.' Bob was looking up and down the street. 'Maybe he's taken a turn round the block.'

Meg was knocking on the door.

'Fred! It's Samantha. Let me in.'

Emma and Edgar exchanged glances.

The door was opened by a large man in a crumpled uniform.

'Thanks, Fred,' said Meg. 'Has anyone else been out this way?'

'Not since you left.'

That meant that the remaining performers were still in the theatre, thought Emma, as they followed Meg along an ill-lit corridor. It smelt of damp and greasepaint. At the end, Meg paused at a landing with three doors.

'Ida's probably still in her dressing room—' Meg stopped. From somewhere above them came the unmistakable sound of a scream.

'It's coming from the stage,' said Meg. 'This way.'

She led the way through the middle door, up more stairs and through an area full of what looked like junk. Finally, with no warning, they were there, on the very boards of the Theatre Royal Drury Lane. The stage was lit by a dim, rosy light and Ida was lying on the floor.

Kneeling next to her was Linda Knight and, in the foreground, glowing strangely, was a platinum blonde wig.

'Ida!' Meg got to the strongwoman first. To Emma's relief, Ida was sitting up.

'He just came from nowhere,' she said. 'He had a knife. If Linda hadn't thrown her wig at him . . .'

'It was all I could think of,' said Linda, who was stroking Ida's arm. 'I think it shocked him. He ran away.'

Emma didn't ask why Linda was wearing a wig in the first place. 'Who was he,' she said, 'the man with the knife?'

'It was Tommy Horton,' said another voice, 'wasn't it?'

'Sam!' Emma swung round. Her partner was standing there, looking the same as ever in her tie-dye dress and knee-length brown boots. Behind her, in shirtsleeves, was Max Mephisto.

'Yes,' said Linda slowly. 'It was Tommy, but I don't know how . . . I mean, he's old, he's in a wheelchair.'

'That's what he wants you to think,' said Sam. 'I worked it out just now. It was something Rex said.'

Emma had to struggle to remember who Rex was. She didn't like Sam coming out with all these revelations. Then she realised that this was hardly the matter at hand. 'Where did he go?' she asked. 'Tommy?'

'The main entrance is locked,' said Max. 'He'll have to leave by the stage door.'

'I'll go back there,' said Bob.

'Everyone else stay here,' said Edgar. 'Max, can you turn the lights on?'

'The spirit lamp's for the ghosts,' said Meg, to nobody in particular.

The stage was suddenly flooded with light; it picked out the two women on the ground, one dark, one fair, Max standing by the wings, the green and orange of Sam's dress.

'Is there anywhere this Horton could be?' Edgar asked Max.

'He could be almost anywhere,' said Max. 'It's a real warren of a place.'

'I think he'll go up into the gods,' said Ida. 'That's what I would do. You can see everything from up there.'

Emma knew that 'the gods' referred to the highest – and cheapest – seats, where you could look down on the action like a deity. She craned her head to look upwards. The Royal Circle and the Grand Circle curved round like a great red mouth. The Balcony was above that and its seats were in darkness. But, as she watched, she saw a tiny movement. A shadow merging into another shadow. She nudged Edgar, knowing better than to say something out loud.

Edgar whispered to Meg to keep watch and he headed towards the wings. Max followed. Sam and Emma exchanged glances and then they, too, exited stage left.

Max must have taken Edgar via some secret staircase, but Sam and Emma took the public route, following the red carpet and gold handrail. Sam switched on lights as they went and they revealed barred windows, thick with grime, framed programmes from the 1920s and '30s. As they climbed, the carpet grew thinner and more threadbare until it was just a strip of maroon between wooden floorboards. They were both out of breath by the time they reached the door saying 'Balcony' in peeling gold letters.

'Do you think he's still here?' panted Emma.

'I don't know,' said Sam. 'Where are Edgar and Max? I thought they'd get here first.'

'Let's go back,' said Emma, suddenly scared.

She turned to find herself face to face with a white-haired man in a blue jacket.

'Tommy?' she said. His face was so mild that Emma didn't feel scared. She tried for a comforting smile, stretching out a hand. And found herself with a knife at her throat.

'I'm going to kill you,' said Tommy. He didn't sound confused any more. His voice had a calm rationality that was almost as frightening as the cold of the blade. 'I'm going to kill you like I killed the others. She left me. You're all the same, you women.'

'Tommy,' said Sam. And Emma could hear her trying to sound calm in her turn. 'Drop the knife. Think of Greta. Think of Heidi.'

At the last name, the arm round Emma's neck seemed to shake. She raised her own hand up to push against it. She remembered Tommy Horton as an old man in a wheelchair. Surely she could overpower him? But Tommy seemed possessed of superhuman strength. He pushed her through the door and they were amongst the rows of tipped-up seats, the floor sloping violently downwards. 'The nosebleed seats,' Max called them. The giant chandelier was at eye level. Tommy pushed Emma forward until they hit the balustrade. She could see the stage, very far below, and the upturned faces of Meg, Ida and Linda.

'Tommy,' said Sam again. 'Let Emma go. She's never hurt you.'

In response, Tommy bent Emma forward so that she was looking over the balustrade, down to the Grand Circle. Would she die if she fell? Emma tried to push against her captor but the knife was still at her throat. He's stabbed two women to death, she told herself. Don't think he won't kill you. After all, Emma had blonde hair too. That was probably why he'd grabbed her instead of Sam.

'Police!' shouted Edgar from the other side of the balcony. 'Drop the knife!'

But the arm round Emma tightened. She closed her eyes. And then another voice echoed around the auditorium. A woman's voice, sweet and slightly sad.

'Tommy? Tommy, it's Gracie. Come to me, Tommy. Let her go.'

With a sob, Tommy dropped the knife. Emma fell to her knees as Edgar hurdled over the seats to push Tommy to the ground. Max was at his heels and he held the old man while Edgar handcuffed him. Not that he was putting up any resistance. Tommy was gazing towards the spot where the voice had come from. Emma was looking in that direction too, as was Sam, who seemed unable to move. They watched as a man in a grey check suit made his way towards them.

'I'm sorry, Tommy,' said Perry Small. 'I just couldn't let you kill another woman.'

'Grace?' said Tommy, uncomprehending. 'Where's Grace?'

Perry turned to Emma, who had got to her feet and was massaging her neck. 'I used to be a ventriloquist,' he said. 'I could always do Grace's voice well.'

'Because she was Geoffrey's sister?' said Sam.

'That's right,' said Perry. 'Poor lovely Grace. Geoff was heartbroken when she died. And Tommy was never the same again. As you see.' He gestured towards the man, shrunken and frail-looking now, being led through the rows of seats. Emma and Sam followed. Sam put her arm round Emma.

'Are you OK?'

'Yes,' said Emma. 'I'll be fine.' She turned to Perry. 'I think you saved my life.'

'Anything to help a damsel in distress,' said Perry.

'Did you guess?' asked Sam. 'About Tommy.'

'Not at first,' said Perry. 'But recently I've had this feeling. Rex King told Tommy that Ted had a new assistant who looked just like Grace. Rex never could keep his mouth shut. Tommy must have come to see for himself and the sight of Cherry was too much. He remembered how Grace had left him for another man and he saw red. Poor Joanie too. Tommy must have come to see the show and waited for her afterwards and . . . well, you know the rest. I'd better get back to Geoff now.'

Perry left the way he'd come but Emma and Sam followed Edgar, Max and Tommy down the red-carpeted staircase. Bob, Meg, Ida and Linda were waiting for them in the lobby, surrounded by posters from the theatre's glory days. Dan Leno in *Mother Goose*. Noël Coward's *Cavalcade*. Emma could see blue police lights outside. Bob took Tommy by the arm and led him towards the waiting car. Edgar turned to Emma.

'I'm sorry—' she began but Edgar wrapped his arms round her and held her tightly. When he released her, she saw that Sam and Max were kissing passionately and Linda had her arm round Ida. The couples sprang apart when Danny Black came bursting through the double doors.

'Meg!' He rushed up to her and took both her hands. 'Are you OK?'

'Where have you been, DC Black?' asked Edgar, repressively.

Danny let Meg go. She looked surprised, but not displeased, at this turn of events.

'Looking for DS Barker,' he said.

'Oh, I think I can help you with that,' said Meg.

CHAPTER 35

At Tottenham Court Road police station, Alan Deacon ushered Edgar into a room where a fair-haired young man was sitting behind a table, a uniformed policeman standing impassively at his side.

'This is Craig Fitch,' said Deacon. 'We apprehended him in Catherine Street, near the theatre. He was in his car, apparently waiting for Mr Horton. Fitch, this is Superintendent Stephens from the Brighton police. He's got a few questions for you.'

Edgar sat opposite the man, who seemed little more than a youth. He was dressed in a blue blouson jacket and there were rings on every one of his fingers.

'Do you work at the Cedars Care Home in Worthing?' he asked.

'Yes, I'm an orderly.'

'And you look after Mr Horton. Tommy Horton?'

'Yes. He's been like a grandad to me.'

Edgar glanced at Deacon but his colleague's face was deadpan.

'Why are you in London today, Craig?'

'Tommy asked me to drive him. They said it was OK at the Cedars.'

'What did Tommy tell you he was going to do?'

'Said he was visiting his daughter. Grace, her name was. I remember his other daughter coming to see him at the home. Lovely girl, she was. Tommy said Grace was in a show at the theatre.'

This was one Freudian step too far, thought Edgar. He leant forward, knowing he'd get more by sounding sympathetic. Establishing a rapport, as Meg would say.

'What did Tommy ask you to do, Craig?'

'Just to wait in the car for him.'

'Has you asked you to do other things for him?'

A slightly furtive look. 'Sometimes. No one else knows that Tommy can really walk. In fact, he's not in bad shape for an oldie. That's our secret.'

How many more of Tommy's secrets did this man know, wondered Edgar. That would be for Deacon to discover. Now he just needed answers.

'Did Tommy ask you to go to Brighton on Sunday 11th May?'

'He just asked me to find a girl called Cherry. That was all. I didn't do nothing wrong. I just had a chat with her.'

'Did Tommy borrow your car that night? And your jacket too?'

Craig regarded him with what looked like genuine wonder. 'How did you know?'

'How did you guess about Tommy?' asked Emma.

'I realised why he'd told his family not to visit,' said Sam. 'It was because they knew that he could walk perfectly well. He'd persuaded the home that he needed a wheelchair. I met his daughter Heidi today.'

'Where?' said Emma. 'You suddenly seemed to know everything about everyone.'

They were in a featureless area of Tottenham Court Road police station. Inspector Deacon had called it the 'waiting room' but really it was just a corridor with chairs lined up by the wall. A WPC had been dispatched to bring them tea and digestive biscuits. Emma disapproved of women officers being given these tasks but the hot drink was very welcome.

'I've been visiting Rex King in hospital,' said Sam. 'He's not a bad old stick really. Tommy's daughter Heidi came in today. Apparently, she looks very like Grace. It was seeing her gave Rex a funny turn and actually killed Pal, gave him a heart attack. I think Pal only saw her reflected in his trophy cabinet but that was enough. Heidi was saying that she and her dad used to go for walks. Then, suddenly, he asks them not to visit and he's in a wheelchair.'

'That implies that he planned it,' said Emma.

'I think he did,' said Sam. 'Rex said that he visited Tommy a few months ago. He must have mentioned Cherry and how much she looked like Grace. He's a bit of a blabbermouth, Rex. That set Tommy off. He pretended to be frailer than he was. Heidi said that Tommy was friendly with one of the orderlies, Craig. She called him Ringo.'

'Ringo,' said Emma. 'Do you think he was the man in the Beatles jacket? The one talking to Cherry that Sunday afternoon?'

'Possibly,' said Sam. 'Maybe Tommy asked Craig – Ringo – to find out where Cherry lived. If so, it's more evidence of planning.'

'Tommy was a good magician in his day,' said Emma. 'Ted English said so. Craig, or Ringo, was a distraction. Misdirection. A double, like Meg and Max tonight. I think Tommy put on Craig's jacket when he went back to murder Cherry that evening. He might even have borrowed Craig's car.'

'I thought Tommy was a bit creepy when we met him at the nursing home,' said Emma, 'all that guff about "lovely young women".'

'They all talk like that,' said Sam. 'Even Rex.'

'At least we've got something to tell Cherry's parents,' said Emma. 'Not that it will help them, poor things. To think their daughter was murdered because she looked like someone's ex-wife.'

'I feel sorry for Heidi too,' said Sam. 'Tommy's daughter. She seemed a very sweet girl. Maybe Rex will look after her. He's longing for a daughter. He even seems to have adopted me as a niece.'

'You've obviously got a secret life,' said Emma. It came out more acidly than she intended.

Sam looked up. 'I'm sorry,' she said. 'I meant to tell you about me and Max. It's just . . . it seemed more fun to keep it secret for a while. Just until I knew what *it* was, if you know what I mean.'

'I do know,' said Emma. 'Is it serious then, you and Max?'

'I think so,' said Sam. 'We make each other happy.'

'That's the most important thing,' said Emma. There was a pause while she wondered if she and Edgar still made each other happy. She thought so, remembering how much she had enjoying drinking champagne with Edgar earlier. They ought to do that more, make time for each other, go out once a week in Brighton. This reminded her of something . . .

'Did you know about Ida and Linda?' she asked.

'No,' said Sam. 'But seeing them together, I think they are lovers. It's sad that they have to keep it secret. That must be why Linda was wearing a wig tonight. She was in disguise.'

'It must have been Ida and Linda who Mario heard in Ida's room that day,' said Emma. 'He said something about a mezzo and a soprano. Linda's voice is deeper than Ida's. I did think they were close and that Ida seemed very much at home in the house. And Linda never forgave Ted English because he made a pass at Ida. That's why they quarrelled. Ida punched Ted but didn't seem to hold a grudge. She even helped him with his act.'

'Maybe it was easier for Ida to forgive,' said Sam. 'I think Max has forgiven Lydia, but I haven't.'

That was something to ponder over later, thought Emma. She said, 'From something Linda said to me I think Pal might have known and even tried to blackmail her. It's hard to feel sorry that he's dead. But I do think it's a shame Ida and Linda can't live together openly.'

'Brighton's a more liberal town than most,' said Sam. 'But, even in Brighton, you get prejudice. Homosexuality is still illegal, although that doesn't include women because, apparently, Queen Victoria couldn't imagine what two women would do together and no one dared enlighten her. But gay women still have to be discreet. Well, look at Astarte.'

'Astarte? Is she . . .?'

'I always assumed she was a lesbian,' said Sam. 'She goes to all the right clubs.'

'Gosh,' said Emma. 'I feel very stupid.'

'A new feeling for the brilliant Emma Holmes,' said Sam, teasingly.

'Believe me,' said Emma. 'It's not.'

'It was like the last act of a Shakespearean comedy just now,' said Sam. 'Everyone pairing up. Do you think that policeman is keen on Meg?'

'It seems so,' said Emma. 'Meg is a bit of a dark horse. Look how good she was on stage tonight.'

'Oh, that was all Max,' said Sam. Confirming, for Emma, that Sam really was in love with the great magician.

*

'Craig must have been the person Logan saw chatting to Cherry in Brighton,' said Meg. 'The one wearing a Beatles jacket.'

For a moment, Edgar wondered who Logan was. Then he remembered. Astarte's cousin, the man Barker had described as 'half-naked'.

'Is Craig blond?' Meg asked Deacon. 'And dressed like one of the Beatles?'

'He was fair-haired,' said Deacon. 'And I'm no expert on fashion but I think he looked a bit like a pop star. He was wearing lots of rings like the drummer chap.'

'Ringo,' said Meg. 'Bingo.' Edgar thought she seemed remarkably cheerful considering the evening she'd had. Maybe she was still wearing her stage make-up. Bob, on the other hand, looked quite haggard. 'We almost let him escape,' he kept saying on the way to the police station. 'We almost let Horton escape again. 'But he didn't,' Edgar told him. 'We've got our man.'

The police officers were gathered in Deacon's office for the debrief. Tommy Horton and Craig Fitch were both in custody.

'Did Craig really not suspect?' said Bob. 'Even when Tommy borrowed his car and his jacket?'

'He seemed almost wilfully naïve,' said Edgar. 'Unless that was an act. He said he thought of Tommy as a grandfather. Maybe you just don't suspect your grandfather.'

'What do you know about this Thomas Horton?' asked Deacon.

'Just that he was a retired magician,' said Edgar. 'One of a group that centred around Gordon Palgrave. Pal. Tommy's first wife Grace left him for a theatrical agent and then for Palgrave.'

'Well, there's no accounting for tastes,' said Deacon. 'I've always thought the man was a creep. God rest his soul and all that.'

'I don't disagree,' said Edgar. 'It seems that Tommy Horton was obsessed with Grace. He never got over the fact that she left him.'

'He was rambling about someone called Gracie just now,' said Deacon. 'It seems he heard her voice at the theatre.'

'That was a ventriloquist called Perry Small,' said Edgar.

'Bloody hell, Stephens,' said Deacon. 'Sorry,' he said to Meg who replied that she didn't mind swearing. 'You live in a strange old world.'

'I don't live in it,' said Edgar, 'I just visit sometimes. Small could imitate this Grace's voice, which turned out to be a stroke of luck for all of us.'

'And you say Horton killed two other women?' said Deacon.

'He admitted it earlier,' said Edgar. 'He killed Cherry Underwood and Joan Waters. They were both blonde and looked a bit like Grace. Tommy seems to have convinced himself that they were being disloyal to him by performing with other magicians.'

'Well, Horton will plead insanity,' said Deacon. 'I'm sure of it.'

'Maybe,' said Edgar. 'But the murders were carefully planned. Sam Collins, my wife's partner in the detective agency, knows some of the background detail. She says that Tommy pretended to be wheelchair-bound so no one would suspect him.'

'I'd forgotten your wife was a private detective,' said Deacon. 'I'll need statements from her and from this Sam Collins.'

'I'm sure they'll be delighted,' said Edgar.

It was past midnight by the time all the statements had been taken. Deacon offered a squad car to take them home. 'You'll have missed the last train, I'm afraid.'

'Do you want to come with us, WDC Connolly?' asked Edgar. 'Or shall we drop you off at the hostel?'

'I can walk,' said Meg. 'It's only round the corner. If I go home, Mum and Dad will be in bed and, if I wake them up, they'll only ask all sorts of questions.'

'They worry about you,' said Edgar.

'I know,' said Meg. 'Well, they won't have to worry for the rest of the run.'

Up until that moment it hadn't occurred to Edgar that the show would go on or that Meg would want to continue in her role. He had underestimated the lure of the footlights. He caught Emma's eye and smiled. He'd have to reconcile himself to being an officer down for two weeks.

'We'll give you a lift all the same,' he told Meg. He didn't want his WDC to take any more chances that night.

'Are you coming back to Brighton, Sam?' asked Emma. 'Or . . .'

'I'll get a taxi,' said Sam.

'Are you sure?' said Edgar. But Emma gave him a look that said, 'Don't ask any questions.'

The squad car, one of the new two-tone Ford Anglias, glided to a stop in front of the station. Meg got in the front, leaving Edgar, Emma and Bob in the back. Edgar's last sight of Sam was of her colourful dress gleaming briefly in the blue light above the porch. Then she disappeared into the shadows.

Sam was not surprised to see Max waiting round the corner.

'Me and my shadow,' she said.

'Have you shaken off the others?' said Max. He was back in his everyday clothes, trilby in place.

'I thought they'd never stop talking,' said Sam.

'Edgar will be pleased,' said Max. 'Case closed. Do you want to get a cab here or shall we walk for a bit?'

'Let's walk for a bit,' said Sam.

Max put his arm round Sam as they headed down Charing Cross Road. 'Has Emma forgiven you for solving the case first?' he asked.

'I was almost too late,' said Sam. 'Tommy could have killed Ida. And Emma too.'

'What were you and Emma thinking?' said Max. 'Chasing after Tommy like that.'

'I don't think we were thinking at all,' said Sam. 'I think we just wanted to be in on things.'

'In at the death,' said Max. Where was that phrase from? wondered Sam. Hunting? It certainly had an ominous ring. After a pause, Max added, 'Well, you nearly gave Ed a heart attack. Me too, for that matter.'

'Was it climbing all those stairs?' asked Sam innocently.

Max laughed but his voice was serious when he said, 'I was just terrified that you might be hurt.'

They walked on in silence, between the shuttered shops and the flood-lit advertisements for shows that never seemed to end.

EPILOGUE

Saturday, 30 July 1966

It was chairs that were the problem. That was the trouble with such a big family, thought Meg. Even the nine of them would struggle to fit into the tiny front room at the same time. When you added Marie's husband Terry, Nanny Kathleen – her dad's mother, who'd come all the way from Ireland – and Declan's girlfriend, Sandra, the whole thing started to look like one of Max Mephisto's magic tricks. The amazing expanding council house.

'We'll have to ask Paul and Pauline from next door,' said Mary. 'They haven't got a television.'

'More fool them,' said Patrick, grumpy from carrying kitchen chairs into the sitting room.

'Love your neighbour as you love yourself,' Mary told him. 'We can't let them miss the World Cup final.'

Meg didn't dare tell her mother that, yesterday, Danny had asked if he could come over to watch the match. Meg had prevaricated – she wasn't sure that she was ready to introduce Danny to her family – but she wouldn't put it past him just to turn up. Danny and Meg had been on two dates since Meg had come back from London. Both had been fun, they'd been to the cinema and the roller-skating rink, but, beyond a kiss hallo and goodbye, nothing had actually happened. Not that Meg wanted Danny to pounce on her, the way horrible DS Barker had done, but it would be rather galling to have to initiate proceedings herself. Meg wasn't sure what she wanted from what Emma would call 'the relationship' but she was conscious of wanting something to happen in her life.

DS Barker had taken early retirement. Meg didn't know if he'd been forced out by DI Willis and Superintendent Stephens, or if he couldn't face the embarrassment of everyone knowing that he'd been knocked out by a strong-woman in a fur bikini. She was just glad that he was gone. Bartholomew Square was a far nicer place without him. There were actually two new WPCs, both of whom were pleasingly deferential to Meg, and, best of all, DI Willis had recommended that Meg be promoted to sergeant. 'I'll outrank you,' Meg told Danny. Come to think of it, maybe that was why he hadn't kissed her.

Tommy Horton had been charged with the murders of Cherry Underwood and Joan Waters, plus the attempted murder of Ida Lupin. The orderly, Craig Fitch, had been charged with being an accessory to the crimes. Emma's name had been kept out of it, probably at her request.

DI Willis thought that Horton would probably plead insanity and end his days in an asylum. He said this like Horton had got away with it, but Meg thought that it sounded like rather a just punishment.

Meg's two weeks as Samantha were still the most exciting of her life. After the last night, they'd had a party and Meg had drunk so much champagne that she'd slept on Max's sofa rather than going back to the hostel. She had woken up to a blinding headache and Sam Collins offering her a cup of black coffee. Meg realised then that Sam had spent the night with Max. Meg felt very daring to be so close to what she would call 'an affair' and her mother would call 'sinfulness'. It explained the choice of the name 'Samantha' as well.

Now things were rather quiet. Number 84 Marine Parade was closed for refurbishment. 'Turns out there's asbestos everywhere,' Linda Knight told Meg. 'That's probably why everyone kept getting headaches. Anyway, it's an ill wind. Gives me time to pop off to Greece with my friend.' The super and his family were on holiday in France. Sam and Max were in Italy. Max had sent Meg a postcard of the Trevi Fountain. On the back he'd written: 'To Meg, the best shadow I've ever had. Love M.' Meg knew that she'd keep it for ever.

Finally, the stage was set. Marie was on the sofa with baby Niamh in her arms. Terry was next to her and then Nanny Kathleen. Uncle Paul and Auntie Pauline from next door had the armchairs, which caused some muttering amongst the younger members of the family. Meg's parents, Declan, Sandra and Patrick were on strategically placed kitchen chairs. Aisling, Collette and Connor were sitting on the floor. Aisling was reading *Jane Eyre* because she said she wasn't interested in football. 'Why take up space then?' said Collette. Aisling ignored her. Meg, coming into the room with a tray of 'nibbles', was surprised to see that a chair had been saved for her. True, it was in the doorway and you could hardly see the TV from there, but it cemented her position as a senior member of the family. Meg's parents had treated her slightly differently after her West End debut, she noticed. She didn't get special treatment exactly, but her opinion was sometimes considered and, once, Mary had actually told Connor (her favourite and a boy) to be quiet while Meg was speaking. It was almost as if they had finally realised that she was an adult.

The teams were coming onto the pitch. England were in darker jerseys and Patrick, who had a football magazine open in front of him, told them that they were playing in red because Germany also wore white.

'Why should we change?' said Collette. 'It's our country.'

'We should always be polite to visitors,' said Mary, with an almost imperceptible nod towards the armchairs.

'I think they tossed a coin,' said Patrick.

Meg was just relaxing – surely Danny would be here by now if he was coming – when Collette, who had sharp ears, said, 'What's that?'

'Shh,' said her mother. 'The anthems are starting.'

Collette went to the window. 'It's a horse,' she said.

Meg slid out of the room and opened the front door. Outside was a dappled grey horse, harnessed to a strange, high-wheeled trap. Logan was holding the reins. He grinned down at Meg.

'Want to go for a ride?'

Meg could hear the national anthem playing from the sitting room. Someone laughed and was shushed. Collette stood, open-mouthed, at the window. Logan was still smiling, almost laughing, his gold earrings glinting as he turned towards her. The horse whinnied and shifted its weight, making the harness jingle. The summer's evening suddenly felt full of possibilities.

'Oh, all right then,' said Meg.

ACKNOWLEDGEMENTS

Thanks, as always, to my wonderful editor, Jane Wood, and all at Quercus. Special thanks to Joe Christie, Florence Hare, David Murphy, Ellie Nightingale, Ella Patel and Hannah Robinson. Thanks to Jon Butler for always believing in me and my books. Thanks to Liz Hatherell for her meticulous copy-editing and to Chris Shamwana for the beautiful cover.

Thanks to my incredible agent, Rebecca Carter. It's so exciting to be on this journey with you. Thanks to my crime-writing friends for all their support. Special thanks to the South Coast Squad, William Shaw and Lesley Thomson.

It's a joy to write these books about my hometown of Brighton. All the places mentioned in *The Great Deceiver* actually exist but the characters are entirely imaginary. Thanks to my neighbour, Mike Laslett, for his encyclopaedic knowledge of local history. Any mistakes are mine alone.

The Brighton Mysteries were inspired by my grandfather, Dennis Lawes, a popular variety performer. This book is dedicated to his other granddaughters: my sisters, Giulia and Sheila de Rosa, and my cousins, Ellie and Katie Slee. Thinking of you too, Roger, wherever you may be. Dennis's memory lives on.

Finally, thanks to my husband, Andy, and our (now grown-up) children, Alex and Juliet. You all inspire me every day. A special mention for our new cat, Pip, who was no help at all.

EG, 2023